Please Fear Me

JENNIFER LOVE

Fairlight Books

First published by Fairlight Books 2024

Fairlight Books
Summertown Pavilion, 18–24 Middle Way, Oxford,
OX2 7LG

A CIP catalogue record for this book is available from the
British Library.

1 2 3 4 5 6 7 8 9 10

ISBN 978-1-914148-61-3

www.fairlightbooks.com

Printed and bound in Czech Republic

Cover Design © Emma Rogers

This is a work of fiction. Names, characters, businesses,
events and incidents are the products of the author's
imagination. Any resemblance to actual persons, living or
dead, or actual events is purely coincidental.

Please Fear Me

I

'Stay still.' She stretches the skin of my eyelid tight with one finger. 'If you twitch again, I'm giving up and you can paint your own eyes on.'

I would nod, if not for the acrylic nail pressing into the flesh beside my left eye socket. I hold my breath, block out the familiar smell of cigarette smoke, hairspray and bubblegum shimmer body mist. She paints thick, careful strokes.

'Okay. Open.' She leans back to inspect her work. 'They aren't even.' She snaps the compact closed, wipes the tiny brush with an already lipstick-stained Kleenex. 'But no one's gonna look at you up close. So whatever. You ready?'

I can only see a sliver of myself in the mirror on the far side of the room. Blink my affirmation with a heavy, unfamiliar eye.

2

Violet treats everything like a threat. She opens both doors to walk into the audition room, green-lidded eyes scanning and darting to every corner, one-two-three-four.

Auditions are easy to get, which I suspect has something to do with the perverse satisfaction of watching other people fail. They're easy to get, and hard to believe in after a while. Violet has dragged me all over the coast to auditions in theaters, dive bars, performing arts collectives and a converted school bus whose owner told us he was cooking up the next big thing, the next great big American traveling showcase with pirates and cowboys and pixies.

Even he didn't want what we had to offer.

Violet stands before the three men sitting behind a fold-up table. There is absolutely nothing on the table.

'My name is Violet Laborde, and this is Smidge. We are living dolls.'

We always perform without music, because neither of us wants to put a target on our backs by carrying around a jukebox, and you never know if these places will provide one.

Violet says it improves focus and coordination to perform without music, anyway. That it adds drama and suspense for the spectator.

I volunteered to be the tied-up one for our new performance. Violet has become adept at the crosses and knots of wrapping my body in a secure network of rope, quickly enough to get the show on the road, and with enough flourish to draw admiration and intrigue before we have even begun.

When she first recruited me, I asked what it meant, which proved to be the wrong question.

'It's performance art,' she had scowled. She'd been filing her newly applied plastic fingernails into sharp little claws.

'But what does it *mean*?' I had persisted. In my head I was thinking, *but what is the* point. I would never say that out loud, though.

'It's about fragility. It's about being bound.'

'Bound to *what*?'

'Bound to rules that someone else made up for you, some people you don't even know, and they're probably all dead by now, and yet here we all are, still listening to them. No one thinks about that, Smidge. They've only come up with the words so far for bullshit like religion and free will. And they don't think about it because they don't have to think about it, and I want to make them. But I don't want to burn shit down to get people's attention, you know? I want to make it beautiful.'

Sometimes I just let Violet keep talking, even if I don't follow. Somehow I always understand the feeling behind what she's saying, even if the words don't make sense to me.

'And tragic.'

'What?'

'Beautiful and tragic. Like Shakespeare.'

*

We finish with elegance and grace, something that Violet will inform me of later while we shop for defective plastic-wrapped sandwiches that we can ask for discounts on at the corner store. The three men behind the empty fold-up table are not impressed.

'Listen, ladies. This isn't a strip club. That's not what we're trying to do here. Why don't you take it to the Poodle? That's down on 14th.'

One of the other ones whacks him with the back of his hand. 'Man, they're like thirteen.'

Sixteen, I correct him. Only in my head.

'Do your parents know what you're up to?' the second one asks. 'Where are you girls staying? Are you local or what?'

'None of your concern.'

'Come on. If you're really underage, this isn't cool. Now you've made us responsible, doing all that, not telling us you were minors beforehand, I don't know. We could be implicated for some shit.'

The first one snorts. 'Yeah, and what are we supposed to do about it? Call the cops?'

Cops. That's the magic word to secure a quick exit from Violet and me. This isn't the first time someone's threatened the cops on us, citing concern and the goodwill of their hearts.

No one has caught up with us yet, though. Sometimes I wonder if anyone bothers actually calling, or whether speaking it into existence is enough to soothe their consciences. Maybe they don't know how to describe what to look for, although it feels to me as if we stand out no matter where we go. Two girls, could be anywhere from thirteen to twenty-five. One of them in a floor-length gown, big hair, big muscles, big eyeliner wings; the other a beanpole in fishnets. Both of them a little ratty, maybe a little smelly depending on their current situation. Bulging backpacks. Makeup smeared on thick. We look like trouble on purpose. Flash our poison in obvious neon-sign signals, just like insects warning predators away. We aren't trying to hide.

Violet doesn't untie me before leaving, just leads me by the wrists out the back door and into the alley. I watch tiny bulbs of sweat populate the space between her wrinkled brows as she yanks me free. She's giving me rope burn. It feels kind of good in the sudden sting of a January evening.

'They didn't get it.'

I shrug. 'I don't know. Didn't you call it "live erotica" once?'

'No. Yes. Yeah, I did, but I was just trying to make you understand that it tells a story, and the point is the story, and the message, not the fact that we're tied up or whatever. If people can't get past that, then they don't get it. You know?'

I nod. I don't know. I just want her to calm down so she can remember that she is hungry, and we can go to the corner store. I want a Slim Jim.

We are accustomed to our act being met with revulsion, confusion and occasional concern. 'Where are your mothers?' someone asked us not three weeks ago, hard-jawed on the word *mothers* so that it only just slipped out between nearly clenched teeth.

Mine is in California, where I left her last year.

I wonder what she would think if she saw our performance; whether she would be horrified or impressed. On the one hand, she was always critical of proper society and mistrustful of the institutions upholding it – she might appreciate the subversiveness of our art. On the other hand, she might say I was a slut.

Slut was what she called me when I wore a pleated skater skirt for the first day of seventh grade, a thrift-store score that I had been so proud of and then never wore again. *Trash* is what she called me later that year, when I bleached stripes into my hair and dyed them pink.

Liar is what she called me when I later reminded her of these moments. 'I would never say that about you, beautiful girl. You're perfect. You know how to take care of me.'

This is what is difficult about loving an addict.

They will assign you nouns and adjectives: *liar* and *slut*, *ungrateful* and *selfish*. They will accuse you of not caring about them, of only wanting to feel like you have control over something. Of using them to feel needed. They will tell you that they don't need you, that they were better off before you. They will cry and remain able to talk through their tears to say that they hate you – no, they will correct themselves, that's not what they meant, they just hate that you exist when they've already been ruined; they don't want to raise another fuckup like them.

The next day, they will say they don't remember anything.

It gets increasingly difficult the older you grow, the more you learn about the world outside of your house, the more acutely you realize that there are other options beyond continuing the endurance trial of loving the addict unconditionally. It becomes so difficult that once those options come into focus, it feels impossible *not* to choose one – so in order to survive, you escape.

3

Violet has never tried to be a stripper, escort or porn star. She wasn't interested in exploiting her body in the name of money and a temporary sense of security, she told me. She was interested only in exploiting herself in the name of art.

I tried stripping when I first got to Miami, but I wasn't very good at it. That was before Violet discovered me. The club owner told me not to look so dead inside, that it was giving his clientele depression and a guilt complex. I didn't get it. I was just trying to look sexy.

One night, though, a customer inexplicably chose me for a private session. I led him into one of the back rooms as if I knew what I was doing. The light buzzed like a hornet when I flicked it on, revealing a rolling tray of condoms, ammonia, baby wipes and paper towels perched unceremoniously next to the tweed sofa. I felt my gag reflex activate, and it almost made me laugh.

Anyway, he wanted me to act like I was his daughter, and I told him I wasn't no actress. I said things that I thought the girl would say to the man if this were a movie, things like *take your ass to Hollywood if you want that shit*. He was not amused. He grabbed my head with both hands and I pretended to be a robot for the rest of the night, mechanical and programmed in advance.

When he left, I sat in the room and inflated all of the condoms in the box, one by one. It made me dizzy, dizzier, until black holes prickled at the edges of my vision. I kept tearing open packets, inflating, tying, tearing, inflating, tying. I closed my eyes and imbued the task with ritualistic significance. Pretended that I was steeped in the indigo of the Peruvian jungle. Blocked out the noise, the light, everything, anything at all, until I passed out backwards with my face upturned to the fluorescence.

That's not what I got fired for. I was fired a few days later, when one of the kiss-up girls busted me to the owner for swiping from the buffet. That was the end of my career in adult entertainment. Soon afterwards, I met Violet.

4

anginophobia – fear of choking

Since then, I've started to get this feeling sometimes. It's like I'm blowing up a balloon but it's inflating inside out: starting from my mouth, filling my throat, then pressing down through my windpipe and lungs. I can't talk when this happens because I'm all filled up already with latex and trapped air. The only thing I can do is wait for it to deflate.

Other times, it's like there's nothing back there. Where my vocal cords should be, I guess.

So something will happen, and I think I should speak up.

So I open my mouth, and guess what comes out?

Absolutely nothing.

5

'Nudity isn't inherently sexual. That's the thing. Everything doesn't have to be so cheap.'

We like to take whatever food we've scrounged up throughout the day and sit on this concrete slab by the train tracks that runs through downtown. Or, Violet likes to. I like sitting next to her. It's late afternoon; the sun has dropped low in the sky and is casting its rays almost sideways. The low light reflects off the waxen leaves on the trees, setting them aflame.

'Also, it's not like nudity is the sole avenue to arousal anyway. Not that it matters. That place was philistine.'

Violet often declares places philistine, and accuses people of enacting bourgeois charades. How she detests bourgeois charades. No trains have come by in a while and if I'm honest, I am past ready for the rumble to drown her out for a second, just half a second. I already know that our act is deeply misunderstood. Violet has explained exactly how and why so many times that I know these lines by heart now. She pauses to take a bite of egg salad, and I scramble for the chance to change the subject.

'Do you think we could ever jump on one of these?'

'One of what?'

'Sorry. The trains. Do you think we could ever just jump on as one is passing? People used to do that all the time. Could we?'

'Sure. 'Course we could. We could just get on one once it's stopped, too, you know. Whatever we want.'

I've also heard of a train that busted right through the wall of the station and fell to the street below. Everyone in the train survived, but a chunk of the wreckage hit and killed a woman selling newspapers. The railway company's way of making up for that was to pay for her two sons' education, and then to offer them both jobs at the railway in the future.

This was in Paris or the Netherlands or some other place where I will never go, but the screech of the runaway train sliding across the concourse pushes every other thought from my brain. It is always too easy to slip out from the present this way; I see concrete crumbling to fairy dust, bricks tumbling and scattering to disappear in the haze. Cartoon physics, the train emerging and bouncing harmlessly to its graceful suspension over the street. The driver had been running a few minutes late. No one knows if the sons took that offer.

'Speaking of. I've been feeling like we've just about exhausted the circuit here. Just no takers – that's not our fault.' Violet leans thoughtfully back, inspects the dandelion pulp wedged under her fingernails. She is perpetually distracted by the little affronts to her appearance that our lifestyle imposes. Split lips, skinned knees, blackened soles, broken nails. The bulk of her shoplifting, other than food, consists of handfuls of makeup from drugstores. Sticky tubes of concealer, press-on nails rattling in their little plastic cages, lipsticks up her sleeves. She could paint over absolutely anything.

I like it in Cary. The days are long and the people seem dully content, like they could watch the rest of their lives unfold from behind a window and smile about it. I know why they're like this, too. You can see wildflowers from the street wherever you are, even in the ugly parts of town. Where it looks like there should just be trash and piss crystals clotting the corners of twisted-up fences. Instead, wildflowers.

'What do you think? I knew someone from school whose brother joined the circus in Louisiana. I still have his number. Our act would be perfect. I feel like there's a lot more of that going on there, you know? I don't even know what we're still doing here.' She's digging under her nails now and flicking the tiny samosas of pulp toward the tracks. I watch carefully to make sure she doesn't draw blood.

The length of time that we ever stay anywhere depends on how many auditions Violet can get us. I never really understand how she finds us so many. She always knows someone, somehow. And we always run out.

The Carolinas are pretty, but I've already caught myself admiring the shadows from the billboards lengthening in the streets.

Even between the slats of the tracks, wildflowers grow. Maybe they are weeds – I can never tell the difference – but they somehow spring up in clouds as if there aren't hundreds of tons of steel bellowing through to crush them on a daily basis. The sky is just starting to fade to a dusty purple haze, making everything look dreamlike. In the distance, the hook of a crane lines up exactly with the top of an ugly high-rise-in-progress. Their outlines nestle together like puzzle pieces. There is order. Sometimes I think seeing stuff like that is what will crush me.

Eventually, the sun drops behind distant mountains and the evening snaps cold, just the way I like it. I smell Violet all over the air, next to me, fuzzy. Something else she swipes: those plastic bottles of body spray that have glitter inside and shining script across the front, sweet plumeria or island breeze. She sprays it into the thicket of her dark curls, telling me it lasts longer that way, then dabs it behind her ears like it's real perfume from France instead of the artificial stink-water it is.

The lights of a train materialize in the distance.

'Should we try to jump this one?'

I look over to check if she's serious, and she's already tying the shreds of her gown into a knot above her knees. This is another trick she's taught me: if you ever find yourself needing to run while wearing a long dress, you can just gather it all up and tie it into a ball. This way you don't have to worry about holding up your skirt and can pump your arms for speed, keep your hands free. I haven't had to use that trick yet. I don't go around wearing as many old ball gowns as she does.

The train is getting louder now, close enough to hear it rattling on the tracks, and Violet runs toward it like she wants to collide. When I catch up, her eyes are darting to every handhold and platform as they pass. It all seems higher up from here, the potential for dangling limbs and broken bones swelling, but if she really jumps on, I know I will too.

She springs up and grabs hold of a rail, legs dangling horribly for a few seconds before finding purchase on a ledge. She's on the train and the train is hers now, and it's already starting to take her away. I have to jog beside it to keep up. I am very uncomfortably aware, as I jog, that I have nowhere to go if Violet leaves for real, nothing to do with myself. She jumps, I jump. You know the deal.

She looks back and holds one arm out to me. I shake my head and motion for her to hold on with both hands, try to make *are-you-crazy* eyes, even though I can't help but laugh when she does stupid shit with a big smile on her face like that.

Violet could make anything look easy. The beams are too high for me; I can tell that my fingers would slip and my feet would have nowhere to go, and before I have to call up to her that I don't think I can do it, she's leaping off and rolling to a stop in the gravel, the sharp planes of which leave a gash in her knee.

I wince at the blood. Not because it's blood. Because it's hers.

Plugging the wound with my sleeve, I give her *you-are-crazy* eyes, which is just a way of saying she should be more careful without having to say it out loud, because saying it out loud always sets her off.

'We should look for one that goes in the direction of Louisiana, though,' she decides as we start the trek back to our concrete slab. 'We'll get on it when it's stopped in a train yard.'

'Sure. I'll go to the library tomorrow and figure it out.'

'New Orleans. That's where we're going.'

I nod. I don't say anything about the wildflowers, but tomorrow I will make her a bouquet and she will put them in an empty Coke bottle, and when they start to wilt because she forgets to change the water, she will take them out and hang them upside down instead. 'This way they will dry out and last forever,' she will tell me, and this tip I will take to heart, because lasting forever is a shiny, unfamiliar concept that sounds extra-special particularly because it is so out of reach.

6

They will tell you they can see right through you. They will tell you they know you are ashamed of them, warn you not to think they haven't noticed that you never have friends over to your house.

This will take you by surprise, because it does frequently seem as if they don't notice anything.

This will also, strangely, make you long to share all the other things they don't seem to notice. *What about the fridge that I scrubbed to get rid of the smell in the kitchen? What about the muscles that are starting to pop out of the backs of my legs, from the long runs I take myself on to keep myself out of the house, give my heart a reason to be pounding so hard sometimes?*

In this way, you know you still love the addict. You are convinced that anything that comes easily isn't worth doing. Loving her is not easy.

But part of loving her is sifting through the noise for the things she notices about you, because you are convinced there must be a reason that these penetrate the haze. This, then – the loving, the sifting, the paying careful attention – is how you find the pieces of yourself that matter.

7

When I was trying to make it on my own, I didn't get very far. Sure, I made it from California clear to Florida, the furthest place I could think of. The problem was that I didn't have Miami money, just part-time-cashier-at-the-small-town-video-store money, and wasn't smart yet. The club owner wouldn't let me stay with the other girls in the upstairs flat after he fired me, and I found myself shaken awake that night by a cop just a couple hours after making my bed on a train-station bench. He asked how old I was and I said eighteen, without an ounce of guilt. Really, I was fifteen and pushing my shoulder blades together to appear elegant and sophisticated. I hadn't packed any ID – no one had ever asked for it – and the cop said he wasn't taking any chances. He vice-gripped my arm on the way to the car and for some reason I didn't try to snap free and run. I guess this was back when I was still afraid of men in uniforms.

There was nothing to do all day in the shelter other than lie to counselors, read old paperbacks and watch the other kids play cards. Violet slept a couple cots over.

I'd impressed her in a group counseling session, when the counselor had asked about the scars on my stomach that they'd written down in my record when they checked me in. Did someone do that to you or are those self-inflicted? Now, why would you do that to yourself?

Feeling theatrical, I'd shrugged and rolled my eyes. 'Because I'm the only person that I'm allowed to stab.'

Violet's laugh from across the plastic-chair circle was a sharp clap of thunder, a panacea.

8

Later on, once we'd migrated into side-by-side cots and started spending every waking moment together, Violet would ask why it took so long for me to leave home.

I was nine when my mother did the worst thing she'd ever asked me to keep between us, and Violet was the first person I'd told. I was already fifteen by then.

'I didn't really think it was an option,' I explained. 'And I still loved her.'

It was the easiest way to answer without having to get into the other reason that I lived with my mother for as long as I did, especially after the worst thing – a reason that was not quite as clean as love.

It was something else entirely: a hyperspecific set of needs and the way I'd evolved into an animal equipped to meet them exactly; a connection infinitely more complicated than lock and key, something that was ours alone.

This element of our relationship was not love, although I loved her too. Not love but compulsion. Not love but the function of two organisms which each cannot exist without the other, so their cohabitation is not a choice but a necessity for survival.

It felt less like love than it did a calling. She needed that which only I could give. As in, I was born to do this. I was born and raised.

That truly is how it felt back then. I didn't think *symbiosis* but also didn't think *parasite*, obliterated that word from my mind when she sat with me at the kitchen table and held her head in one hand, eyes buried in her palm, and reached for me with the other. Her touch was always cool and I knew in a moment she would lift her forehead and support her head from the side instead, so that she would be facing my way with spent eyes that fixed on mine, bloodshot with tears or dull with oversleep, but either way tired, always tired, hungry and needing everything from me.

To be able to provide the eye contact she needed, I often tried to imagine what was beyond those eyes. Behind the eye stems, in the fluid lubricating the sockets, then within the crunchy calcium of the skull. I descended her vertebrae like a staircase. I traveled through my mother bone by bone, hollowing out the marrow, placing sleeping families within each freshly empty enclave. This was why she had to remain so still so often, I reasoned – she couldn't disturb them. But she also couldn't tell me all about them, because she feared I would call her crazy or a liar or both. With no space for tiny cribs, I imagined the babies nestled firmly between their parents, rice-sized fingers curling over a father's bean-sized thumb. I imagined how warm they must be in there. I longed for our secrets to be as innocent as this.

9

A purple flyer showed up on the bulletin board in the shelter that Violet and I checked daily. 'You always have to be on the lookout for opportunities,' she'd told me by way of explanation. 'You never know what's out there unless you go looking for it.'

According to the bulletin board, what was out there were meal programs, Christian youth groups, entry-level jobs sealing medical equipment into sterile plastic bags at warehouses, and random lost dogs, which I don't know how anyone expected us to find. The day of the purple flyer, it was revealed that what else was out there was a seminar to unlock our true potential.

We asked Victor at the front desk what he thought that meant.

'It's like a professional development program,' he said. 'You kids don't need that – I don't know why they bothered posting it up here. But I mean, if you don't have anything better to do...'

We didn't.

I'd never had a reason to be inside a hotel's conference room before, and the chunky white perimeters made it feel like we had entered the belly of a birthday cake. We sat in chairs snuggled too close to each other. The room was not well populated and the rows of paper cups to fill with water were untouched. When they asked us to partner with someone we didn't know, Violet and I turned to each other and introduced ourselves like we were strangers.

'Hi, I'm Buttercup.'

'Nice to meet you. I'm Swath.'

We hid our stupid smiles as they gave further instructions. 'Think about what brought you here,' the man holding the microphone encouraged us. We could hear his voice perfectly well without the microphone. 'Think about what brought you here, and what you would like to take from your time here. Now, with your partners. Share what your pivotal moment was, your moment that made you realize you were not operating at your full potential. That you needed help.'

I turned to Violet and waited for her answer. She told me to go first, so I thought as quickly as I could of everything that had brought me here.

'I was fired from my illegal job as an underage stripper,' is what I came up with, a sentence that was so transparent in its intent to impress her that I wanted to take it back.

'Nice.' Violet approved. 'I was some dude's sugar baby, which meant essentially exchanging my dignity for money and a place to live.'

My eyebrows stitched into a knot against my will. Why hadn't I known that? She knew all about my trials and failures as a stripper. Why had it taken attending this trashy seminar for Violet to share this with me? An unfamiliar sting of betrayal was suddenly coiling over my head.

'Is that why you left? To preserve your dignity?' is what I asked instead.

'I'm just kidding. I wasn't his sugar baby. I was just, like, his live-in companion.'

'So...?'

'He was old. It all went to shit.'

It felt like more than was appropriate or possible to get into in two chairs with coffee-stained upholstery, within earshot of strangers, so I dropped it. The microphone man spoke up just then anyway, directing our attention to the whiteboard at the front of the room where he'd drawn a circle. He asked us what it was, and corrected the person who said *circle* by launching into an explanation of how what we realize is outside of our knowledge is still not everything that there is to know. He kept drawing circles as he spoke, each one larger and swallowing the previous circle inside of it.

He talked for a very long time. To be honest, I don't remember a lot of what he said, because the way he was talking matched his drawing with its never-ending circles. And the circles made it very easy and comfortable to tune him out: ripples gliding over my head, meaning nothing.

I do remember spying on Violet for the last exercise, for which the man handed out clipboards with blank sheets of paper attached to them and passed around a bucket of pens. The man encouraged us to abandon all our preconceived notions about what was possible. 'If you could do anything. If nothing was holding you back. If all of this was so – what would your dream be?'

I stared at my blank paper when he told us to put our heads down and write it out. My mind raced, but the paper remained blank. My eyes couldn't help but creep over to Violet's paper beside me.

She had chosen a thick green marker. Her handwriting was huge and loopy.

I dream of ascension out of this void and into the next, where we're each suspended separately, close enough to see but not to touch. Finally making sense, and the astronauts they send do not find us, and the history books they print do not recall us, until we fade into a gradual stillness, a shrinking mote on an ever-expanding timeline, till collapse do us part, amen.

She wrote all of that in like three seconds, hand moving purposefully across the page.

My dreams sounded nothing like that. I thought about my life and everything I'd ever wanted, and it all boiled down to stubby little sentences that paled in comparison to Violet's vision: *I dream of being safe. I want to feel uncomplicated. By that I mean: I dream of a world that makes sense.*

None of it was worth writing down.

I watched Violet's hand draw outer space swirling all around her dream. Later, she gave her dream to me, and I taped it to the wall between our beds. It hung there at a height where I could kneel before it to read and reread and will it to come true before Violet came in for the night with two mugs of ginger-lemon tea for us.

I looked at her hand on one side of the cup and my hand on the other for a second as she gave it to me. And that second was all I had ever dreamed of, I realized on my knees. And that was my life. So I guess that was my dream. I probably slept like a baby.

10

When we were getting ready to leave the seminar, I knew I wouldn't be able to focus on anything until I got some answers. I confronted Violet as soon as we left, dodging the flyer-wielding door attendants who wanted us to sign up for a six-week course. 'You were... what, a live-in companion for some dude? What does that mean? Why didn't you ever tell me about it?'

She shrugged, walking just quickly enough that I had to half-jog to keep up. 'You never asked.'

'Were you really a sugar baby?' Sometimes I needed to double-check when Violet said she was joking.

'What does sugar baby even mean?'

'Come on. What you said at the thing. Just tell me.'

'I know. Well, I don't know what to call it. I wasn't, like, prowling for a man to take care of me, obviously. Basically, when I was working at the donut shop, he was a regular who was super into the idea of supporting me as an artist and student, because he believed I was a high-school student even when I was there at eleven on a weekday, but that just goes to show what level he was operating at. Anyway, he was trying to teach me chess, because he was a chess guy. He would get just coffee, not even any donuts, and sit at a booth with his practice board. We'd get interrupted by customers coming in, obviously, so he invites me over to his house, and I'm not an idiot, so I go but take my gun with me. He was

33

cool about it, but he made it clear that he'd figured out I was, you know.' She paused. 'He said I could live in his house for free. So I did. And I could tell he got something out of my being around that was, like... I knew it wasn't going to last and it would all come to some kind of breaking point, but for right then it was a roof over my head, you know? So, yeah. I don't know what to call it.'

'You don't have to call it anything,' I reminded her. Violet liked to categorize. Sometimes she categorized to a fault.

I knew she had worked at a donut shop in Miami. She'd told me the story of her boss instructing her not to ring up at least fifty dollars' worth of orders every day, and to set aside the cash in a tray above the cash register instead. He came in at the end of every shift to retrieve it. She thought that was a clever trick, so she started setting some aside for herself, too, and when the owner noticed the numbers were off for the quantity of donuts made, her boss put it together that she'd nicked his trick, and when he threatened to tell the owner, she made photocopies of the Bible pages that talk about original sin to slip into the bag with the cash deposit, and she never heard another word about it after that.

I'm saying I knew that story, where she had won. But I didn't know about this customer, and I wondered what that meant about how it ended.

'Did he teach you chess?'

'He tried. I couldn't tell you anything about it now.'

'And he scorned you?'

She laughs at me. 'What do you mean, scorned?'

'Why aren't you still living there?'

'Well, it had nothing to do with scorn. He was old, like my grandparents' age probably, and it was, like, kind of a lot of responsibility to be the only other person in a house with someone that old and who was... I don't know, unable to accept that they were old and couldn't just do whatever they wanted all the time anymore. He had stairs in his house and every time he would go up and down them I had to brace myself for what to do if he fell, you know?'

'Did he ever fall?'

'No. But he could've. And I still had to be ready for it even if he never did. The tension was always there.'

I knew I'd met my mother's parents when I was really young, but I barely remembered them. They lived in New York. The country-side part with cows behind long white fences. At least, that's how I imagined it. All I knew for sure was that I'd never worried they were going to fall down any stairs.

'That didn't end up being the problem, though. He started forgetting things all the time. Like, he'd forget that he'd already gone to the donut shop that day – he'd go again, maybe thinking it was the next day or something. I mean, in the end he kept mistaking me for his granddaughter. He called me Jo. So then I knew he had family somewhere, at least, and tried to make him give me anyone's phone number, because I didn't know what I was supposed to do. I literally had to strip-search his house for a crusty address book and just called random numbers in it. Finally, I got ahold of his daughter, so she flew in and was honestly acting annoyed that she had to deal with this, which pissed me off. Like, where was she while her dad was losing his grip on reality? Selling real estate in Texas, apparently. And she was grilling me about what I was doing in his house, and he was confused, still thinking I was her daughter, and then remembering I was me, so he kept giving different stories, and she basically told me to get out or she'd call the cops.'

'Oh, shit. Did she?'

'I don't think so. I just left, didn't want to risk it. She, like, supervised me packing and went through all my shit to make sure I didn't have a key, and then she just drove him to the hospital.'

'What happened to him?'

Violet shrugged. 'I mean, they probably put him in a hospice or whatever.'

I thought about the man in the hospice, alone, and Violet on the street in front of his empty house, also alone. I thought about the space that the daughter had put in between them.

'And now he's probably dead,' Violet finished, and the way she said it made it clear: that was that.

I I

Our train is thrumming toward Atlanta and Violet's showing me a solo piece she's been working on, after making me confirm four separate times that I wouldn't be upset that she'd had an idea for a performance that only needed one person.

It was easy to sneak onto the train when it was stopped. We'd climbed into the divot in the roof at 4am, in time for the 5am departure, and if anyone in the train yard saw us, they didn't care enough to do anything. The buzz of the train seems to power Violet's movements now.

She practices everywhere, all the time: at bus stops in a void of self-consciousness, in one of our many rooms, quietly in the dark so as not to wake me. As if I'm not staying awake on purpose to catch what I can from whatever light leaks through the window. Hear her footfalls at least, her breaths.

Sometimes when she performs, even in practice, I feel like I can see right into her. Right through the skin and guts and everything. Knowing that everything she is doing holds some great Violet-decided meaning makes her strange language translate somehow; I can see it, the little pearl, carved from somewhere deep within Violet, heavy and rich from having been carried inside her for so many years. She gets this longing in her face – it softens her so that you can almost imagine what she looked like as a baby girl.

The truth is, I wish I could have seen Violet when she was a baby girl. I wish I could have crawled into her house and stolen her from her crib, and led her quietly away into the woods to nestle into a deer bed and wait for our mother deer to come. She's proud of being born in Jersey, can recall the tiniest details of Piscataway; wherever we are reminds her of it in some small way. When we ran into a guy doing stick-and-poke tattoos for free, she even got an 848 on her ankle, her hometown area code. They'd turned to me next, all drunk and wild-eyed, *what do you want, Smidge, what do you want*, and I got overwhelmed and ended up telling Violet to decide for me, and she took my hand and told me with sudden focus and the utmost solemnity that if I couldn't decide for myself, I shouldn't get anything at all, so my skin is still just skin without ink in it.

The other truth is that Violet's fondness for her hometown is something I understand and don't at the same time. She had two parents and one dog, but while staring down a scrappy butter-yellow terrier tied to the bars of a storefront across the street from us back in Miami, she told me this story where she was trying to help her mother wash the dog, and the dog freaked out and bit her mother on the right hand, so she slapped Violet with the left and accused her of agitating the dog. Later her mother had come to her room all soft and said she would give Violet a chance to apologize, and when she didn't, her mother slapped her again and said she wasn't sorry either. She told me her father called her a faggot even when she brought home girlfriends, and how those were the only times she could remember him looking her in the eye. She spoke about these things the same way she spoke about her years at the high school for the arts they'd paid to send her to in Brooklyn. Violet can make anything look easy.

She lifts her palms to the air, thumbs hooked and the rest of the fingers spread wide. The eagle of her hands crosses the length of her body and becomes an egg in her now-cupped palms, which she extends toward the sun like an offering. Her face sweats in the direct light, and the squint of her eyes, which I'm not sure is intentional, makes her appear uncertain about whether her gift will be received. Whether it will be taken or ignored, whether it will become just another thing she will be made to carry alongside all the other pearls ripening in her gut.

Art school taught her that she could choose whatever she wanted, which for Violet meant dropping out of art school. She described the beautiful chaos that she'd imagined New York City to be: freaks in the streets, outlaw artists like her running the place. Instead, she found ugliness and desperation, and it drove her right out, away from trouble, down the coast. I secretly thought she must have been happy about this, because it meant that she was special, after all.

There is always this barely perceptible friction with her, between how she longs to be seen and heard and how she feels when someone actually starts listening. Sometimes I worry she only keeps me around because she knows I will never steal her spotlight. Because why has she chosen me when I am me and she is she?

But I don't need to worry, because the last and final truth is that even if I don't understand her fully, the parts that I do, I understand deeply and attentively, and in the end that is all Violet has ever wanted. And I know exactly how that feels.

The egg dissolves from her hands and she clasps them in front of her chest in an exaggerated display of humility before dropping to her knees, then to all fours, panting and licking the God-knows-what-has-touched-it-and-when-and-where surface of the train car. And when she's right at my feet and turns her eyes up to meet mine, she doesn't look like no baby anymore.

12

April in Louisiana is sticky unlike anything I've ever felt before. Long, slow days that stick to your back and dribble down your spine. From my official swan-boat lifeguard post, I can plunk down and dip my feet in the water whenever I want. My swan-boat boss calls me Chelsea on the rare occasions that we cross paths, because that's what I put down on my application. Chelsea had worked in an ice-cream shop before this. She lived on Deerfield Drive and was lifeguard-certified, high-school-educated and twenty-two years old.

We have an audition tonight. Apparently, Violet has contacts in Louisiana too. As Chelsea, I am responsible for taking people's money and putting them into the swan boats, then locking the boats up at night. Then I am free to be Smidge again, still the living doll. I don't know much about this audition other than it's supposed to be the real circus this time, and it pays in cash. I hope I'll have time to visit Dusty in between work and then.

Dusty is the living statue who hangs out on the main wharf, coated in silver paint, entertaining tourists and freaking out the occasional child. Back closer to when we first arrived in town, they offered me a flyer for something when I was walking past on my way to the smaller swan-boat dock, but didn't let go when I tried to take it mid-stride.

'I'm Dusty,' they introduced themselves. 'My pronouns are they/them. I'm in town with Holy Toledo, the greatest show on Earth, only here in New Orleans for the next couple weeks. Will I see you there?'

The flyer said something about inheriting the wisdom of ancient times, and I dropped it like a hot potato. No thanks. I had current times to worry about.

My next shift, they said they had a present for me. It was a seashell. 'Look inside.' Their phone number was painted in red lacquer. 'I had to use nail polish because the ink from the pen just rubbed right off. I had to buy the nail polish special, because I don't wear it, and guess what? I learned that I like having red fingernails after all.' They flashed the backs of their hands in front of my face. 'So I have you to thank for that, kid.'

I didn't call them, or whatever it was they wanted me to do, and they tracked me down like clockwork the next time I was heading down to the dock.

'Swan girl,' they called, 'I just broke my illusion by calling you. I just lost a dollar, probably. A hundred cents. I deserve to learn your name.'

That night they found me after my shift was over and all the swans were chained in place. They brought me a big pink cloud of cotton candy that I tore into pieces and pressed into melted sugar crystals between my fingers while we walked down to the shore. When I licked them clean, the saltwater on my skin dissolved with the sugar on my tongue; it tasted like something you could get addicted to.

'So, what's the point? Or, you know, what does it mean?' Dusty asked.

I'd just finished describing our act to them in nervous detail, which ended up being mostly describing Violet in detail, and then explaining everything that she said and all the ways that she was.

'Well, it's... performance art.' I scraped the folds of my brain for a better answer, something Violet would say. 'It's about being bound.'

Dusty nodded solemnly, apparently satisfied with this explanation. All the paint had cracked and settled into the creases of their skin, imperfections visible even under low moonlight.

'That's cool. I think you guys would be a great addition to the show – you're exactly what we've been looking for. Seriously. You've got this way about you, too.'

I felt my face heat up against my will and shifted my eyes to behind their head, where a seagull was eating vomit off the wharf.

'What do you mean?' I asked, and immediately hated myself for asking.

'Well, you're an enigma, aren't you?'

I didn't know what *enigma* meant, but the way they'd chosen that word so deliberately made it sound like something that was a problem and a solution at the same time. I liked it instantly. Liked them, against my better judgment, chipped red fingernails suddenly looking kind of fun.

'What's the show?'

'I thought you'd never ask.'

I recognized the flyer they pulled out as the same one they'd tried to give me the first time we crossed paths, covered in faux-glowing text. *Holy Toledo*, it read, *the first and last and always of art, life and light.* It was crammed with words. *Gravity-defying acrobatics. Daredevils. Expanding your mind to access the secrets of everyday life hidden in plain sight. Clowns.*

I didn't even know which question to ask first.

'What about the living statue thing? What does that mean?'

'I guess it's performance art too, but I don't know if I've ever thought about it that way. It's more like... Have you ever noticed how people avoid eye contact with you if you look a little different, but they still look? They'll look at you when they think you aren't looking, and look away as soon as you look back. Have you noticed that?'

'Yeah. Of course.'

'Right. Well, I've always looked a little different. I didn't get diagnosed with Marfan syndrome until I was seventeen, but I've been taller and skinnier than the kids around me for as far back as I can remember, stretched out to the point that I could feel people trying *not* to look at me too long. So there's this weird thing where as soon as you cover yourself in silver paint and stand perfectly still, you've given those people license to just go ahead and look. They'll look right into my eyes. They take pictures. And all these people still know I'm human, not statue, right? They finally look me right in the eyes, knowing full well I'm human and that we're just playing a game of pretend together. They leave as soon as I break it and lunge at them for a crowd-pleasing jump scare. It's convenient that it works that way, that they leave as soon as the statue gives up the jig.'

I considered this the same way I considered the people who came down to rent a swan boat to themselves. I'd had one earlier that day, an older man who was quiet and cold while I took his money and handed him his life jacket, but waved at me over his shoulder as he paddled away alone. I decided Dusty knew something about life that I didn't.

'Are you only here for the summer?' they asked.

'I don't know. It depends how many auditions we get, I guess, and whether we land anything.'

'Right. Well, show that to Violet. You'd have to audition, but I can pretty much guarantee you'd be in.'

I'd already folded up the flyer and shoved it into my shoe. I would show it to Violet, but I already knew there was no way it would come that easily. I wasn't ready to explain all of that to Dusty yet, though.

'What about you?'

'I don't know either. They keep saying we're going to take off soon and be a traveling circus, but at this point I think I live here.'

'I thought you said the show was only in town for the next couple weeks.'

They laughed. 'You got me. That was a trick to make you come see it. No, we've been stuck here for a long time. I've gotten to know New Orleans real well.'

'Oh. Well. You're lucky you're not a real statue, at least.'

'You're right, kid. I forgot to be thankful for that this whole time.'

We stared out at the flat black water then, in perfect silence, and the only thing I could think of that it reminded me of was the video store I used to work at after school and the security guard who would tap on the glass to invite me to smoke breaks on the concrete wall over the dumpsters facing the parking lot. I didn't want to talk to the security guard, but this wasn't unusual because I never wanted to talk to anyone. I'd go out there and listen to his stories about girls who wanted him bad when he wore a cap and how much chiller it was to be a security guard than a bus driver, so I ended up not having to talk much after all, and I respected him because he never asked how old I was, and never once touched me. There was a Fastsigns store connected to a Flooring America store beyond the parking lot, and after that some low-income housing bunched around the train station, and after that the suburbs, and none of it was going anywhere and neither was I. The security guard smoked a cigarette while I held a candy cigarette between my lips and did not bite down because I wanted it to last, and I thought: *there is the world*; thought: *here is my life*.

13

Violet and I are staying in something that she calls an *artists' community* and I call the attic of some lady's house. We are deep, deep in the suburbs and far from the water, but the rent is nominal and the walls are all painted with overlapping murals from decades of other artists who stayed before us. The lady had told us, when we first got to town and found her ad on the bulletin board of the natural foods co-op, that she was just so passionate about housing artists of all disciplines. 'Performance art? Amazing!' she'd declared. 'Show me what you got.' And after we'd done our act she just clapped her hands and did not ask what it meant.

One of the other rooms is occupied by a folk musician who we often see swaying around the kitchen. Her neighbor is a single father whose kid is obsessed with her. I tried to get Violet in on my theory that the folk musician and father would fall in love eventually. She was not on board, and instead delivered a speech about the modern conception of love being almost purely circumstantial. 'That's the point,' I said. 'It's a charade,' she said. 'Don't fall for it.'

We have another audition this afternoon, then the folk musician has invited us to join her this evening at something she called a psychedelic meditation. 'Absolutely,' Violet had said while I was opening my mouth to ask what the hell that was supposed to be.

Violet pulls the ropes around and around her elbow into a neatly coiled snake. She got the afternoon off from her job across town in the animal control department. Her job title is Roadkill Cleanup Specialist, which according to her is a whole lot of sitting around interspersed with a few long drives and horrifying scenes out on the edges of town.

'You want to know something, Smidge?'

'Sure.'

'Back when I was auditioning on my own, I carried a gun with me to every single one. Because you never know. And you know how much I hate guns.'

I do know. I know her father hung one over the headboard of her parents' bed, too, as if it were something beautiful.

'They said they'd have to confiscate it before they could let me stay in the shelter. So I pretended to get rid of it. But I just buried it at the beach. I carved a V into the tree it was under, like a huge one. And then I thought I'd go dig it up when I needed it again. But then I met you, and guess what?'

'What?'

'I didn't think I'd need it again.'

'That was stupid,' I tell her unconvincingly. I can already feel a blush taking over my face, so I slam it into the quilt.

'Yeah. Do you think that makes me soft?'

'Yes,' I say into the quilt.

'Because I never wanted to have a gun in the first place, you know. I've had a gun pulled on me. That's some shit I'd never want another person to feel.'

I lift my head, the warmth gone from my face. 'What? When?'

'Like right before I went to the shelter. It was someone who… They thought I was someone else.'

I can feel myself staring at her like a five-year-old. 'Someone else?'

'Like, a boy,' she clarifies.

'Oh.' It feels like something I should have known. She didn't make eye contact with me when she said it and I feel inadequate simply in being unable to have prevented that from happening, inadequate in not knowing what I could do to fix it now.

'You won't say anything about this to anyone else.'

'Of course not.'

'Good.' She zips up the duffel, pushes herself to her feet. From where I sit on the floor, the light from our small window casts a glow through her legs. 'Because rats with loose lips get cut.'

We saw that scrawled on an underpass once and have never gotten it out of our heads. Now it's what we use in place of a pinky promise.

The producers – or whoever they are – at the audition receive us politely. The woman who waves us back out the door says they will call us, without an ounce of sincerity in her high, clear voice.

Rope burn again.

Sometimes – and only sometimes – I wish Violet would ask before she touched me, so that I could say no.

14

Everyone already knows about sea turtles and how the babies have to run like hell seconds after they're born to make it to the sea alive.

Evolution gives turtle babies an egg tooth and a brain that knows they have to jam that sucker into the smooth, white, curved room in which they are born. Their brains can sense that there's something beautiful on the other side, so they pound away at their shells, which they somehow know are not expensive, even though they look like they could be. They dig their newborn bodies out of the earth, slowly, painstakingly, and when they break the surface and blink the sand from their eyes, the first thing they see is the ocean.

Or the sky.

Both beautiful.

Basically, as soon as they see something beautiful. That's when they know to run like hell.

And if it's nighttime, it's the same. Into pitch darkness they gain consciousness; into partial darkness they run for their lives. They orient themselves to the brightest glitter they can find in the dark, which is the glass of black waves reflecting the moon at its seams, and they know what they need to do.

So they run, all of them bubbling up at once and beating the ground with their flippers to get themselves propelled down the slope of sand that stretches between their birthplace and the sea.

They're running like hell and barely getting anywhere. Basically crawling. I mean, they're babies. But can you imagine working that hard to move that slow? And having that be the best you could do?

The baby turtles run, and the seabirds swoop from the skies to scoop them up. The wild dogs emerge from the mangroves to crunch them down. Some of them make it to the water.

I don't remember being born. But I know I didn't have to run away from anything immediately. I waited fifteen years for that.

One of my teeth is sharp enough to bust myself out of an egg-shell, though, should I ever find myself within one.

It's because I won a third-grade spelling bee at school and as a reward my mother took me to the library. I picked out more books than I could hold, even ones from the reference aisles about UFOs, which I couldn't possibly comprehend. Just knew that UFOs meant aliens and aliens meant great possibility outside of the mediocre cluster around which I seemed to be orbiting.

My mother kneeled on the ground and followed me down the aisles on her knees so I could stack more books on top. Then I browsed the CDs, not because I cared about music or knew what any of it was, but because the clacking sound of the plastic cases as I flicked them back made me feel like my hands were the hands of a sensible grown-up who knew exactly what she wanted and just how to get there. I selected the one that spoke to me the most to place upon my book tower, the oozing maraschino cherry on top of my afternoon's worth of labor.

It was Jane's Addiction. *Ritual de lo Habitual.*

My mother told the librarian how smart I was as we were checking out. 'You watch,' she said when the librarian smiled tamely, patted the book pile and agreed that it seemed like that was the case. 'You watch, she's going places,' she insisted, harder than she needed to. 'I bet,' said the librarian underwhelmingly, and my mother snatched the receipt from her hand. It took her a long time to get the books stacked up in her arms again. In hindsight, I don't think she got to have the snappy exit she was going for.

I put my new CD into the slot in the car and immediately hated the sound that came out. My mother laughed and rolled down the windows and turned the dial so the ugly music stumbled out of the car and into the street, making people turn their heads and glare at us at every single stoplight.

The guitars sounded like nails scratching through acid, jagged and horrible, building to a crescendo with no catharsis as we approached a stop sign too quickly. I saw the man on the bike from what seemed like still far away and didn't scream STOP, even though the word was ringing fire-engine-spinning-siren-stop-sign-red-hot-emergency red inside my head. My voice wouldn't have been loud enough over that music, anyway, I told myself later, no matter how violently I'd screamed. My voice could never get as loud as other people's. It always felt like there was something missing from the back of my throat.

So I did not scream, but my mother did as her foot crushed the brake pedal to the floor. Her hands yanked the wheel sideways, but that just made us lurch into a forward-moving arc. We were too late. The bicycle looked like it was levitating in the second that I saw it suspended before my face made contact with the dashboard.

The car kept skidding forward until the front corner crumpled against a telephone pole, something I didn't register as having happened until after we'd left the scene. All I sensed in the moment was my mother's silence once the car was still.

I registered motion a few seconds later, but couldn't see anything with the airbag pushed into my body, enveloping me. Smooth white walls all around and pressed up in my face.

She was driving away.

Like she'd informed the librarian, I was smart, even if I knew it was only a particular kind of smart. So even though no one had ever told me, my brain could sense that we were supposed to stay there and make sure the man was okay. But we were driving away.

Blood mixed with saliva inside of my mouth, and was seawater foamy when the airbag deflated and I spat high tide into my hand. I fished a tiny shard of tooth out of there and laid it on the slope of flesh that connected my thumb to my palm. A seashell for my miniature beach.

The first moments of a turtle baby's life are pitch black in an underground egg. The turtle baby has one tooth and four pathetic flippers to dig itself out and drag itself to safety, in a wide-open space with no defense from the many predators drooling over the meat tucked inside its shell.

Even after all that, they return to where they came from when it's time to lay their own eggs. They find the section of beach where they were born, marked by nothing but their memory.

The first thing my mother asked me when she started talking again was if I was okay. I looked at the beach precariously cradled in my hand and said yes. I had a feeling there would be no hospital or anything if I said that I wasn't, and that feeling was true, because the second thing she asked was for me to keep this a secret between us.

Secrets were supposed to be delicious, from what I knew of them by then. They were supposed to be precious, invisible treasure that only existed inside the minds of the most special people, and they were absolutely fraught with meaning. Nothing like the cold, terrifying experience that was already flashing back at me in violent freeze-frames. I did not want it, but I accepted it gracefully, as gracefully as one accepts something as important as a secret, and sealed it by swallowing that whole ocean right back down my throat, seashell and all.

*

The next day, my mother said she was playing hooky from work and that I wasn't going to go to school; that we were going to have a fun day off together.

I said I'd rather just go to school.

'Don't be an ungrateful bitch,' she said. 'Just kidding,' she said. Then she went out onto the front porch to smoke.

The dark coolness of the movie theater made me nervous, and I couldn't focus on the movie. It was animated. It was about robots. When it was over, we went to sit at the dog park, but I thought we weren't allowed to go inside the gate without a dog and was certain my mother was lying to me when she said it was, indeed, allowed. So we stood just outside of the dog park and peered through the green gate, shaped to look like extra-tall blades of grass. There were two dogs in there. I watched them intently. I waited for either of them to do something for me to watch already.

The bruise was still deep purple the next day, and the next. My mother kept calling the school and telling them I still wasn't feeling well. 'Yeah. It was a pretty bad fall,' she said on one of these calls before noticing me in the door. 'Poor thing,' she said into the phone, her face pinched and misshapen like someone had run a needle and thread all through it and pulled.

I didn't think about running away back then. There was no destination in sight, even if I could crawl. And the survival rate of baby turtles is not encouraging. It's something like one in a thousand.

So with no other frame of reference, I had a one in a thousand chance of surviving if I tried to pull something like that.

If nothing else, I was newly armed with a razor-sharp egg tooth.

If nothing else, I was alive, which meant that I would grow, which meant that I would, eventually, flee.

I just didn't know any of that yet, wandering through the Dollar Tree with my mother on our second day of hooky, feeling slimy when she told me I could pick out anything I wanted. She had already given me a dirty, sorry excuse for a secret; I didn't want any of those toys, and the yellowed beams of fluorescent light-bulbs above our heads reminded me of the sunlight blurring the suspended spokes of the bicycle wheel. So I closed my eyes, tried to tell her we needed to leave, but I couldn't even get my mouth open; the back of my throat had gone missing again, felt cold, felt tight, helped me realize the gravity of the wrong we had done.

We left the Dollar Tree empty-handed when I wouldn't open my eyes or tell my mother what was wrong with me. It was going to get dark soon, so she drove us up into the hills to a different park to watch the crappy sunset.

We ate supermarket cake on the swing set. I wanted to choke on it.

15

amaxophobia – fear of riding in a car

I got my driver's learning permit as soon as I could. After my shifts at the video store, I would drive out to the water park to sit in the parking lot and watch the flags at the top of the highest slide slap each other above the fence.

It would get late and I would go home, or I would just keep driving north, most of the time not knowing what the plan was until I turned back onto the street. I crossed the state line more than once. The first time I saw the *Welcome to Oregon* sign appear in front of me, I remembered that other places were not nebulous concepts for me to dream about all day and night. Other places were distinctively different from the various fantasies I sustained myself on as I stayed in the one place I knew. They had signs marking them; they had roads leading to them; they were real, and they were waiting for me.

Most of the time when I'm in the passenger seat, though, I have to close my eyes.

16

The folk musician gave us bus directions to the meditation. Violet is silent the whole way.

When we arrive, the folk musician is flirting with a man coiled over her like a willow tree, gnarled curls spilling. Over the chatter of the bar I hear him explaining the original meaning of the swastika. *Not a lot of people know this, but it actually doesn't have to do with the Nazis at all. It's a symbol of well-being in Sanskrit.* He rolls up a sleeve and the folk musician's fingers trail curiously over the tattoo embedded in his pale forearm.

Long tendrils of plants curl down from hanging pots, the benefits of kava are written in chalk on the wall, and everyone is pressed up against the bar and the windows and each other. Violet and I settle into the rug that's been rolled out in front of the stage. A woman leans back almost into my lap, beaming up at me. A pipe and lighter balance precariously on her pregnant belly.

'Hello.'

She presses the pipe into my hand, but I don't want any. I try to balance it on her forehead, but she keeps laughing.

'Stay still, it's gonna spill everywhere.'

She slaps a hand over her mouth and speaks through the hand. 'Is it your first time here?'

I think she must be really high, but I will realize later on that maybe this is just what someone overflowing with love and absolutely free from secrets is like. She points to which tea we should order off of the chalkboard, which I get up and order as both a thank you for her sunshine energy and a reason to keep her talking to us. The tea tastes like hot dirt but is served from a carved cast-iron pot that feels heavy and important in my hands. We learn that her name is Tina, and that she comes every week. She tells us that women don't need God because divinity is already inside of us.

I can't keep eye contact with her, and place my hands in different arrangements on the teapot, trying to figure out which way makes them look like they belong there. Press my fingertips into the carved grooves, willing them to burn hotter and leave an imprint on my skin. She's talking about how we should never be afraid to walk alone at night because nature fears us; she doesn't want to say it but, you know, men, men fear *us* because our wombs are embedded deep in a protective cushion of vital organs and shrouded in mystery beyond what science can explain, decidedly out of their reach. We carry the power of creation around with us every day. We take it to the grocery store.

Violet stands up while Tina's still explaining all of this to us. 'I'm going to have a smoke.'

Tina rocks back to turn her face up to Violet. 'It's going to start any minute now.'

'I think I'll be fine.'

Tina keeps talking while Violet punches into the throng of people behind us and two gauzy figures pad barefoot onstage. One of them sits cross-legged on an amp and balances a synthesizer in her lap.

'If we could have all cell phones off, please. We're going to get started.'

I don't know where Violet went and can't see her through the wall of bodies closing in toward the stage. I don't know if I should try to go get her. They're telling us to get comfortable and people are laying their heads on each other's stomachs.

The music starts low and hollow, some sort of pipe I can't identify. It makes me think of mountain cows, the kind with thick cables of hair running all down their bodies and over their eyes. 'Let your mind go anywhere,' someone on stage quietly reminds us. 'Allow your subconscious to explore. But focus. Focus on the music.' The music sounds like tubes, is what I think after focusing on it. The music sounds like tubes that run underground and pick up the echoes of everyone's feet and carry them to the bottom of the ocean, where they distort into these hollow growls that terrorize the innocent fish.

I want to see what Tina's doing but feel like I shouldn't open my eyes. Like it would be sacrilegious, not that this is religious, it's… what? Probably something Violet would class as a bourgeois charade. Or would fall right into and devour and love to her white-hot core. Maybe it's for the best that she left.

Staccato notes rain over my head and make me shiver; I can't help but recall the night we left the shelter, feeling just as electric. Violet had been talking about it for weeks and I just kept looking at the heavy red blanket bunched up on my bed and the hot mug of ginger-lemon tea in my hands, heard myself trying to convince her, again, that we should wait until the time was right.

Violet had been there a lot longer than I had, by a couple months at least. 'Look, Smidge, I get it. What we have here is tough to let go of, but guess what? This isn't real life. This is an in-between. And with things like this, waiting until the time is right just means waiting forever.'

'Not forever. They'll kick us out when we're eighteen.'

'Fine, yeah. How long is that for you, anyway? How come I don't know how old you are?'

'I'm fifteen.'

'Me too. Anyway, that's three years of real life that I don't want to lose.'

We didn't have the bound act at that time, but Violet had made me her voice for a spoken-word piece that she was constructing from everyone's diary entries and group counseling confessions. I spoke the stolen words with minimal inflection, at her command, while she interpreted wildly with her body. She thought we were on to something. I figured it was high art, way above my head. Either way, she was fixed on leaving and wouldn't go without me coming with, something that ignited a little ember in me.

She'd come up to me after the counseling session where I talked about stabbing myself, and asked if I'd ever shanked anyone. I said yes, even though I didn't know what shanking meant, so when she asked what happened I had to admit that I didn't know what she was talking about, and she laughed again the same way, bang bang thunderclap. *I like you*, she said. *You have something to you, you know?* I still didn't know but shrugged like I did. Figured I would learn by being close to her.

I saw right away that Violet was smart. She taught me about how performance was woven into our everyday lives, and how her craft was only a mirror held up to what she already saw all around her, exaggerated so other people could see it like she did. For example, she taught me how everyone puts different names to the same faith. How in order to be worshipped, something just had to be invisible and untouchable, and the worshippers did the rest of the work. The performance was the work.

She taught me that girls are not as helpless as men want us to be. That being a girl playing the part of 'girl' next to a man who got to play the part of 'man' was a performance too, that the world conditions us to participate to the point that it just feels natural. 'Which it isn't,' she told me. 'Think about how it really makes you feel, and you'll start to notice it everywhere. And once you do, it won't feel natural at all.'

Without Violet, I didn't know who I would hang out with in the shelter. But it wasn't just that. Without Violet, I wouldn't know where to go when I inevitably got to feeling restless again. Because I'd had a go in my bones for years. She supplied what was missing: a direction.

And she was a person. Something to hold on to.

'Okay,' I decided softly, mostly to myself.

'What?'

'Okay. Let's go. You have a place for us to go, right? A plan?'

She sprang from her cot and landed next to me. 'Of course.'

Her eyes were too hot and close to meet, so I stared at the sediment swirling then settling at the bottom of my mug.

'So. I trust you,' I half-lied.

Victor at the front desk called out to us as we were leaving. 'Where you girls going with those big bags?'

Violet spun around with her hand on the door handle.

'Goodbye, Victor. Thank you for your accommodation and guidance, but it's time for me to go.' She said it like a presidential announcement, before flinging the door open and sailing through.

He shook his head, eyes lowering back to the TV on his desk. 'You know we can't guarantee you a spot if you come back,' he told the TV.

Violet was gone. I placed my hand where hers had been and looked over my shoulder at him, tilted my chin up, tried to make my voice sound like the devil cared or didn't, couldn't remember which was the scary one, tried to make my voice loud enough that it would echo on the tile. 'I know.'

'We had to jump through mad hoops to get you in here, especially. You didn't make it easy.'

No ID, wouldn't talk and lied on every rare occasion that I did open my mouth. I know I didn't make it easy. *I know I didn't make it easy*, Violet would say, but I couldn't pull the words out. I looked out to the street where she was already at the end of the block. She barely glanced to each side before crossing the street without breaking her stride, one foot swinging to land hard in front of the other. I wondered what interpretation of this performance she would deliver later, what she would say it revealed about the triumph of the human spirit or the downfall of authority or whatever else. I'd have to catch up to find out.

Victor still hadn't looked up from the TV, and I stepped outside without saying goodbye.

As soon as the door shut behind me, I started running, and the world pushed up vibrant against my vision. Violet was one grey figure among many in the distance by then, so many coats and coats and coats, and the sidewalk melted over with rubbery black puddles of long-discarded gum, venetian blinds broken and smashed up against windows like piles of bones, buckets and bags of trash congregated around the parking meters, overflowing. In a moment I would catch up to Violet and her face would crack open into the biggest canyon smile I'd ever seen; she would scream like a banshee and grab my hand and take off running. I would feel my body grow miraculously weightless the further we ran, would watch everything below us grow smaller the higher we ascended, and with the buildings as specks and people as pinpricks, I would realize that I was screaming too. I would think, then, that this must be our masterpiece already, that we had activated magic by our own shared hand and put it on invisible, untouchable display. There was nothing left to do but await our worshippers.

17

I can't find Violet when the meditation is over. The folk musician is gone too, and I figure she's wrapped in the drapes of the willow-tree man. Why she would go home with someone else when a man absolutely free from swastika tattoos is right there in her own home is beyond me, but I don't pretend to understand people.

The cord on the bus home has been yanked free from its metal trappings, and raps against the window at every speed bump and pothole. There's only one other kid on the bus, taking up prime back-corner real estate, transferring candy from his sweatshirt pocket to his mouth with a hand engulfed by a baggy sleeve. I want to tell him there's no need to be sneaky, that the drivers don't really care if you eat. I want to ask him for a piece. Violet hasn't returned any of my calls. There are a lot of things that I want.

I shift my stare out the window so I don't freak out the kid, and think about my mother in California. I used to lie in the empty bathtub and pull the shower curtain between us to peel at the ugly decals, restless and hungry while she put her makeup on. The sun wouldn't be up yet, so all the light through the curtain came from the incandescence buzzing overhead. She liked having me there, I could tell; liked that I pulled myself and my fuzzy blanket out of bed to be near her while she got ready for work. She would make me promise to be good before she left, and those days, having something to promise her felt absolutely sacred.

Sometimes, even when she wasn't at the bathroom mirror, I'd lie in the bathtub just to have a place to be. She kept breath mints on the soap shelf for some reason, the kind you could hold in your mouth until they melted down spiny and cut your tongue. It felt like I could sense everything from there, all the plumbing snaking through the house, gathering its wisdom and secrets and centering it in a knot of pipes below me. I could see a rectangle of tree and sky through the small window near the ceiling. I could hear her in the other room, watching *Judge Judy* or crying softly to herself, sometimes both at once. Sometimes emptying bags from the freezer onto a tray and closing the oven on it. It was often hard to tell if she was happy or sad. I could hear everything.

When I get back to the boarding house, the light in the front room is off and Violet is sitting cross-legged on the floor, soft glow from the television screen flickering across her face. She doesn't say anything to me when I come in and set a plastic mug of lukewarm water on the floor next to her.

She's watching some sort of nature documentary. Ugly brown birds sloppily wading out from shallow shores.

'You didn't answer my calls.' I don't want to sound needy and desperate, but I am needy and desperate, and there is never any use in trying to hide anything from her.

She takes a sip from the mug and hands it to me. 'How was it?'

'I don't know. Why did you leave? Why didn't you tell me you were leaving?'

'You really don't know?'

I feel the little ember light up in the pit of my stomach. Was she jealous of Tina? Of Tina and me?

'Tina?'

'Yeah. All that shit about wombs.'

Oh. Something melts. I look at her profile straight on, curve of her nose and chin half-illuminated in the dark, every moment we've spent side by side like this flooding my memory. I remember when we got kicked out of the apartment we were squatting in back in Miami after leaving the shelter, even though no one was trying to live in there. The water didn't work, we were sponge-bathing in public restrooms and the walls were yellowed with nicotine. It was a shitty little place and we weren't hurting anyone. Still, they busted in and threatened the cops. Violet wanted to fight, but this was back when I was still scared of the type of performance that the rest of the world has named authority, and somehow I convinced her to choose flight with me.

Later, she fell asleep on the bench where we were waiting for a bus to take us away, even though it was the time of night when you couldn't be sure that one would be coming at all. I cradled her head in my lap, bundled her rain-soaked hair into a tangled wet knob that I clenched in my fist. Made it disappear. Waved my hand over her body like a magician. She did not disappear.

We were out of tricks that night. No bus came by, and I knew that they must all be sleeping in the lot somewhere on the other side of the city. Still, I kept my vision trained on the furthest speck on the horizon that my eyes could reach before it melted into black sky. I felt like every teenage girl I had not been, lying in her bed and writing in her diary, gazing out the window, waiting for something to happen to her. Someone's corner-store coffee cup had disintegrated on the curb, leaking coffee into the leftover rain glazing the street. Violet felt heavy. I felt heavier. We could walk a hundred million blocks to the train, but I saw stars in light pollution and felt safer than I should have where we sat. I prayed to the invisible untouchables that, if we survived here until sunrise, everyone would leave us alone.

It had occurred to me that even if a bus were to come, it wouldn't really matter because it wasn't like we had somewhere to go. I knew we would've gotten on it anyway, though. Violet and I were the same in this way, something I understood even back then. We were always reaching for anything that would take us somewhere else and absolve us of all that had happened where we had already been, as if departing from ourselves could be perfectly physical. As if other places had anything that would make us different from what we were.

Our life now is here, huddled together in the darkened living room, and I'm just grateful to still have her beside me. I rest my head on her shoulder. 'I'm sorry.'

'Nothing for you to be sorry for.'

I know she knows what I meant. I pretend like I can feel the tension in her body easing beneath my temple as we watch the National Geographic documentary hum quietly on the screen. They're in the rainforest now. The elegant rise and fall of jaguar shoulders intermittently visible between the trees.

A while ago, closer to when we had first met, I asked to see pictures from when she was a boy. That was back when I was still stupid. 'That's not how it works,' she had told me. 'I was never a boy.'

But from when you *looked* like a boy, I had persisted.

'I never looked like anything.'

The single dad's kid busts in a few jaguar-attack scenes later, cranes his neck to look at the screen. 'Are you guys high? This seems like something you would watch when you're high. So that meditation thing worked?'

'Yeah, man, it worked,' Violet says without breaking her gaze from the screen.

'Where's Jamie?'

The folk musician. I'll take this one. 'She's learning all sorts of interesting new history facts right now. Why don't you watch this nature stuff with us?'

The screen fills up with lightning bugs. It's a chemical reaction inside of their bodies, says a voice that melts over my head, hydrogen and something else. I don't catch it. I'm not really listening. Instead, my mind drifts to Tina again, with her belly full of baby, who told me afterwards that the meditation had guided her mind to a scene of her daughter and herself dancing in rice fields. She'd felt her baby kicking from the moment the music started, she told me. She knew that she loved it.

I imagine, briefly, that my heartbeat has tiny feet attached. I hold a hand over my heart, watch monkeys tear open fruits, envision the dark caverns of my body miraculously illuminated by fireflies. I think about my own mother in the same place I left her in California, how she had never seen rice fields and we would never dance. I think about how easy it had been to leave when I was fifteen, how I was so concerned with the logistics of pulling it off that I'd forgotten to consider all the empty space I would be leaving behind. Hand on heart, I pledge nothing to no one and swear to never call anywhere home.

18

oneirophobia – fear of dreams

I don't have nightmares the way I know some people do. The way I know Violet does.

She told me about this recurring nightmare she has where she's suspended in a clear substance that she can't see but can feel all around her, holding her limbs in place. She fights to free herself, but the more she pushes against it, the thicker it congeals, until it's hardened like sap.

I think about the keychains glittering in every souvenir shop in the world whenever she tells me she's had this nightmare again. Scorpions encased in amber. They really do look just like her.

'Maybe you have this nightmare when you feel stuck,' I once interpreted brilliantly, and she assured me what a brilliant interpretation this would be if she had ever, ever, even once in her life, felt that way.

I don't always believe her when she makes sweeping statements like that. I mean, her subconscious was kind of giving her away in that case.

But Violet is undoubtedly very good at becoming unstuck. She is the first to suggest we get back on the road. She decides our destinations. She gets us out of trouble.

Some people who have a fear of dreams are really scared of something else. They're scared of losing their minds. They have a dream so crazy that they think their brain has unhinged itself and they are in a terrifying new world where nothing makes sense and there's nothing to promise them that they will wake back up into anything rational.

Violet was born into a world that perceived her incorrectly. She corrected the world. She did not need to correct herself. That's the meat of it: she could be deeply misunderstood, at odds with everyone else, a tortured artist as much as she wanted – but she was never stuck.

19

The church downtown has its doors thrown open to the daylight. I hear they let anyone into those things, and I have two hours until my shift at the swan boats.

Someone standing near the door gives me a knowing smile as I walk in, which I try to return like I know what they know and we're all in the same club here. Just inside is a pool of water in a stone fountain protruding from the wall. Somehow, I know to dip two fingers into it and press them to my head. I must have seen it on TV. The water slithers down my forehead and dries in a cool patch.

The church looks even more foreboding from the inside, brawny pillars extending to a ceiling far beyond my reach. Light pushed through the stained-glass windows looks syrupy-thick, enough to fill up your ear canals and stick there.

Rows and rows of pews separate me from the priest, his little body looking like a weary mule under layers of robes, his neck bent dutifully over his book. I want to go up there and help him out or something. Take some of that shit off of his tiny body. Find his flashcards in one of his pockets somewhere. He stays cemented there, very still, small voice working its way through what I assume is a Bible passage, and I wonder if this is what a prayer sounds like.

The line to enter the confessional box snakes along the back, and I find my place at the end. The priest is talking about his recent trip to the grocery store now, where he saw coffee without caffeine and milk without lactose, and almost broke down crying in the aisle because he realized his people had become Christians without faith. I tune him out then and start wracking my brain for anything I've ever heard about confessions, any book, any movie, until it's my turn to push back the red curtain and step inside.

The cool patch on my forehead whispers in the sudden stillness of the interior, and some memory of what I'm supposed to say bubbles up from source unknown.

'Forgive me, Father, for I have sinned.'

A voice comes through from the other side, pronouncing each word with a meticulous cadence that makes my voice, in comparison, sound like a chihuahua. 'How long has it been since your last confession?'

'Well... this is my first time.'

'That's okay. I'm glad you're here. What are your sins?'

'I mean, I've talked to God before. It's not like that. I think I've done a lot of sins, though, but I don't exactly know them off the top of my head. I guess you can help me figure out if this one thing I did is a sin, because I'm trying to fix it right now.' My throat catches there, and I take a sharp mouthful of dusty backwash air.

'Quite all right. Go ahead.'

I try to deconstruct the pattern on the veil between us. Not quite a lattice.

'Well, I left my mom behind when she needed someone to take care of her while she was sick. Like, left her alone in the house. Just packed a bag and left her there. She doesn't have anyone, and I knew that when I left. No other family or anything.'

'I see.'

'I mean, is that a sin? Can I repent for that and be... you know, covered?'

'That's between you and the Lord. He tells us, honor your father and your mother, that your days may be long in the land that the Lord your God is giving you. Perhaps you have done your mother a dishonor in failing to take care of her when she was sick.'

Dishonor. I don't think I've ever even thought of that word before. It feels shiny and strange, a river pebble at the back of my throat.

And not *sick*, exactly, I want to correct him, before realizing he's just repeating the word I used. I know what to call it and I don't. I thought I knew what to call it, and I checked with Violet, and she agreed, but I don't want to use that word in this place. *Sick* could mean anything.

Sick like alternating between scared and scary. Sick like I never knew what I was going to get. Like the summer when my mother would bring me to the park almost all the afternoons that she was awake. It was always a little too far of a walk, and it would be pitch dark by the time we were coming home. I'd be sweaty and tired and seething. But she walked like the air was carrying her on an invisible throne. *That fresh air*, she would call it. 'Doesn't it feel nice to get some of that fresh air?' At the park we'd eat pieces of cheese right out of the plastic, apples that she peeled and cored and sliced into perfect expressionless bites. 'We gotta get you a glove,' she said more than once, staring at the empty softball diamond as we chewed. 'We can play Heads Up.' We never got me a glove and she never stopped saying we should, so that became its own game.

I had another game, just for me, where I focused on the whitest, brightest part of her when she wasn't looking. The whites of her eyes. The further the sun fell in the sky, the whiter they seemed to glow, and at the time all this meant to me was that we needed to get home soon.

Sometimes I would start packing up around her when she wanted to stay a while longer. She'd let me gather everything into the blanket and sling it across my back, start stomping homeward. She'd move aside to make it easier. Sing something about love and mercy as she stretched out belly-up like a kitten and settled into the grass.

'Yes. Okay, so, forgive me, Father, for I have sinned. I... I confess my dishonor. I've dishonored my mother.'

'Very well. You will love and honor her going forward. Remember that love covers a multitude of sins. For your penance, you'll say one Our Father and one Hail Mary for your mother.'

That's it?

We had cable for a while and she never missed an episode of *Judge Judy*, even the reruns. I would drag my blanket into the front room to watch with her and eat my dinner wrapped in its folds.

One night I was eating Cheerios out of a mixing bowl. A commercial for Meow Mix came on: the cat calling its owner in the middle of his important business meeting. The cat meowed the Meow Mix song and I lost it, laughing so hard that the milk coated my chin.

My mother didn't laugh, and I turned around to see why she didn't find this shit absolutely hilarious. Her head was rolled forward, chin pointing to her collarbone, eyes glazed. I knew that meant she either couldn't hear me anymore, or could hear but couldn't understand; either way she wasn't going to be saying anything that made sense for the rest of the night and her Hamburger Helper was going to solidify on her plate so that we would probably get ants again.

I remember only being worried that this meant she wouldn't see who won the case. A woman suing one of her baby daddies for the value of a donut-shop gift card he'd given her then taken back after they broke up. We were rooting for her. And she won. Not that my mother would ever know. We never talked about it again.

The priest clears his throat politely.

'Right, okay. I'll do that,' I promise, trying to remember what he told me to do. 'I guess I'm trying to see, though... trying to see how I could even start to fix it. Make it up to her. I need to do that too, right? How do I do that?'

'The Lord will advise you once you've done your penance. Now, have you shared everything you need to confess today?'

My eyes fixate on the almost-lattice again, brain slashing through every time I've stolen, lied, cheated, hated, envied, lusted. I don't know where to start.

'Yes. That's everything.'

'Very well. God, the Father of mercies, through the death and resurrection of His Son, has reconciled the world to Himself and sent the Holy Spirit among us for the forgiveness of sins. Through the ministry of the Church, may God grant you pardon and peace. And I absolve you from your sins in the name of the Father, and of the Son, and of the Holy Spirit. Amen.'

'Okay. Thank you.'

'Now you say "amen".'

'Oh, sorry. Amen.'

I wait to feel an incandescence take light in the river of my throat, a golden new understanding descend upon me. These do not come, and I'm starting to get self-conscious about how many scabs are visible all over my summer legs.

'Okay, so... that's it?'

'That's it.'

*

I don't know how to do an Our Father or a Hail Mary, and there's no way I could find the right thing in one of the Bibles slotted behind every pew. I just sit there staring at the heavy-lidded Jesus who seems miles above my head, waiting for him to say something.

Unable to process the sheer decadence of this place. Waiting to be swallowed. Whichever comes first.

Maybe I'll try bowing my head instead. *Are you there, God? It's me, Smidge.* I read that Judy Blume book cover to cover, over and over, when I lived in a group home. This was when I was thirteen and the state of California had determined that my mother's care was unsuitable. It was my first couple weeks and I had made a friend named Michael. The hands that had tried to strangle his mother gripped chalky markers then, sitting next to me in art therapy, so sinfully close that they scooted our chairs apart while we were still in them. As if we were toddlers. I laughed inside my head, drawing spirals of waves, thinking about the girl I shared a room with at night. She was my first kiss.

Michael was released back to his parents' house soon after that and promised he would call me all the time. It would be a cliché of tragicomic dimensions to say he never called, but I'm saying it, because he never did. I read that are-you-there-God book six times in waiting. I fucking hate that story now.

Still there, God? Were you listening to that?

It's a beautiful building, something that cannot be ignored as I turn my back on it to head to the dock where my fiberglass swans will be waiting for me. It is a significant place on top of being overblown gorgeous, heavy in a good way, purpose and consequence lacquered into the bones. I scratch a scab on my cuticle until it bleeds and drips down the back of my hand and onto the holy tile. And I feel the big glass Jesus eyes behind me, watching me not clean it up. Bringer of spirits, healer of ailments, flanked by glowing red glass roses blooming taller than I am. I feel him watch me walk away.

20

Here's something else about my mother: most of the time, she was asleep – or pretending to be – behind a closed door. She had long periods of sweating and shaking, and then not sweating, not shaking, perfectly lucid to tell me you couldn't believe anything out there.

And then I came home late. I had been sitting in the parking lot at the water park. I had gone through the drive-through at McDonald's on my way home. She was in the front room with a jigsaw puzzle, except the puzzle wasn't anywhere close to put together. The pieces were scattered like protective salts in a circle around her.

She sat with her arms wrapped around her knees, glaring at me.

'Where were you?' she spat out sharp, and I shrugged like the teenager I was. Wondered what she was worried about: boys? Underage drinking?

'You think you're so cool,' she said. 'With your chicken nuggets.'

I wanted to laugh. And maybe my face showed it, because she stood up then and left her jigsaw circle to pick up the fire iron that I'd never seen her touch before. She didn't say anything else. She walked toward me in swift, deliberate steps, calm as a predator, and raised the iron above her head.

And she made a motion like she was going to hit me. But she didn't hit me. And when I didn't flinch, she made another motion like she would hit me, and when I still didn't flinch, another, and another.

I wasn't looking up at her from below, because I was fifteen and almost her height by then. She was small and I wasn't. I had taken after a father I'd never met. Her arm holding the fire iron was so skinny I had the thought that I could snap it like a twig and make the danger go away.

She was trying to scare me and it worked, though not in the way she intended, because I had this ugly thought and found myself unable to push it back into the trench from which it had surfaced.

So it was only almost fear. Because it was only almost violence.

21

atychiphobia – fear of failure

The secret is that I was having a lot of thoughts like that. Looking at something and seeing how it could be broken. Knowing that I could be the one to break it if I wanted to, that I was capable. I could smash the TV with my fists; the glass wouldn't even sting after I'd steeled myself with razors on my stomach all those years. I could incinerate the trash piling up on every surface of our house. It was when I started eyeing my mother's knuckles like a stack of jawbreakers that I got worried.

It started to feel like everything was held together much more tenuously than anyone else was letting on. Like I was seeing the other side, the underside, and maybe that meant something. The house felt smaller every day and my mother was everywhere. The slow-dawning conviction felt handed down by God: if I stayed in there much longer, one of us was going to get hurt.

22

'You wouldn't believe what happened at work today.'

I've just got back from the swan boats. Violet puts a bowl of noodles in front of me and sits in the other chair, cracking her knuckles.

'Was there a call?'

'Yeah. For an opossum, not even that far outside town. We got there so quick and when we did, it was still alive. Its legs were clearly twitching. And its eyes were wide open. So I thought we were going to take it to the vet.'

I don't tell her that some animals can still move after they die. That it isn't uncommon at all. I don't tell her their eyes can stay open until they rot out, and that, more relevantly, a vet probably wouldn't know what to do with an opossum. I fill my mouth with broth.

'But Brian – I've told you about Brian, right? Yeah, him – he agrees with me that the opossum clearly isn't dead, but instead of taking it to the vet, he says he'll just *take care of it*. And he goes in the van and gets a *sledgehammer*. So I try to grab it but his grip is like, there's no way, so I go and basically shelter the opossum with my body instead. And he's super grossed out, but like, what the fuck? He wants to smash it with a *sledgehammer*. He literally wants to commit *murder*, and he's acting like I'm the crazy one. He goes, "It's our job," but I'm pretty sure my job is getting dead animals off the streets so they can rest with dignity. Not killing them, you know?'

'What happened to the opossum?' I ask.

'Well, it died. Like, as I was there and Brian was saying he couldn't leave without me getting in the van, and I was saying I wouldn't get in the van unless we were taking it to the vet. It stopped twitching at some point, and yeah. It was dead. But it wasn't killed,' she says, her voice lilting with pride on the final sentence.

I've never seen anything die up close. The closest I've gotten was when I hit a deer on my way back from the state line.

It made a sound like the earth was shattering when it hit the front of the car, then rolled and landed on the roof, crushing the metal toward my head. I screeched to a halt. Threw the car into park, then ran back to where I was sure an almost-angel would be lying in the road. There was nothing on the road for as long as I walked. The deer must have run off, been somehow untouched, somehow fine. I searched the trees at the side of the highway, pushing my vision to the point where everything looked perfectly black and still. No signs or sounds of motion. The only thing moving was me, just me wondering if what I'd seen had been real. I thought I'd throw up the whole way home.

I knew it was real because the dent that the deer left in the roof of the car was enormous. The next morning, when my mother saw what I'd done, she said she was going to kill me. Said it just like that: 'I am going to kill you,' staring at the gaping dent collecting its shadow into a puddle. She asked where I'd been driving – something she'd never asked before. I made up a story about a friend's house. If she didn't believe me, she didn't show it; this was the way it always was.

'People are going to think I'm...' she said, still staring at the dent, the ruined car, one of the few small symbols of normalcy and having it together that were in our lives. She didn't finish her sentence because she didn't have to. I knew what she meant.

And I knew it was my fault. But she was talking to me. She wasn't talking a lot those days.

'At least it missed the windshield,' I pointed out. 'That was lucky. It would have smashed it. I could've been cut up pretty bad.'

And she was back to not talking. *Trash*, I knew she was thinking, *trash trash trash trash trash*.

'And that would've been expensive to replace,' I added, and she nodded, and I'd take it. That was the first time I'd seen her outside in weeks. The rising sun threw the red deltas under her eyes into sharp relief, and I wondered what she thought people were thinking of when they looked at her face.

The woods were pitch black when I searched for the deer between the trees. A poem bubbled up, the one about the woods being lovely, dark and deep. But having promises to keep.

Be good. That was the promise I could not keep: it felt sacred when I was little, but kept getting harder with age. I'd already drawn blood. And I would draw more. That deer must have been sent from somewhere in the sky, so that I would stand at the edge of the woods that night and be reminded there was another way. And that it was always there, so that whenever I was ready, I could wander to its edge and claim my dominion.

'So, I have a plan. Do you want in?' Violet asks.

I roll my eyes like, *of course*.

'Okay. We're going to send a message. I'm going to get a ton of fake blood, and we're going to coat the office with it.'

She really does get the blood from somewhere by the next day, and convinces me to join her in unlocking the door of the animal control office after hours and coating Brian's desk with that blood, flinging what's left at the walls.

The next day, her boss will ask if she did it. She will say yes – unblinking, I imagine – and get fired, and walk out knowing that even if they think they've won this battle, she has won the war.

When she tells me the news, I will briefly wonder what she'll do next. Scan my mind over the businesses around the wharf and gauge which other ones seem like they'd hire without a background check.

Turns out it won't matter.

23

I need to go back to California.

Outside the smoke-stained window, a swan is slowly crossing the lake toward me. I squint. Father and son. The boy had a chocolate stain around his mouth when they got on the boat that I'd wondered why the dad didn't wipe clean.

Redding, California, where I was born and where my mother was born and where she never left for all I knew, was 2,000 miles away from New Orleans. I'd looked it up when I was figuring out how we were going to get to Louisiana from Cary, without knowing exactly why I was doing it. A premonition, maybe. I had no idea how many miles 2,000 was, what it meant other than far, far away.

I was thirteen when I first got it into my head to run away from home. I mean, deep enough into it to start making plans that felt concrete to my thirteen-year-old self. I stayed up late on the computer poring over planes and trains and departure schedules and dollar amounts, lines and lines of numbers that I copied meticulously into a spiral-bound notebook and stuffed under the part of my bedroom floor where the boards dipped and I'd ripped the carpet free. I did that instead of my homework, then, because I knew homework wouldn't matter soon. The school called home after a while, but my mother was passed out when the phone rang. I erased the voicemail they left. Declining academic performance. Lack of focus in the classroom. Growing concern.

This repeated until it didn't and she picked up the phone. Not long after the appointment with the school counselor that followed, some strangers turned up at our door to take me away.

My mother was furious, more furious even than when she'd finally gotten the call from the school in the first place, and I'd thought that was bad. She was using words with the strangers that I'd never heard her use before, like *baby girl*, like *that's my baby girl and you have no fucking right to take her from me, that's my baby girl and she needs me, fuck you, she's my baby, you don't understand, I'm her only family.*

It might have been true that they didn't understand, but I already knew by then that there was no use in trying to make them. There must be words out there somewhere for what my mother was trying to express, but these weren't the right ones, and I didn't have them either. So my mother said *fuck you* and I said nothing, and neither of us won.

I was the one who'd opened the door for the strangers in the first place. They knew my name.

If you take my baby girl away from me she doesn't have no one, that can't be right, you have no idea. I'm all she's got.

I didn't feel like a baby girl. Whenever I searched within for any little glimmer of what it was like to be a baby-toddler-child, sweet little untouched girl, it all went dark and fuzzy.

Underwater cave brain. Squid ink.

We hadn't been expecting visitors, and with the strangers in the house, I saw my mother suddenly illuminated through the window by passing headlights.

I saw her wearing a sleeveless sundress, exposing every bone in her arms.

I saw her thin hair plastered upward against her head, the trail of saliva dried against her cheek, the ketchup stain near the hem from dinner three days ago.

I felt the heat of one of the strangers next to me and saw her and saw her and saw her until an unfamiliar revulsion rose in my stomach. This was not all I had, I decided then. She was stupid or something; she was a liar.

A cry brings my attention back from underwater to my box on the dock, and I look up to see the father waving at me.

'Did you guys have fun?' I yank the boat too hard with my swan-fetching pole and cringe at the too-violent thud when it hits the dock.

'Yeah!' The son raises both fists in the air like he's just won something. His mouth is still ringed with chocolate. Maybe it's a birthmark.

Wrapping the chain around the cleat, I rearrange my face into a smile. 'That's great. Thanks for coming.'

The father pulls the son up out of his seat and hoists him onto the dock like it's the easiest thing in the world. He smiles without looking at me as they leave. 'Take care.'

That's the last thing one of the strangers said to me before I never saw her again. The strangers had brought me to what I would learn was a group home for in-between kids whose parents needed to get their shit figured out. In the car, my mother's words, her face, her body dragged their claws deep and slow. Her hard, bony body. Her almost-nothingness. If she was really all I had, then I had exactly that. Nothing. Almost.

In a banana-yellow room, the remaining stranger asked me questions that I didn't have the answers to. Some of them were easy, like did I know what my mom was doing. Some of them should have been easy, like did I know when it had started. Like did I know where my father was, any other family. Some of them were impossible, the ones about how I felt about myself, my life. I knew that I wanted to be a different person, with a different life. It would hit me all the time at school, seeing the other kids just sitting at their desks, leaning heads together to share earbuds, tying their shoes. I wanted to be them, any one of them.

After school, a snake of cars would wrap around the block and I often imagined myself just picking one. Opening the door and sliding in to be taken somewhere warm and sturdy, with a neatly mown yard and maybe even flower boxes under the windows. The fridge always full, and not with moldy or rotten shit that had formed a pool of water so pungent you'd have to hold your nose while pouring it into the big garbage can outside. Instead, a shelf of cookbooks. A bird feeder. Sometimes I'd throw in a dog, or some younger siblings stirring up trouble and noise and warmth.

I had a blueprint to work from. Libby's mom made her invite everyone in the sixth grade to her birthday party at their three-storey house in Quail Hollow, so she invited me. They had hired an exotic bird man for the party, who swooped around with parrots draping his arms, and at one point we were all supposed to line up to receive a kiss from the star of the show, a big red macaw. I sat where I was sitting on the grass, pretending to be fascinated by their tabby cat perched on the fence, and Libby's mom came to coo at me: 'You're scared of the bird? No need to be scared of the bird. Well, it's okay if you're scared of the bird. Come have cake.' I wanted to tell her I wasn't scared of the bird, in fact how dare she, I particularly loved birds and how their bodies moved so effortlessly across a sky that was entirely their domain, how they made the most of it, and I desperately craved a kiss from the macaw, but somehow getting into that line with Maddy and Aaron in front of me and Dinah and John behind me was just not going to happen. Where would I look? Straight ahead? What would I do with my hands?

Then it was three o'clock and moms were coming to pick up their Maddys and Aarons and Dinahs and Johns one by one and two by two, and then it was half past three and mine still hadn't come. I petted their fat orange tabby cat for what felt like an hour. It pushed its fat self into me over and over, twisting its head into my ribs like it was trying to excavate something. 'Why don't you give her a call?' Libby's mom offered politely when it started nearing four o'clock, and I clenched the cool plastic of their phone until it warmed from the hot flush of my skin. I waited for the dial tone to turn into the voicemail message telling me that my mother couldn't come to the phone. When I hung up, Libby's mom asked me my least favorite question, which is *are you okay? Are you okay* meant that something from my guts was showing on my face, and bodies aren't supposed to work like that. 'Are you okay?' she asked, sounding surprised. And then she said, 'Why don't you let me take you home,' sounding less surprised.

At first, I was embarrassed about how far she had to drive, making small talk past the grassy green contours of the golf course sloping outward from the edge of her neighborhood, chatting aimlessly through town and its stoplights and umbrellas in all the same colors on the tables lining the pavement, then finally silent on the long stretch of road before my house came into view. I was embarrassed until I wasn't. Listening to her chatter was just like overhearing the bubbling of a river, unpredictable and consistent at once, and I marveled at how it melted away the last reserves of self-consciousness coursing through my awkward limbs, and at how the car smelled like absolutely nothing but car, instead of the funk of stale cigarettes that I wished I wasn't used to, because I hadn't even thought my mother's car smelled like anything until I'd gotten into this one, and finally – the biggest secret pleasure of all – at how anyone could look through the window and mistake us for a family.

If I were a different person, with a different life, I never would have ended up in that banana-yellow room at the group home, something that I realized after they asked me whether my mother had ever expressed guilt about her use of substances. Tears brimmed up against my will and I could tell they thought it was from the question, which it wasn't, but I didn't care because it meant they let me go back to the room they'd showed me earlier and described as mine. The girl that I shared it with would come in from the common room later that night and introduce herself as George. She had short red hair, a lazy eye and track marks all over her arms. When she sat me between her legs to braid my hair, a counselor exploded in to yell at her for touching me. 'There's no touching here,' he said. 'She knows that.' He stabbed a finger in her direction. 'I ain't mad at you, cos you didn't know,' he said to me, 'but George here knows damn well.'

Later I would question why one of the counselors always touched my shoulder, then, without fail, whenever he talked to me. His name was Richard; he was apparently studying psychology at the nearby community college, and most of the girls exchanged hushed whispers about the crush on him they shared – especially Sabs, who seemed to care less about ever leaving this place than she did about making him her boyfriend. His face was symmetrical and his lashes were dark and he touched all of our shoulders, only the girls, except Abby who had a genetic disorder and weighed 194 pounds. George once bragged at lunch that he'd fingered her in the room where they take our vitals, which I knew couldn't be true because she was teaching me how to kiss at night. 'That was a lie, right?' I asked her to confirm that night, heart pounding when she didn't answer right away. 'It doesn't matter,' she finally said. 'It was just to shut up Sabs, always running her mouth about him treating her special.'

'So it was a lie, yeah?' I pressed, and she just kissed me until I shut up too.

The truth was I thought it was a dumb question, whether my mother had expressed guilt for her actions. Of course my mother had expressed guilt. Guilt flowed from her like a river, although one shallow enough to evaporate by the next day. Blossomed from her like a rose. Thorns just prickling. Sometimes she would ask me to stay with her at night with enormous fearful eyes, and I would lie there wrapped in the cage of her limbs for hours before her body stopped shaking and the room emptied into quietude. *I'm so lucky to have you*, she would tell me all the time. On her good days, or at her most vulnerable moments. *You're the greatest blessing of my life, you're my angel, you're perfect, I don't know what I would do without you.* I'd be wiping dried vomit off her chin with a warm washcloth, pulling off her soiled T-shirt to scrub under the sink. *I don't know what I would do without you.* I figured I knew something about guilt and shame then, love and pity, and back when I was stupid and without many options, those words all sounded a whole lot like love to me.

I was in the group home for seven months while my mother was rehabilitated. They told me she was learning how to function without substances and doing an incredible job, that we could live together again just as soon as she had finished learning all these powerful new tools. It always sounded like a script when any of the adults talked to me in there. In hindsight, maybe it was.

When they started taking me to visit her a few weeks in, all I could ever focus on was her haircut. They'd cut her hair to shoulder length, two dark panels on either side of her slowly swelling cheeks. 'You look like the moon,' I'd told her the first time I saw it, and she laughed harder and longer than I'd ever heard her laugh. I knew she was laughing too much and my eyes darted to the people supervising our visit at the door, but I quickly discovered that I could also close my eyes for a second at a time and steal fleeting shreds of pretending she was fine and this was normal.

Richard was assigned to take me on one of these visits, and Sabs pissed on my pillow while I was gone. 'That was quick,' he said when I came back into the waiting room where he was reading *Fear and Loathing in Las Vegas*, or at least holding it open in his lap. I didn't want to tell him that my mother and I had run out of things to say to each other, that I was trying to leave before stumbling on something that would set her off and ruin the illusion that we were so good at generating when we needed to, how that illusion was our job right now, and we were both working on it so hard that it felt real even to us sometimes. So I just shrugged.

Richard didn't start the car when we got inside, only asked me what I wanted to do with all this extra time. I asked if we were allowed to get milkshakes and he said no. He said, 'Well, technically no.' He said he had other ideas about what we could do, though.

'Have you ever been with an older guy?' he asked me, then: 'Have you ever thought about it?' and he slid his hand from my shoulder to the tender meat on the inside of my elbow while I stared straight ahead out of the window. 'Take me back,' I ordered, and he said, 'Oh come on, I know you've thought about it,' and I said, 'Take me back or I'll kill you,' and he just laughed, and I said, 'Take me back or I'll kill myself right now while I'm under your care and you'll be fired and probably charged,' and he was silent as he turned the keys in the ignition.

When we arrived at the group home and parked, he bent toward me and said, 'Hey, let's put what happened back there behind us, let's just not mention it again, deal?' He offered his hand to shake and I could not look him in the eye so I concentrated all of my hatred on that hand, a *fuck you* for every finger and an extra one for whichever finger had been inside George, something I couldn't convince myself had been a lie anymore.

'Sorry,' I said, 'I have rabies.'

Then I spit on that hand and he made an ugly noise, recoiling so quick that you'd think he'd been stung by an actual fucking wasp. 'Narcissistic whore,' I heard him hiss before I slammed the door behind me, and I had to pretend he'd said *sacrificial lamb* to keep myself out of worse trouble than I was already in.

So I knew about guilt. Guilt and shame, those came easy as breathing, easy as fear when I felt hands pressing into my skull again. Love and pity were hard-learned. I knew they were difficult to conjure in the face of violence sometimes, and other times they gurgled up simultaneously from that pit in your stomach that you never filled with solid rock the way you meant to. And I knew that sometimes, love and pity – they feel exactly the same.

After the strangers decided my mother had been fixed, the first weeks back in our house together felt like something new. As if the illusion had come true. To celebrate, my mother baked our favorite cake, Pillsbury yellow mix with chocolate frosting, and sat us down to eat it with forks at the kitchen table. 'We'll have one slice each,' she said proudly. 'We'll put the rest away for later.'

She plugged in the vacuum and did the whole house. She replaced the curtains. Cleared the trash from the kitchen counters so the pink tile underneath was visible again. She started packing lunches for me to take to school every day, like I was seven years old, and I didn't mind it one bit.

Then it was spring and I heard her wailing from her room, and my insides all turned to stone again. 'Are you there? Come here, I need you.' Tread quietly down the hall to find her face glossy with tears again, eyes wide with fear again, that drowned-woman look that I wished were less familiar than it was. As in, I wished I could look at my mother when she was this way and see a stranger. But I looked at my mother and saw my mother. And my mother could tread water for months at a time, but in the end she was always drowning. I'd carry her image with me so that years later, when I tried to picture her, sometimes the first version of her face that I'd see would be wet and dark.

Because I had become stone again then, my heart was not allowed to break. I climbed under the covers so she wouldn't have to ask. Her arms were steel beams across my back. I felt like a thousand-year-old gargoyle destined for failure, because it was someone's bright idea to make me protect a castle whose cannons pointed back inside itself.

The ice in my stomach that these memories create doesn't belong in New Orleans, on this swan-boat dock in the early swamp of summer. I'm still holding the chain and realize my knuckles have tightened to a vice grip; I drop it with a clank.

It shouldn't be allowed to get this hot. I head back to the office, feeling like I'm pushing my body through sludge. I feel tears coating my cheeks, two wet sheets – didn't realize I had cried, hope I look nothing like she did that first night. The first time I saw the hard-beaten bible of recovery fail. The first time I let slip the one and only thing in my life I was responsible for, the only thing I was supposed to protect. Shame flashes hot and the sun feels too close and the light reflects from the water in blinding streaks, so I turn around and run and run and run like a child, run and run until I get to the end of the dock and fly.

Everything is familiarly quiet under the water. My body is an embryo in a cool, unfeeling womb. Bubbles flutter out of my nostrils and mouth, and surge toward the surface and the light, and I will my impatient limbs not to follow them even as goosebumps prickle and pressure crams the small caverns of my lungs. The worse I can make this hurt, the better. The longer I can stay under, the better, because I've done enough testing of my survival instincts by now to know that I won't let myself drown.

This will be my second gestation, ripe with possibility, no limit to what might happen when I break the water and return to the world again. What will I want now? What could be different so I could shed the crust I'm still carrying around me and capture my share of the light? I need to go back to California, that's the only thing my brain can formulate in the shape of an answer, and there's no space for anything else as I start to go starry-eyed dizzy. I need to go back to California, apologize to my mother for failing to protect her, make sure she's safe. I don't know how to do any of these things, but I'll do them.

In a few seconds I will break through the surface for air and pull myself onto the dock, trying to piece together the experience as a baptism with a still-starry brain. I need to go back, to reconcile, to protect. If I still don't know how when the time comes, I'll learn.

24

haphephobia – fear of being touched

Some touches mean more than others, of course. You can tell by which ones leave ghosts that come back.

Big hands on either side of my head. Even though I pretended to be a robot, another secret is that I was betrayed by my skin. Which means I felt them then and I still feel them now, sometimes, when I'm looking for an answer and can't find it right away.

And I didn't tear them off. And I don't tear them off. I'm certain that if I ever tried, the bones would crack and collapse under my grip, and then there'd be no one but me to clean up all that blood.

25

'No more swans for you, baby girl.' Violet is buzzing with joy, wet brown eyes gleaming. She and Dusty are sitting on the front porch. Neither of them questions why I'm soaking wet.

'Dusty? What are you doing h—'

'We're booked,' Violet interrupts.

'With the thing? Holy Toledo? We didn't even aud—'

'That's the thing, we didn't even have to! The ringleader totally got it just from the concept, which is why I'm always telling you it's so important to have a strong message behind everything you do. See? He loved it. He got it. They're only in town for another week, so we need to hop on right now and get up to speed for the next show.'

I stare at Dusty with all of my hundred million questions in my eyes. 'You're really leaving?'

They nod. I turn to Violet. 'You didn't even... We aren't going to audition?'

'Smidge, why are you going to question this? Dusty introduced me to the ringleader and I was trying to just set up a time and date to audition, like usual, whatever, and he made the offer on sight. I already signed our contract.'

I need to go back to California.

'I trust you, Vi. I just—'

'Just what? Would rather be sharing a mattress with two other strippers in Miami?'

My face flashes hot. That story was supposed to be between us, although I guess I never said that out loud. I resolutely avoid eye contact with Dusty and look up at Violet, towering in a blaze of golden wheat-field light from the last of the afternoon rays. 'Well, where's the next stop?'

She drops to a kneel in front of me and hugs my legs. 'Baton Rouge. We're heading west.'

'West? Are they going all the way to the coast?'

'I don't know. Probably. Why?'

'Yes, darling,' Dusty cuts in. 'All the way to the coast.'

I weigh my options and, as always, being without Violet is not among them. Before Violet, I wasn't doing so well on my own. The thudding club comes to mind, the grease-smeared window of the studio upstairs where I shared a pull-out with two other girls. One of them kept liquor bottles in her pillowcase, and they'd leaked enough times after she'd drunkenly screwed them on crooked that the nights smelled like a permanent chemical void. When she'd wake up the next afternoon, she would open a compact and scoop concealer into her hands, then smear it across her cheeks like she was splashing her face with cold water. She didn't use a mirror. I think her name was Jackie.

And anyway, if anything, it sounds like a free ride west.

'Okay, I'm in.'

Violet breaks into a sunbeam of a grin and screams, burying her head in my knees.

I can't help smiling back. 'Can I at least meet the guy?'

26

Lying is a strategy and, of course, an art. It's storytelling.

A year ago, we found our place in Daytona Beach near the swamp. It was the ultimate swamp. Mosquitos circled lazily in it. Cicadas screamed in it. People probably died in its goopy quicksands. Best of all, I liked to think alligators lurked in it. I was always watching for an island of eyes in the water's surface haze.

A low fence ran along part of it, backyards pushed up in a row with a clear view all the way into their kitchens, into the TVs playing in the living rooms. People stapled plastic to the fences there, big orange mesh that I always half-expected Violet to rip off and fashion into a dress or something. The backyards were all the same design of concrete and grass, and each one equally sparse. A rickety barbecue in one. Two plastic baby-bikes shaped like unicorns shoved in the corner of another.

Our shoes sank into the sludge on the other side where we would cut through to get to the taqueria with the neon macaw in the window. Violet had found a kid who would give us food in exchange for nothing more than stories of the grand adventures we pretended we'd had. He'd assumed when he first saw us that we'd had grand adventures because of how Violet introduced us – *traveling modern performance artists*. I didn't blame him. And Violet could make up anything on the spot.

She told him about a time we'd outsmarted a bank robber in Paris, how he'd kicked open the door and swept his gun across the whole lobby. She went into detail about the lamps, running her tongue over the ridges in the twisted bronze and every little vine in each perfectly carved bolt holding the sconce to the wall, until he was doubled over, begging her to get on with the story without saying that out loud. He'd already learned what happened when you said things like that out loud to Violet.

Anyway, Violet didn't drop to make out with the floor along with everyone else in this story when the robber came in and announced himself. She pretended she didn't speak French even though, she assured the kid, she totally did; she pretended she didn't understand what the robber wanted and made a big show out of not understanding to distract from me crawling on my stomach across the floor, toward a pillar that I would scale like a spider monkey – I'd find purchase in the molding near the top, then leap off and grab the chandelier, swing myself down to pluck the gun from his hand and render him absolutely useless.

I often wondered if the kid really believed shit like this, but then it would get so quiet in the alley behind the strip mall when she was telling her stories, and her words would fill the space with invisible light. It was invisible, but I knew it was there because I could feel it eggy-warm in my eyes. I knew because I would look at the kid and see it reflected in his, too.

Violet would never make fun of the kid. He was miraculously spared from her usual acutely critical eye on every person we encountered. She would never declare victory, either, as we squelched back home with bellies full of beans. Maybe he was too much of a kid – it was just so kitten-milky-soft that all he wanted was to hear a story. And we just needed to eat. Our transactions happened several times a week, and the scales did not tip. It didn't feel like either party was taking anything from the other.

27

During the time we lived by the swamp, I worked in a laundromat. It was near the edge of town, where the bail-bond places blended the sleepy part of the city into the palms.

Taffy had the night shift and I had the day shift. The night shift apparently got more action. I mostly spent my days staring out the window and polishing the machines with a cocktail of cleansers, water and bleach. She got to handle the locals and their laundry drama into the wee hours. I was jealous of her.

There was one woman who I came to recognize as a regular for even as short a time as we were there. She came in early in the mornings, when the sky was still coming to life. I admired her for her stories without morals that revealed bleak realities about the world. For her belief that horses were sad when they looked at all the cars, because humans used to rely on horses for transportation, and now that their necessity had faded, the horses felt useless and didn't even want to breed anymore. She'd get so guilty that when she'd drive on highways that passed by fields of horses, she'd pull her hair down to cover her face so the horses couldn't look through the window and resent her specifically.

She also warned me to watch out for the skunk apes, which sounded a lot like the bigfoots that hung out in the forests where I came from. I told her this – hairy monkeyish thing, bigger than a person, smaller than a giant? – but she vehemently disagreed.

'The skunk ape has intelligence,' she corrected me. 'They communicate with us. I met one once, and it spoke to me. Not in English. Not in no telepathy neither. Something else. I smelled it before I saw it. It came out the water and told me not to be too afraid, but not too confident, neither. That humility makes you an alpha dog. I believed it, you know. No reason not to.'

I took her seriously. I understand why people want to believe there are intelligent creatures in swamps. It's a different kind of air, a kind that can make you feel like you're one organ nestled among many in a sleeping body.

And there are so many places where someone can be watching. Not in a creepy way. I just mean there are someones who care about you, even if they aren't people. And when it comes down to it, isn't that all anyone wants? Isn't that what I want?

28

We join the circus a few days after Violet told me we'd made it in. We quit our jobs, tell the boarding-house lady and the folk musician and the kid. Dusty emphasizes again and again that they're leaving, finally leaving, and if we don't join now we'll be left behind forever.

That doesn't make any sense to me. I mean, if anything, we can just find out their next few destinations and catch up if we need to, right? Dusty doesn't have a good answer for that. Just pats my head and tells me how lucky they feel that I'm along for the ride.

The ringleader's caravan is just like Dusty had always described it. Every inch covered in weather-beaten color, moons and stars and animals spilling out from behind oversized flowers and symbols that I can't place. A flash of orange under the back door catches my eye: California poppies. As it turns out, though, the ringleader is the only one who stays in the caravan. It's off-limits to the rest of the crew, only to be entered by direct invitation from the man himself.

When we turn up with our backpacks, Dusty shows us to the accommodations for everyone else: a big sleeper bus that one of the contortionists drives. Well, almost everyone. Mazzy the daredevil drives a truck with all the big-top pieces and rigging, and she gets to sleep in a California king with October, her husband and daredevil-in-arms. I guess there isn't enough money to put us in motels or anything. I wonder aloud if that is a bad sign as we shuffle down the narrow row between the seats, and Violet accuses me of not appreciating the authentic experience.

In our authentic experience, we'll keep our few belongings – costumes, toothbrushes, socks – in plastic bins wedged beneath our bunks and mesh bags that dangle from the bunks above. It looks like a flea market inside the bus. There will be just enough room not to touch anything while we sleep if we keep our arms at our sides and lie perfectly still.

The ringleader hardly introduces himself, emerging from his caravan in what I think is an appropriately theatrical cloud of thick smoke. He wears a long sequined cloak with a turned-up collar over a dingy white button-up with a Victorian ruffle down the front. I admire these choices. Wouldn't take him seriously if he were wearing anything else.

He says very little, but presses thick packets into our hands with great reverence and uncomfortably intense eye contact, so for a second I'm tricked into thinking I hold an ancient religious text instead of a stack of printer paper held together with a staple. The Xerox lines are faint but definitely visible.

The Holy Toledo introductory packet tells us how important it is to adhere to the Holy Toledo code of conduct, and how spreading the good word of Holy Toledo is the only way to ensure that Holy Toledo can continue to spread its good word. It's all written in circles, none of which make any sense.

The packet also tells us that when we have a show or, even better, a run of shows in any town, we are expected to commit the rest of our non-performing waking hours to fundraising and outreach efforts. This means penetrating every Internet forum out there if you're a tech whiz, recruiting from the streets if you're charismatic, and, for the rest of us, papering the town with flyers to fill the seats.

Before returning to his caravan, the ringleader tells us that it is an honor to have us along, and there's that word again, *honor*. *Dishonor*, I think, I have dishonored my mother, and *honor*, I have somehow honored this strange man. I dishonored by leaving. I honored by joining. I wonder if these things have anything to do with each other – if they mean that the hum of my often barely perceptible existence in the universe has some sort of gravity, after all.

29

Something else about my mother: after she was fired from her job at the Kmart, we drove three hours to get to the beach. It was going to be dark by the time we got there, I'd protested when she announced our destination. I had just gotten home from school. She had piled beach things by the door: the faded neon towels that had only ever seen the community pool, the folding chairs from our backyard patch and a big rainbow umbrella that I didn't recognize. There were sunglasses on top of her head, even though outside the clouds were swelling with threats of rain. She said the longer it took me to change into my swimsuit, the darker it would be when we got there, and since that was technically correct, I went to dig it out from wherever it was stewing in the back of my closet.

She put a Beach Boys CD on for the drive, which I thought was a little on the nose.

A Beach Boy told me I was his Miss America. My mother told me that when I grew up and got a job, I shouldn't be tricked into thinking my coworkers were my friends, and I should not even for a second believe that my boss was someone to be trusted. 'The things you keep to yourself are your power,' she told me. 'The second you share anything about yourself, they can take it all away.'

I stared at the dead flowers on the dashboard and thought of everything I did not share with her. The Beach Boy reassured me that my heart was made of gold.

'Your teachers,' she added after a pause. 'Don't confuse them for your friends, either. Nobody really cares,' she reminded me, 'no matter how much they say they do. Unless they can prove it. So if they say it, make them prove it.'

Make them prove it, I thought as the car snaked into the pine forest for the long, dark stretch that lay ahead. The elastic from my bathing suit dug into my neck.

Make them prove it, I thought again as we entered the quiet narrow streets of the seaside town. Everything was closed. There were no other cars out, just people wandering corner to corner laughing to themselves. *Prove it*, I thought as the coast finally emerged, silhouettes of warehouses and cranes rising into view against the night sky.

Prove it, I thought years later when the strangers on our doorstep insisted I could be honest with them.

Violet never had to tell me I could trust her. I just do.

My mother didn't have to tell me, either. I did and I didn't. I'd gotten real good at knowing, for any given moment, which made sense.

The ocean was black and mostly still. Driftwood looked like gnarled limbs washed up on the shore. I approached a gigantic twisted leg and couldn't understand why it smelled so vile until I made out the lump rolled up against its side. A dead seal.

'Poor thing,' my mother said. It was the first thing she'd said since we'd gotten out of the car, so I was secretly thankful to this seal for unknowingly sacrificing himself to the rupture of silence and tension. We walked further down the beach to get away from the stench, the ocean fermenting into a probiotic stew.

I pretended that the sound of wind pushing the tufts of grass against each other was soothing enough to make us feel warm inside. She hadn't brought any jackets. Just the umbrella. Watching her cling to herself only made me colder; it was like she was trying to push all of her outer body into a soft inner core, some reserve of warmth that had already been used up.

I watched the earlier determination drain out of her eyes as she looked at the water. I watched the questions that she had for herself materialize. Like: why had she dragged us here? Like: why had she done this; and now that we were here, what was the plan; and after that, and in general, what was the plan? What was she going to do?

So I decided to pretend the cold didn't bother me. I pretended to be excited about going swimming anyway, and ran into the tide to prove it.

She ran in after me. 'Do you feel that?' she asked as the water swirled around our legs.

I considered the feeling. Not quite groundedness, not quite levity, but somewhere in between. The water taking hold of my limbs and pulling them in a reminder that this was the ocean, the big big bad, but I could pull them back. I felt solid.

'That's your body and the ocean, and how they interact to make magic inside of us. That feeling, if you feel it. No one can take that away from you.'

And I did feel it. Electric, like we were doing something wrong and getting away with it. And then I really didn't care about the cold. It felt witchy and delicious. The sand was collapsing beneath our feet, proof that the earth would change without anyone's permission, us having made it all the way here to feel it happen; we were witches, and I was so proud of us.

She was scream-laughing, so I did too. It felt like releasing myself from the responsibility of the lessons she had laid upon me on the drive, lessons that had already started to drag heavy behind me on a chain.

No one can take that away from you. I was young and very stupid at this point in my life. I didn't feel like anything had been taken from me, because it didn't seem like there was anything to take. I felt that life was unpredictable and mine was especially fraught with secrecy, both spoken and unspoken. I felt gaps, certainly – intermittently in our family, like when the concept of my father came up; most of the time at school; and constantly at the back of my throat. But I felt like I had been born with these gaps, and had grown soft and spongy around them, had arranged the shape of myself to quietly cover over the missing parts that might otherwise have felt like aches, and to keep myself whole.

My mother ventured deeper into the water, beyond where my feet could still reach the sand. I stayed where my legs could anchor into the earth below and watched her head become smaller in the distance. The earth and sky melted together, misty waters blurring the horizon line, and for all I knew she was disappearing into the edge of the world.

30

Russell called a hitman on himself, once, to see how long he could outrun his own killer. He tells me this before he introduces himself as the sword swallower with a small demonstration. I politely do not mention, as I watch the blade disappear slowly between his wet and eager lips, that there was probably no hitman and he likely just made some scammers very happy that day.

Deva is the ringleader's daughter; he claims she was immaculately conceived. She is convinced that she left our astral plane and visited other worlds when she was a small child, and her time back on Earth is just part of the journey to return to the ones she remembers. She always walks around looking lost, wearing this expression of having just woken up from a dream. Some of the others suspect drugs. I suspect the ringleader.

'It's surreal – all the colors are different from the ones we have here,' she explains about her travels, voice soft and pleading. 'But there's no way to create them from the colors we have, from mixing paints or anything. They're a whole different set of shades. And the beings look like us but they have powers – they can fetch medicine from the sky. It doesn't even feel like a special power to them, it's just how they are. I hope I can show you one day. I'm going to find them again.' Deva had dreamed of being a lion tamer, apparently, but there wasn't room for a lion in this circus. She'd settled on charming snakes.

Dusty and I have come down to the waterfront one last time before getting on the road tomorrow. I have never seen them without their statue makeup before and can't stop tracing my eyes over the contours of their face, as if I will need to remember so I can draw them from scratch later.

'Is it often that the ringleader accepts acts before even seeing them?' I ask. 'It feels weird to me. We've been to so many auditions, you don't understand. Like, I know how it's supposed to work.'

Dusty doesn't answer right away.

'And is dinner always that long? I think we got about four hours of sleep last night. No way do we have to do that every night.'

The ringleader had announced that it was Violet's and my welcome dinner. At first it felt nice, all of us ringed around the fire, passing around pots of various stews that the ringleader had cooked in the caravan. Everyone introduced themselves, so many people that I forgot their names immediately and settled on remembering them by their roles in the show.

Hours later we were still in that circle, and the ringleader was passing around torches for us to light. 'We are the light,' he said, 'and light is truth.' Others carried out reams of golden cloth stacked in their arms, long red candles, a heavy brass gong. A green-haired clown handed us cloths from her stack, which unfolded to reveal themselves as robes of a sort, their material papery. Everyone pulled theirs on to display a symbol of concentric circles on their chests. I followed suit as the ringleader came to stand in front of Violet and me.

'What is light?' he asked with no expression visible on his face. He seemed ten feet tall in front of us.

I waited for Violet to answer.

'Truth,' she said, nodding agreeably.

He did not nod in return, but swept down to the trapeze artist beside us. 'What is light?'

'Light is what only we understand. The more they try, the less they will ever be able to understand it.'

Who are 'they'? I wanted to ask as the ringleader smiled approvingly and moved on to Dusty. *And who are 'we', for that matter?* The sounds that the robes made as we moved around within them were not unlike the crunchy snaps from the fire.

Dusty said light was the product of true communion and absolute trust, which is what would save us. *Save us from what?* I was almost going to lean over and whisper as the ringleader moved on, but then the gong was struck and it was time to dance.

The ringleader warned everyone to mind their torches and the candles, which were now lit and surrounding the fire, and the circle erupted into a cacophony of whirling bodies and flames. 'The dancing,' Dusty screamed over the drumbeat, 'is a spiritual practice. You move as vigorously as your muscles will allow. Until your body thinks it's drained. Which it isn't!' they insist, index finger to the barely visible sky. 'It's a trick your mind plays on you to keep you from getting to the new place, the place beyond that feeling, like' – they take a breath of smoke-blackened air – 'like *oh my God, I'm going to die.* Trust me,' they said, dropping their torch to take each of our hands, 'trust me, you won't die if you just keep moving. Keep moving and' – they squeeze their eyes shut – 'you'll feel it, and when you do, that's light.'

'What does it feel like?' I screamed back, but their eyes were closed as they jumped up and down, dragging our bodies with them, coughing from the smoke. 'You'll know when you feel it,' and it was Violet screaming back to me. 'Do you feel it?' I asked, and she pressed her torch to the reluctant stars. 'We'll know when we feel it,' she announced, and seemed to like the sound of that, so she said it again and again, punctuating her upward bounds. 'We'll know when we feel it! We'll know when we feel it!'

I don't know what time it was when we finally stamped out all the flames, but we were up the next morning before the sun.

I realize Dusty still hasn't said anything. 'Sorry,' I concede. 'I can't even bring this up with Violet, she'll get so mad. I just don't want her to lose anything. Like, if this turns out not to be what she's been working for, what's that going to do to her?'

'Hey, calm down.' Dusty laughs. 'You'll feel better once you start performing. I know we're weird, but that's also what makes us cool, what makes people come see us. If it's not exactly what she's always dreamed of, it certainly isn't as if she's going to be permanently scarred. People are disappointed all the time, kiddo. They live.'

Violet is not people, I want to say. Violet does not experience disappointment. She is too big to have her feelings captured in a jar and labeled like that. I try to think of how to explain this to Dusty, though, and decide it's beyond any words that I could put together.

I haven't yet told Violet about my realization that I need to go back to California and my mother, either. I figure it can wait until we're further west. Figure also that a few more weeks or months, however long it takes, can't make that much of a difference to my mother after all the time that has already passed. There are a lot of things I don't tell Violet these days.

Dusty also does not know that I am, in fact, permanently scarred. The night I left my mother, I put a note on the kitchen table after she'd gone to work, changed my mind and put it in my pocket, changed my mind again and put it back on the table, then got on the bus to the airport instead of going to school. The note was barely more than an apology, after I'd spent hours poring over and rewriting it, unable to express what I needed to say further than *I'm sorry, don't look for me, I'm sorry, I love you I promise*. I didn't say that I'd be back, because I didn't know if I would. At that time, I had survival on my mind. I thought I needed to form a hard crust over everything that had happened in my life so far and crawl out the other side as a clean sardine, unblemished in the sudden clarity. I thought I just had to run so hard that nothing could catch up to me, had to burn down everything in my path.

When I arrived at the airport, I didn't really know where to go or what to do with my luggage and my ticket and my body. I had the thought that it wouldn't really matter if I got on the wrong plane. I just needed to be anywhere far away and, gazing up at the big electronic screen of departing flights, I felt for the first time as if I had options. Hundreds and hundreds of destinations in blinking orange letters while my ticket to Miami, bottom right corner, furthest possible place, burned a hole in my back pocket.

I figured out where to go and found my place on the plane, where a gentle hum slowed the race of my heart. My heartbeat was still flickering back then, two or three beats per minute too fast. Still dropping out of my ribcage sometimes. I had taken to making small incisions on my stomach, just deep enough to wince, to help me in moments like this. Those scars wouldn't drop out on me once they'd scabbed over; I could press them through my shirt and count on them to deliver a steady, dependable throb. Something to match my breathing to. Kind of a trick.

One day, though, I'd pushed the blade in perpendicular, straight like a dagger. The blood erupted right back up like a geyser. My vision flashed and suddenly I didn't feel like a tough motherfucker anymore; suddenly I hadn't outsmarted anyone. The blood had soaked the corner of the mat that we had on the floor next to the shower to dry your wet feet, give you traction, so that you wouldn't fall and hurt yourself. I'd rolled up the mat and stuffed it in my backpack that night. The next day, I'd thrown it in one of the dumpsters behind the school. My mother never noticed it was gone or, if she did, never said anything about it to me.

I recall Violet being very impressed with all this, when she asked about where I'd come from back in the shelter. She asked to see the scar and traced her forefinger over its whitened ridge, gentler, softer than I'd ever seen her.

'You're so strong.'

I squirmed under her enormous, awe-soaked eyes, half her face glassy from the warm yolk of the lamp. I hadn't expected her to touch me. Little rat feet pitter-pattered all up and down my spine.

'I knew you were special from the first time I heard you speak. Before that, even. When you got here, I could just sense it in you.'

My heart started to run off course again and I willed her to press down, but of course she wouldn't. Then when she leaned even closer and kissed the scar with a soft, warm mouth, I thought my heart had just fallen out.

Dusty is looking at me expectantly.

'Sorry, what'd you say?'

'Nothing, just that it'll be fine. You worry too much, dear. And you don't want to make me have to start worrying about you, do you? Why should we worry, huh? You're a star.'

After bandaging the wound and taking care of the blood-soaked mat that afternoon, I calmed myself down by promising that there would come a day when I would forget I had ever done this. That I just needed to survive these long years before I became rock-fucking-hard, tiger-striped and invincible. I had tried to find out how long it takes for a scar to disappear and ended up scrolling through rows and rows of images of other people's mutilations: the missing limbs, leaking stitches, big gaping-jaw wounds of war vets, burn victims and other strangers who all had it worse than me. I drank these in, like penance, and crawled into bed that night with both eyes bleeding and raw.

The next night, I tried again. *How long does it take for a scar to disappear*, I typed, then scrolled past the medical advice websites and hospital FAQ pages. I was just looking for answers, I told myself as I clicked the video of the man exploding after being caught in a lathe. I was just making my own crystal ball. I was just trying to take care of myself, I insisted as I squinted to make out where the pieces of his body had gone after it happened. There was all the blood, but where did his skin go? Plus all the other parts, like his liver and bones?

Just wondering, just looking. Just seeing what was possible out there in the world.

Violet is not the second thing I've been given to protect. I know this in part of my brain, but another part remembers the full weight of her head in my lap when the night was long and the moon was new and the trust she placed in me was all-consuming. That feeling was sweet and heavy in my throat. As in, it was too much to swallow. A whole new way to choke.

31

hemophobia – fear of blood

Blood itself is nothing to be scared of. It's why you're seeing it that it's scary.

My scars are healed over and I crave wholeness that feels long out of reach. The harm I've done is evidenced in my body, sealed with the same blood that paves my vessels and veins, always reminding me that I'm an alive animal with a heart that beats for many reasons – I am capable of survival, I am capable of hurt, I am capable of love.

32

Performing for a full audience feels different. In some ways, the pressure to impress that clouds the room during auditions is lifted in front of people who have already paid to see us. Captives. *Ow-ow-ow-ow.* Familiar burns spread over the rawest parts of my skin as Violet ties me up like always, but this time with even more achingly vaudevillian flourish.

Ow-ow, she finishes the knots on my wrists and, *ow*, pulls me into center stage. I pucker my lips now like she taught me to do. I am meant to look pretty and lifeless, she always reminds me. Small and pretty like a doll. That's what the painted-on eyes are for. The streaks of pink paint on my cheeks, and the painstakingly applied dots of freckles.

I can't see the audience through the stage lights but will myself not to squint, not to blink my doll eyes and ruin the illusion. Are they getting it? Are they missing the point? I can't help but shift my eyes, just my eyes, over to Violet on stage left.

A flicker lights up my stomach. She's brilliant like I've never seen her, face flushed and expression hardened with determination as she executes the motions with razor-sharp clarity.

This is what passion looks like, I decide. And I wonder if I finally have a name for this flicker that wakes up when I look at her sometimes, that climbs the walls of my stomach lining when I can feel the heat of her breath as she leans in close to apply my freckles.

My eyes snap back forward and I see nothing but white light. I remember a dream that I had not long after the priest in New Orleans assigned me those prayers that I never prayed. An altar sat burning inside of the sun, and I whispered my penance for all the terrible things I had ever done to myself and the people who'd come close enough to touch me. I didn't know how to leave when I had finished my confession, so I just curled up and waited to be burned to a sinless crisp of poetic justice. It didn't happen. The sun cradled me in its core. I don't remember if my eyes were open or shut, but I know I could see everything at once, white-hot and blinding.

It is suddenly very important to me to convey the message perfectly to this faceless audience, drowned in light. I need them to understand exactly what our performance means. I need them to understand so hard that it scares them. I widen my eyes and open my mouth in a perfect, orgasmic O when Violet spins me by the wrist. *Look me in the eyes, the whites of my eyes*, I dare them. *Fear my tonsils.* When she starts to drag me offstage, I really let loose. The screaming, I mean. It's easy to scream into the light, a brilliant void that receives the rage I've been harboring for all kinds of things that I didn't have the language for, and turns it into nothing at all. I don't realize that I'm still screaming offstage until Dusty busts through the backstage doors and Deva is suddenly kneeling beside me with half her fist in my mouth.

'Let her keep going,' Violet says, beaming down at me with pride. 'She sounds amazing.'

'Is she fucking crazy?' Deva does not dislodge her fist from my patient doll mouth. Above her head, Dusty nods proudly.

Violet and I lock eyes and we laugh hard, until she flops down beside me and starts screaming too. I look back out at the stage and can see the faces in the audience from here, without the lights beating directly down on us. They all look dead to me, basically motionless in the dark, dead compared to the brilliant rage and joy that surged through Violet and me. These people have no idea what they've just witnessed.

Later, Violet will explain our behavior to the ringleader as method acting. She will tell him that I am a genius and to please respectfully refrain from doubting the authority of my voice, then sit back and await his thanks for the privilege of having us in his show. I will nod along, as I always do when Violet gets to talking like this. It comes just as naturally as the screaming did, this complicity. Like breathing.

'Amazing. She was incredible,' Violet says before I can pipe up. My mouth is still a little sore from Deva's bony knuckles. 'She totally sold the angle of femininity being bound up with violation, totally showcased what makes female rage unique and so... so powerful, but even that's too weak a word for what Smidge just did out there.'

My face is roaring hot and I feel like I'm still screaming. I snatch one of the brochures from the sheaf tucked under Dusty's arm to hide my smile.

The words come into focus. *Congratulations*, it says. *Your help has been solicited in de-contaminating this area of the universe. It's your duty to make this planet safe not only for us, but for the billions of others also in danger.*

Well. These aren't the brochures for the show.

'Don't worry about that,' they say, reaching for it. 'You guys don't need to see that stuff yet.'

I turn around so they can't grab it. *We did not create the human mind nor the human body. We did not place this planet, galaxy, nor universe here to involve human life.*

'Seriously, kid. It's dangerous for you to see that before you're ready.' Dusty grabs me by both shoulders, making me jump, and my eyes dart down the page as I pull myself free. *On the reverse, you will find the drills that you are expected to complete and report on.* I flip the paper. *Once you are in luminous mind state, observe each person and perceive their relationship with touch until you experience a Sighting.* I turn away from Dusty, toward the truck.

Their hand slams on the metal from behind me, and they tear the paper from my hands. I turn around but can't look them in the silver-painted eye.

'What's dangerous?'

'What? Nothing.'

'You said it's dangerous for me to see before I'm ready. What's the danger?'

'Oh, nothing. I didn't mean it like that! Relax. Always worried about something. That's my Smidge.'

I study their expression and wonder if the paper is bullshit. I wonder if they secretly wanted me to see it. Behind their head, the trapeze artists dart in from the stage, which means the show will be over soon. The ringleader will be giving his closing remarks, which he'd mentioned in passing but never delivered in full during rehearsal. I push past Dusty to go see what he has to say, which suddenly seems pretty important.

He's already talking by the time I get within earshot. Behind him flutters a curtain-height tapestry of his own face overlaid by concentric circles.

'Our artists are inspired by the beauty and purity of the Divine Plan in their works. Tonight, we hope we have succeeded in sharing our vision with you.'

His top hat and coat glitter like a golden sun under those lights. A fake golden sun.

'What brought you here tonight? Curiosity, maybe? Coincidence? The reality is, you are already a part of it, too. All of humanity is evolving toward the realization of the Divine Plan.

'You see, history cannot be justified simply by its own existence – rather, it demands a greater reason for its being. Why else have humans been searching for the meaning of life since the dawn of recorded thought? This is a spiritual process that we all undertake, although few see it through to completion. Pursuit of this greatest truth is natural, which means the innate divinity of humans is the driving force for all actions that create the events of history. Transcendence is vital to the further evolution of humanity to the next plane. This is the Divine Plan.

'Each of the acts you've seen tonight hold some of the esoteric wisdoms necessary to achieve this transcendence. If you weren't able to discern them, don't worry; we'd be honored to help you do so.'

Not ours. Where's Violet to set this motherfucker straight? The ringleader is directing the audience to give their contact information to any of the ushers in red velvet suits all along the back wall, flanking the exits. Violet would not stand for our art being misrepresented, but she's not around, so I summon up all the rage in her place. I feel the heavy-lidded stained-glass Jesus staring down at us, and he is just as pissed. I know Jesus has his own ideas about a divine plan, too, and I bet he never told the ringleader any of this either. Maybe we are on the same side, after all.

33

My mother was home a lot more after getting fired from the Kmart, which meant she noticed me a lot more. This could be a bad thing some days. It could also be good, like when she saw the hole I'd torn through my sneakers.

'Why didn't you show me that?' she asked in disbelief the first time she noticed it.

'Because I don't care,' I lied. The truth was I didn't know if she would blame me for ruining my shoes. Her reaction to things like that could vary so wildly, it was never worth bringing anything up on my own. Failed tests, an upset stomach. I usually just kept everything to myself and waited to see if she would find out.

'We'll go get you a new pair. I can't believe I've been letting you walk around like that,' she muttered, jamming her own feet into the plastic flip-flops she'd been wearing ever since she stopped leaving the house. 'Your teachers must think we're trash.'

I didn't think my teachers thought anything about me, but my mother was always very concerned about us looking like trash. Anyway, I'd take any reason to get new sneakers that didn't let the dew on the grass of the field seep through and soak my sock. We couldn't go to Kmart, which sucked because I knew they had the light-up sneakers that I wanted. It was going to be tough if my mother stuck with the Kmart boycott she'd initiated after getting fired, because pretty much everything we owned that wasn't secondhand came from there. But the wound was fresh, so we went to the mall.

The last time we'd gone to the mall was Christmas. It looked shrunken and bare without the fake pine garlands and fat red ribbons streaming down the aisles. We scoured a bin of shoes marked down to five dollars a pair in a dimly lit store with grids on the walls displaying the clothes, some still sealed in stacks of flimsy plastic bags on shelves below. Club music boomed through the speakers. None of the shoes fit me.

We drank Slurpees on a bench facing the Victoria's Secret. I averted my eyes from the posters flanking the entrance and laser-focused on the rack of bras with no bodies inside them.

In the parking lot, my mother's face flushed with indignation. I followed her gaze to a dog in the backseat of a car, gazing out with big brown pit-bull eyes.

'Someone locked their dog in their car? Are you kidding me?'

She whirled around, looking for the owner to come unlock the door, and stomped up to the window.

'They rolled the fucking windows up?'

She tried every door. They were all locked.

'You never leave a dog in your car unattended,' she told me.

The idea of having a dog or a car to worry about seemed very far-off to me, but I nodded in sage understanding.

'Now we have to wait for the stupid fucking owner to come. If they're not here in ten minutes I swear to God I'm going to break a window. This is not okay.'

Swearing to God was also a far-off concept to me, but breaking a window wasn't. I eyed the pit bull nervously. He seemed fine in there.

Unfortunately, she stuck to her word. When no one came by, she went back to our car and dug the lug wrench out from beneath the floor of the trunk.

'Does anyone know whose dog this is?' she shouted into the parking lot, pointing the wrench at the passenger window where it stared out at her. A man looked up briefly from his phone at the far end of the row. His other arm was filled with a potted plant, cradled against his side like a baby.

My mother looked at me and shook her head, as if to say *these people*, as if to say *do I have to do everything myself?* I'd lived enough by then to have become accustomed to figuring things out on my own, so calling for help didn't surface as an option in my mind. It was break the window or that dog died. Break the window because no one else would, otherwise we basically killed him. The choice was so obvious: better to be in trouble with people than to have dog blood on our hands.

She circled around the car to the trunk window, the furthest one from the dog. She raised the wrench with both hands and slammed it down, and it bounced off the glass, so she slammed it down again and again and again until the glass split into a spiderweb, and again and again until it fell away from the frame and rained down in a glittering pool around her feet.

The car alarm screamed at us. Some lady screamed at us, pointing, looking around for anyone to confirm that what she was seeing was not allowed to happen. Then the owner of the car screamed at us, running out of nowhere to ask my mother what the hell she thought she was doing.

The finer points of their argument went over my head, but she was talking about *animal cruelty* and *jail*, and he was talking about *property damage* and *lawsuit*.

The security guard took his sweet time making his way over, and my mother folded her arms and waited in defiance for him to arrive. Nobody addressed the dog, who was chained to the passenger seat but threw his shuddering bulk over and over toward the open space where the back window had been. I found myself entranced by the snapping jaws. I'd never been that close to some-thing that, for all we knew, was ready to kill.

'She's crazy. She broke my window – look at this!' The owner gestured at the shards scattered between them as if the security guard wouldn't notice them otherwise. 'She's crazy!' he repeated when the guard didn't handcuff her immediately and ship her directly to prison.

The guard looked at my mother, then at the wrench in her hands, then the glass, then the pit bull making a sound like the world was being torn in half. He addressed the man.

'You left your dog unattended?'

'What? I was just running in.'

'It's seventy-six degrees out. You know it can get up to three times that inside a car with the windows rolled up?'

'If I rolled the windows down, my car would've gotten jacked.'

'If she hadn't broken them, your dog would've cooked.'

'You can't be serious.'

'Dead serious. Dead as your dog would've been if...' – he addresses my mother now – 'What's your name, ma'am?'

'Carrie.'

'If Ms Carrie hadn't come along. There are plenty of witnesses. So. I could call Animal Services, or do you want to figure it out?'

The man stared at the security guard and the security guard stared back. I wondered how the man had envisioned this playing out when he'd looked up the number for mall security on his phone and then punched it in, waited for someone to pick up, given his location and description of the incident over the sound of his dog losing his shit, while my mother and I stood by, her with folded arms, me with holey shoes, everyone knowing they were partly wrong but believing they were mostly right.

I wondered if most things had gone how he'd expected in his life. I wondered what that was like.

To have expectations, I mean. And then to have them fulfilled.

We all looked at each other until the security guard told us he would walk my mother and me to our car, and he did, and we drove to Walmart where my mother bought me a new pair of sneakers full price, and those sneakers lasted me the next three years.

She sang under her breath all the way home. Something fizzled to life for a second, electric and new – I was proud of her.

34

gynophobia – fear of women

Tina said that we are the ones to fear. But it isn't our wombs that they're afraid of: palpable organs that anyone could locate and excise if they really wanted to.

That which is to be feared: a flash that becomes an always-burning ember. A drop that becomes a storm. A hunger that threatens to eat you back if you keep leaving it unfed.

So we grow over choppy waters, and no one can tame that which is to be feared. And no one can touch it if they don't quite know what's there. We are good at keeping secrets. And this one is ours.

35

There isn't a waterfront where we are in Dallas, just a whole tangle of wide-open streets that seem to trail off into nowhere. Violet and I settle for climbing onto the roof of a hardware store, hoisting ourselves up from the dumpster. We just left opening night behind us, snuck out to celebrate on our own. That's how I presented it to Violet, anyway. Really, I wanted to be far away from the circus before getting into things.

The stars are dim with light pollution; crisscrossing freeway overpasses rise like rollercoasters over the glow of buildings in the distance. It seems darker where we are, Violet and I feeling well hidden and far away. She pulls out a bottle of wine that she got from who knows where. I don't know how to begin.

'Violet,' I start warily, 'I need to tell you something.'

'Sure.'

'That thing Dusty had? It was this weird worksheet. It said all this stuff like, oh, you've been chosen, so now you need to complete these tasks to clean the universe or something. Then at the end of the show, the ringleader came out and started telling everyone how there's a big plan that we're all a part of, and everyone at Holy Toledo is guided by that plan, and all the performances are only intended to share that plan, and the reason for the plan is like, imminent danger, and the people watching have to join us to be saved from it.'

She peels the foil from the neck of the bottle and stabs her pocket knife into the cork. 'So what?'

'What? That has nothing to do with our act. Well, that's not the point, though. The ringleader is fearmongering to get people to join his movement. You know what that sounds like, right?'

Violet laughs a quiet half of a laugh, shaking her head.

'Do you hear yourself? All that shit is part of the performance, the experience for the viewer. It gives everything higher stakes. That's what good art does, it raises the stakes.' She rolls toward me to offer the wine bottle. 'Like you did tonight. That was incredible.'

I can't believe Violet is going to sit here and accuse me, as always, of not understanding art.

'How can you know that? What makes you so sure?'

'Because, Smidgey. Not everything is so sinister, okay? Something good finally happened for us. We have to see it through. And I get it – I love being on the road too, just the two of us. I wouldn't trade that time for anything. Honestly, I don't think you understand how much I love you. I've never had anyone like you in my life, not even close.'

I can't look at her. We don't usually say *I love you* in so many words, and after our performance, those words glow Venus-hot and dangerous.

'We'll get away like this once a day, okay?' she offers. 'No Dusty. No Deva. Just you and me.'

You're missing the point, I think and do not say out loud. Because maybe she has the point. Maybe she is the point by which I set my course. She said she loved me so casually, as if it were an obvious truth, and I can't think of when I've ever said the same to her.

What if she's right? That I'm just jealous and needy as always, and I'm trying to fabricate trouble to get us back to where I want us. Nothing bad has happened. Everything is fine. Since when do I care so much what people think about our performance, anyway? What am I scared of?

I look over at Violet and place her back on the side of a train in the slow-thawing dusk, imagine that this is the last time I'll see her. I know exactly what I'm scared of.

I feel myself acquiesce and it's almost physical: melting myself down to fit into the world that Violet has created for us.

'Okay, once a day. We'll find some time to at least not be around the others for, like, an hour.' I can't make myself add *and I love you too*, as badly as I want to say it. It feels too late already.

The little sound of happy agreement she makes sometimes is almost like the purr of a cat.

'Whatever you need.'

36

belonephobia – fear of pins and needles

In sixth grade, we were supposed to dissect frogs. I forged my mother's signature excusing me from the need to dissect a frog, even though I knew she would have signed it in a heartbeat.

There were a select few areas in which my mother and I were on the same page. The inexcusability of animal cruelty was one of them.

Mrs Portnoy slapped a thick packet of worksheets onto my desk and sent me to the library with my textbook to fill them out. 'It won't be nearly the same learning experience,' she warned me, 'as the hands-on activity. Not even close. You're going to miss out on a lot.'

Her disapproval fueled me. I finished the packet in ten minutes and spent the rest of the time reading about a deep-sea diver who thought he saw a fish that was supposed to be extinct on one of his expeditions, and then devoted the rest of his life to trying in vain to find it again. I remember thinking that was noble. A life well spent.

I returned to the classroom to turn in my completed assignment before the bell rang. Tommy and Nojan followed me out. They asked why I hadn't been there for dissection, which made me instantly suspicious, because I knew for certain that no one noticed, or cared, where I was at any time.

I told them anyway. I said it was unethical. It was animal cruelty, and I would not partake in it.

They looked at each other. 'That's what I thought,' Tommy said.

'Poor froggies,' Nojan said. 'We didn't want you to miss out on anything, though.'

He pulled his hands out from behind his back and whisked away the top hand to reveal a pile of organs and guts in the other, like a servant presenting the master with his meal.

I stared hard at his wrist instead of his hand, so I would look brave, so I would look truly above it all, without having to actually take in the wreckage of a perfectly good and innocent animal that was already starting the proverbial lump, that was already going to make me cry.

I looked at his wrist and I looked in his eyes, and they were hard and mad because it wasn't the reaction they wanted and I knew it and they knew I knew, and I was proud of that, and me being proud made it even worse when Tommy said *think fast* as he hit the back of Nojan's hand. He hit it really hard, so all the guts and organs flew out of his hand and landed on my face, and I smelled it everywhere and yeah, then I was sad about the stupid frogs in full force, then I was angry, I was grossed out, whatever they wanted me to be, so I delivered. I opened my mouth for once and I screamed. I screamed over the lump still quivering in my throat, threatening to make me messy when I needed to be big and horrible, needed to handle this like a boy would.

I squeezed my eyes shut because I thought that would give my mouth more room on my face to open up wider and make the scream louder and in doing so scare them worse, because the louder the scarier, and until then I had been the quietest person I knew.

When I opened my eyes again, Tommy was still laughing, but Nojan had stopped. He was looking at his hand, slimy with left-overs. Then he was looking at me, and at Tommy, and then down at the frog lungs that had bounced off of my face and landed on the floor between us.

Glove, gauntlet, it had been thrown from his hand, but it was Tommy who had made his hand move, and technically I'd been the last to touch it, so who'd actually thrown the gauntlet, who was responsible for this? I don't know if that's what he was thinking about, but his mouth was shut.

He was the quiet one now.

If someone didn't know any better and saw his face, they might say he was almost scared.

He was looking at me like I was a wild animal.

And my jaw had been loosened.

And I smelled blood and guts all over my face, like I had just killed something with my mouth.

I mean, he was looking at me like I was going to bite.

So I did.

37

Deva has invited me to watch the feeding of her snake in the truck. The snake eats white mice – live ones, she specified, explaining that what makes the meal satisfying for the snake is the need to capture and kill it.

The mice sleep on top of each other in a twitching pile in a corner of their cage. Deva's named each and every one of them, she claims, and truly loves each. She said in her whispery, serious voice that she didn't expect me to believe her, when I said there was no way she could tell them apart. She said maybe if I stuck around long enough, I'd understand. Something about Deva's detachment from the need to be taken seriously captivates me; she floats far above the urgent rampage for recognition that has defined my life since Violet.

'Elliot couldn't make it,' she informs me now, gazing into the mouse cage with slow-blinking eyes. 'He has to do some fundraising stuff.'

Elliot is one of the clowns. He joined the circus fresh out of juvenile detention for getting caught with weed in his backpack in a seventh grade pre-algebra class. This earned him a sexy bad-boy status, and a place as the object of Deva's affections, although she won't admit it to Violet and me. I don't know why. I think it's cute. Deva is thirteen but seems even younger than that most of the time: the way she trails after Violet and me in her perpetual dream state, sleepy voice bubbling with questions, index finger forever holding her place in whatever vampire romance novel she happens to be rereading.

'That's too bad,' I tell her. 'We could wait until later, if you want.'

'No, she needs to eat now. Otherwise she'll be pissy.'

I wonder how someone can tell whether a snake is pissy, but just nod in deference.

'Maybe we can find Elliot later, then. You can show him what you have so far on your performance.'

Violet and I are giving her lessons on choreographing a perform-ance art piece. Not that her snake charming isn't magnificent – it absolutely is. Violet just wants to show her how to use her body to tell a complex story, and sees great potential in her to do so.

The story Deva has proposed is about unrequited love.

'No way,' she says, pulling her hair in front of her face and then inspecting the strands as if it's the first time she's ever seen hair. 'It's not even close to ready yet.'

'Well, he could probably help, with all his clown experience. Not that you actually need help, but I bet he'd love to have an excuse to work with you.'

She shakes her head, but her face comes briefly awake with a smile as she turns away to retrieve the snake from its warm glass cell.

'Do you want to hold her?' she asks shyly.

I roll my eyes like *duh* and reach for the snake, and she delicately lays the length of its silvery body along my outstretched hands. The snake is cooler to the touch than I expected. It writhes slowly, its intestines discernible in its weight, scales petal-soft against my skin.

'Does she have a name?'

'Of course. Thank you for asking. Manasa. Named after the snake goddess. If we were in India, the whole show would be all about worshiping her. America doesn't have the same respect for what's actually important, unfortunately.'

'Total hellscape,' I agree. 'Were you born in America?'

Deva shrugs, gaze wandering skyward. 'I don't know exactly where I appeared. All I know is that I'm here now.'

'But you don't remember where you grew up?'

She doesn't answer, just drags a blue plastic bucket in between us and motions for me to put the snake inside. 'She's going to act quick,' she warns.

I don't want to let go of the snake now that she's coiling herself around my arms – kind of like the feeling of being the tree.

'How does the snake charming thing relate to the... like, the light thing?' I ask, half-stalling and holding on to my time becoming one with Manasa, half-curious and testing the rules of this place a little.

In the ringleader's world, there is a planet of light orbiting the sun that we are all destined for. Like an afterlife, except he just thinks of it as life. Everything we are doing here, he has explained, is just to get there. To bring as many people as we can. To save them.

That planet doesn't exist in the world of Violet and me, but we've discovered that it does for a lot of the other people here. I try to ignore it, mostly. Of course, something else has crossed my mind: we are here to convey Violet's message and not the ring-leader's, and what makes ours so much better? What makes ours the truth? I try to ignore those questions, too.

'Oh, it doesn't,' Deva says matter-of-factly. 'Most of the show has nothing to do with the mission, really. It's just a way to get people to pay attention, and to care, so that they'll join the move-ment and be saved alongside us when we move on.'

'Right. Do you really believe in that whole part of this? That we're going to...?'

'Yes,' she interrupts softly, smiling at the sky. 'Yes, I believe we have a destination. Whether it's another planet where we're free from earthly ailments, or him deciding he's over it and moving us to Ohio so I can go to high school already.'

I consider this simple clarity, from the ringleader's daughter, of all people. 'So that's what keeps you here?'

'I mean, he's my dad. So this is my home. Where else would I go? But I'm also bound by my duty – even when I'm grown up, I'm afraid I can't think about leaving until I've at least done something to make sure the beings are safe.'

I'd almost forgotten about the little aliens. Or whatever they were – Deva only referred to them as *the beings*. 'How old were you when you saw those, again?'

'I was nine. Too young to fully understand what exactly the danger was that they were in – I just knew it was there, and I can still sense its presence after all these years. It's hard to explain how danger can be felt through the multiverse, but I'm afraid it's been an unwelcome companion of mine over these past years... I just need to figure out how to get back to their plane. My dad's helping me hone that, and it's like anything else: better with practice. Like snake charming. Or... what do you guys call your thing again?'

'Performance art.'

'Oh, yeah. It's like performance art.'

I wish she could hear herself.

'But if there are other planes, or other worlds, why wouldn't it be certain that the planet of light exists too?' I don't think I'm trying to test her anymore. I really want to understand the dream logic that everyone here seems to be operating under, maybe even find my own comfort in the promise of a destination.

She shrugs. 'Well, that's what I mean: it might. For those of us who believe in it. But I've never felt its presence in my travels, personally. And just between us – isn't it convenient that the only way to get there is to dedicate oneself to the teachings and practices of Holy Toledo?'

It feels like a trap to agree to this. 'So you think your dad might not have really seen it?'

'No idea. I think no matter what he's truly seen or not, or whatever divine messages he's received, all he really wants is for people to listen to him. Don't you think?'

'Sure,' I respond, thinking of all the places Violet and I have traveled to perform our act. Begging with our bodies to have our voices be heard.

'Hello, girls.' It's a voice that I recognize as the ringleader's before I look up.

How long have you been standing there? is what the person would say if this were happening in a movie. I say nothing. I forget to even say hi back.

'What are we spending our time on here?' he asks, looking only at Deva and not at me, but in a way that still makes me feel silvery-cold inside.

'Just feeding Manasa. Smidgey's helping me,' Deva says coolly, turning her back to him to lift the lid from the mouse cage.

I relinquish Manasa to the bucket, and Deva spends a long time selecting a mouse to scoop into her hand and carry over.

'Very interesting. You never needed help feeding Manasa before,' he replies, smiling and cocking an eyebrow. This is the cartoon pirate expression that he always does when he makes some little comment he is proud of.

'Well, I'm teaching her about snake care. In exchange for the lessons they're giving me about performance art.'

'Isn't that nice? I didn't know you were interested in snake care, Smidge.'

'I like animals,' I say, and don't know why my voice sounds so high-pitched and fake when this isn't even a lie.

'Well, well. I'd love to learn more about what you're interested in. You certainly brought new life to the show when you joined, really unlike anything we've ever seen before. You've been incredible to watch.'

I hate myself for blushing, again. Before he can continue, Deva cuts in with a mouse in her palm. It nibbles on the little crescent of flesh below her index fingernail, but she doesn't seem to notice.

'Never pick up a mouse by the tail,' she instructs, 'except for this purpose. It's actually the least traumatic for the mouse to simply drop in, because it's going to be dead in a second anyway.'

When she lifts the mouse by its tail, it emits a squeak, and I know that with Deva's palm no longer securely beneath its feet, it can see the snake below it and knows the end has come.

I'm convinced it thinks it's unleashing a bloodcurdling scream in response, because the only other thing it can do is dangle, and tremble, and nothing that could save its life.

It makes me think of newborn turtle flippers again, pounding the sand and logging inches per hour. Shriek reduced to squeak, sprint reduced to crawl, making violent efforts while being so small, and imagine – just imagine – if that were the best you could do. I feel a sudden duty to crush everything in the truck to dust.

'Goodbye, little mousie,' Deva says, and then lets go.

Manasa clamps onto the mouse razor-quick, whacking the bucket with her body so hard when she strikes that it sounds like a gunshot, sending my heartbeat off course as I watch her wrap herself around the mouse's body and squeeze. The hind legs of the mouse twitch and struggle, then thrash with final reserves of violence and vulnerability, paws scrambling for purchase against the slippery-smooth scales. I guess the mouse doesn't know that every time a snake meets a mouse, the snake is destined to win.

The ringleader did not start when the snake lurched forward, did not wince at the gunshot sound. His arms are crossed, muscles relaxed as he gazes into the bucket like it's a Malibu sunset in there. I want him to forget any performance I've ever put on. I want him to forget what I look like. I want him to go away. He glances up suddenly and sees me looking at him and smiles; it feels like a knowing smile, and I blush again, against my will again, because my will is telling me to make him leave us alone, to crush something with my hands, to put my egg tooth to work again, but instead my mouth is smiling back, and it feels like a transaction that I did not authorize.

The snake rests quietly for a moment after the mouse goes limp. Then she opens her jaw and swallows it whole.

38

ophidiophobia – fear of snakes

We are hard-wired to be afraid of snakes.

For eons, the only predator to primates was the snake, and this imprinted on the part of our brains that carries impressions through generations, so that even today, the modern man with guns in both hands still sees death in a snake.

So we're born with innate fear, and it isn't fair. But fear has a purpose that we don't want to admit up here at the top of the food chain – it keeps us safe, keeps trouble at bay. Here I am: these are supposed to be my fearless, tiger-striped and invincible years, and all I seem to be finding is more trouble anywhere I go. Wasn't such a distance ago that I never thought I would live this long, never thought I would go anywhere, but here I am, here I am, here I am.

The fear we inherited from our ancestors. The design of the brain. The course of evolution. None of it is fair.

But neither is the reputation that snakes have been saddled with through centuries of folklore.

And you don't hear them complaining.

39

The day after the snake feeding, I receive a note from the ringleader summoning me to his caravan first thing the next morning. Other than for announcements and shows, he stays holed up in that caravan all the time. 'How are we supposed to ask him anything, then?' I once complained to Dusty, but they just said I could ask them whatever I wanted to know. But all the things I want to ask are things I don't want anyone else to know I'm asking.

As the days pass here, I'm learning that the circus is a great place to be if you don't know what you want. It spoon-feeds everyone all kinds of lessons and promises that know how to puff up and sound important without actually meaning anything at all. A lot of the people had been floating before, and landed here like specks of dust settling. They were blank spaces waiting to be filled.

The trapeze artists, for example, are militant vegans who took jobs as gator wrestlers when money was tight, their freelance ghost-hunting venture had failed and things were getting desperate. Not even real gator wrestlers, but the kind that sat on their backs and held their jaws open for a paying audience. I had tried to laugh about this with Violet, and she just asked me what the hell I thought a real gator wrestler was. Anyway, the ringleader had scouted them out in Orlando and promised them better things in his circus, where every cage is empty, except for Manasa's.

I've been too intimidated to approach the ringleader about what he said on opening night. If I'm honest, I was counting on

Violet to confront him, and never expected that she would submit to someone else's idea of what our art should be.

The tender caves below my eyes are sinking southward. The dinners and fire dances are getting old. These, along with getting up early to get what the ringleader called *a fighting start* on flyering before rehearsal and showtime, mean we keep clocking about four hours of sleep a night. I don't know how everyone else keeps up with this, other than chugging the weird dandelion coffee that is brewed in a gigantic vat every morning. It doesn't taste like dandelions. It tastes like crappy instant coffee. Like, crappier than the kind you'd get at the dollar store.

I can't find Deva anywhere before reporting to the ringleader's caravan, which is odd, because usually she's everywhere. She hangs around Violet and me like a trailing wisp, asking Violet how she gets her makeup so perfectly pointy, telling me she could teach me how to tease my own hair into a glittery double bouffant if I wanted so that Violet wouldn't have to. Offering palm readings. Asking when our next lesson will be.

The inside of the caravan is surprisingly blank and lifeless compared to the outside. It's all white walls and messy stacks of books and binders, with a plain curtain dividing the makeshift front office from the rest of the caravan's interior. A desk lamp with some sort of crystal hanging from its neck is the only thing on the ringleader's desk. A lava lamp is plugged in at the far corner of the office, with the warning label tag still on it and visible, which kind of ruins the effect.

'Thank you for meeting with me, Smidge,' he says, pulling out a chair at the desk for me as I judge his lava lamp in my head. 'I'm really looking forward to elevating the show to the next level with your help. You know you have a real gift.'

He pauses, walking around the desk to sit opposite me without breaking eye contact. He sits forward, as if expecting some response from me as the grating silence presses down. I'm considering complimenting the glitter he's streaked through his ratty black beard when he starts up again.

'I'll tell you, a lot of performers come through here and bring their unique vision to the show. Every one of them is valuable, of course, and it wouldn't be the transformative vision that it is without such a vast collage of varied talents coming together under the big top. But every once in a while, a true visionary comes along.'

'Oh, you're mistaken,' I stop him. 'Violet is the visionary, not me. She taught me literally everything. I just follow whatever she tells me to do.'

'Not Violet. You. Believe me, I've heard it all before – no no, I owe it all to my teacher, or my guru, and so on and so forth. But when you have a true, natural gift, the way that you do, at some point you need to start taking responsibility for that.'

I shake my head. 'No, you don't get it. *Everything* is her, down to every last detail. Like, every time my top lip moves a millimeter up or down my face. She told me to do each one of those movements. Plus, she does all the choreography, and both of our costumes, and the makeup and hair.'

He's letting his smile unfurl slowly on purpose as I talk too much, I can tell, resting his chin on the hammock of his laced fingers.

'So.' I know I've given too much detail. 'It really is all her in this case. She's the one you should be meeting with. Actually, speaking of, why are we meeting?'

'We'll certainly talk about the influence that Violet had on you, okay? You are simply the most interesting person to me at the moment. Wouldn't you agree it's always best to focus on the most interesting thing?'

'Well, sure, but I'm not...'

His expression halts me, pirate eyebrow again like he already knows what I'm going to say.

'...going to fight you,' I finish, a last-minute attempt to throw him off. He is not thrown off. He leans back in his seat, clearly pleased with himself, pleased with my reaction to him, everything probably going exactly as he planned.

'You are the most interesting one here, Smidge,' he declares in a tone of voice that says he's the one who makes those kinds of decisions, so I am correct in not fighting him. 'The most talented. The most fascinating. I believe that under my tutelage, you have the most potential to ascend to a leadership function here. I've decided to take you on as my understudy.'

The way he says this, I'm not sure if I'm allowed to decline.

'Oh. Wow.'

'The understudy is granted special access to higher-level teachings. You've demonstrated that you're capable of grasping these, synthesizing them and producing art. Do you understand this, Smidge? Your art will save lives.'

I've barely spoken to the ringleader. He's seen me in a handful of rehearsals and two shows. What could I have done to convince him of this? How much of my conversation with Deva did he over-hear? Where is she?

'Where's Deva?'

'Right now? She's studying.'

'Studying where?'

'I put her on a special program. She needs to complete it on her own.'

'What's the special program?'

'That's confidential between her and me.'

'But I'm your understudy now. I accept, by the way.'

He grins again. 'That's excellent.'

'So what's the program?'

'I can't share details.'

'What's the point of being your understudy, then?'

He's still smiling the knowing smile that I hate, but I can see the muscles tighten around his eyes.

'You'll come to learn. You'll appreciate it more if you give yourself a chance to absorb these lessons holistically, with no agenda. On your journey to understanding all things in the universe, you can't expect yourself to know all of it at once.'

What a fancy way of saying there's no point to it, I do not say out loud, and instead try the feminine little smile and head-tilt maneuver that Violet knows how to make look natural.

'You're right. I didn't think of it that way,' I offer. 'How do I get started?'

'Well, first I'll need to get to know you a little better. Every experience in your life has a say in how you translate meaning to art. Tell me, as best as you can, the events that led up to your joining Holy Toledo.'

'Uh, like starting from birth?'

'It can be easier to work backwards. So, what brought you to New Orleans, and where you were before then, and before then, and so on.'

I think about what brought me to New Orleans: Violet; and where I was before then: the Carolinas with Violet, and Florida with Violet; and before then: without Violet.

Then I tell the ringleader the story of my life. Except I give him the version that I used to imagine for myself, skipping over Miami, placing myself at a loggerhead rescue in the Keys instead, and at Violet's art school before that, and at my parents' house in the suburbs where I had a dog and a little brother. I elaborate on my lifelong passion for the performing arts, and my family supporting me in my pursuits at the community theater, until the ringleader puts up a finger to stop me.

'What's the name of the community theater in Piscataway? The Tabard?'

'Yes.' I have no idea.

'No, sorry, I'm misremembering. It's been a few years since we passed through. It's called the Julius, isn't it?'

Fuck. 'It's the Tabard.'

He doesn't nod or anything, just looks at me, and my mouth suddenly feels too dry to continue. I can't tell if I've been caught in a lie.

'Thank you for sharing, Smidge. We'll revisit all of this later, of course, in much more depth. I just wanted to get a sense for your molding.'

I make a mental note to memorize everything I've just spewed. He opens a low drawer on the echoey metal desk and flicks through file folders, pulling a yellow sheet out of one and smoothing it against the surface.

'As I mentioned, the universe of knowable things is vast, and your coming into understanding of it all will take time. What we can get started on now are your tasks.'

He slides the paper toward me, and I look down at a neatly organized table with a row of blank boxes to check off.

'Tasks are not to be shared with others,' he explains, 'as the influence of others will invariably change how you approach them. I'm after your unique interpretation here. You are to read the tasks and complete them as you see fit, and keep a log of your observations during and upon completion. Do you understand?'

I read the first task on the table. *Observe your reflection as you recall: a) a memory that induces deep joy; b) a long-held anxiety that causes fear; c) a question to which you have sought, but have not found, the answer. Write a record of your observations in your log.*

'I understand,' I say with every ounce of reverence I can muster while sitting across from him surrounded by all those walls. Who knew the caravan would be so lame inside. I wonder what the ringleader looks like on the inside.

My fingernails skitter involuntarily over the runs in my tights, producing a cricket sound that feels appropriate for the moment. I'm ready for this meeting to be over already. I can't wait to show the tasks to Violet.

'I'm grateful to trust you with this, Smidge. I know you would never do anything to endanger future generations of humankind. You understand that defying anything I have said to you today would be endangering them.'

'Of course.'

40

Divine what you must forgive yourself for. Note it down in your log.

Observe the colors and determine whether they match the objects that they inhabit. Note down any discrepancies.

Violet isn't around when I leave the caravan with my list of tasks. The ringleader gave me deadlines, pulled down a screen and projected so many words and images onto that thing so quickly that I felt like I didn't catch any of it, opened a book and snapped it shut in front of my face, and told me all the while how okay it was that I didn't understand yet.

Don't fucking try to hypnotize me, is most of what I thought the entire time, eyeing the crystal hanging from his desk lamp suspiciously. Chinatown score or malicious tool of deception? The ringleader is one of those dudes who thinks he's a magician, as evidenced by the over-representation of velvet in his wardrobe, and the dress shirts he leaves overly unbuttoned with collars undone to rise into a lily around his neck. I knew all about hypnosis, thanks to Violet.

She once had it done at a magic show that had turned down our act, not because it was bad, the man assured us, but because it wouldn't be accessible to the magic show's audience. *And because*, he'd added with a shrug, *I hate to use the term 'family-friendly' or anything like that, but our type of show can't help but attract the little ones. You know what I'm saying?*

He could sense that we were not content with this explanation, so he called it *art*, and we still were not content, so he called us *beautiful*, and little did he know that was exactly the wrong thing to say to Violet. She'd explained it to me before: how she'd had to work so hard to look like a girl so people would take her seriously, only for the world to use her beauty as another reason to continue dismissing her. Sharp on every side. It was simple and absolutely bulletproof.

This man was a people-pleaser. We'd never had a kinder rejection. I wondered where Violet had even found him. He wrung his hands at us while Violet stood there glaring and not saying anything, me still tied up and stretched out on the floor, and finally offered us a couple of passes to that night's show. *You might see what I mean*, he told us, *and hey, you might even enjoy yourselves!*

Violet wanted to have the usual dramatic exit, I could tell, but I wasn't one to turn up my nose at a free magic show. My hands were still tied behind my back, so I told him to put the passes in my mouth. He averted his eyes while crouching down to do so and backed away quickly, big basketball head reddening over with blush.

When we left, she held her hand out for the passes as we approached a trash can.

'No way are we going to go to some kiddie magic show.'

'What better ideas do you have for our evening, Vi?'

She couldn't answer me.

'Why did you have us audition for that place anyway?'

'It wasn't what I thought it was going to be.'

'What else could it be?'

'I mean, I don't know exactly. But definitely something more sophisticated, some sort of multi-experience show that just happened to specialize in magic.'

'What kind of show would that even be? Something you've ever seen? Like what?'

'Lots of shows.'

'But like what? Name one.'

'Like... Criss Angel.'

'You thought we were auditioning for a Criss Angel Mindfreak spinoff?'

'Shut up.' She was smiling.

'No, Criss Angel is cool. I just didn't know that was your speed.'

'I just can't think of another example off the top of my head.'

'You said what you said.'

The sting of rejection, even from a family-friendly people-pleaser, wore off of her then, and we went to the show that night.

I loved it. The small theater was decorated with glitter-everything inside: glitter backdrop on the stage, glitter signs over the doors, glitter cutouts of stars gently spinning on their fishing line around the perimeter of the room. The opening act was a performer with a puppet. The puppet was a dog. It was wearing a cape: silver, like a wizard's. I would call the performer a ventriloquist, but his lips were totally moving the whole time the dog was talking. He didn't even try to hide it.

He kept pulling things out of the dog's mouth, though, to an increasingly impressive effect. First just quarters that he tossed into the audience, which delighted the scrambling children but looked like a recipe for a lawsuit to me. Then swirly lollipops that kept getting bigger and bigger. Then, finally, a bolt of rainbow-striped fabric that he pulled and pulled and pulled feverishly but it just kept coming, and I understood that the crappy ventriloquism earlier was just to get everyone's expectations real low and this finale was the real trick, made more incredible by comparison, and he was completely pulling it off. Subversive. I made a mental note to discuss this tactic with Violet after the show.

She was eating caramel corn out of a cellophane cone, crunching extra loud on purpose – I could tell by her teeth clacking together in her jaw next to my head. She didn't usually chew like that. She was enjoying making a tiny ruckus, and I left her to it, because she was in a mood. I had known she was in a mood when she hadn't wanted to make fun of the ticket taker with me earlier, who had asked if we were witches while tearing our passes in half, and seemed to believe me when I said yes. Violet had gazed vacantly at the line of families in front of us.

The next performer that came on had a mustache like Salvador Dalí, and I made another note to check on Violet's reaction to this after. Was this allegiance to a great artist, or simply derivative? His face was wholly unlike Salvador Dalí's. It was the kind with peanut-butter-colored freckles that faded into nothing at the edges, and which cascaded into his neck and the rest of his body like a soft-serve ice cream cone on a sunny afternoon. He introduced himself as a hypnotist, taking advantage of that mustache by pinching the ends and twisting them between his fingers. He, of course, needed a volunteer from the audience to assist him with his act.

I knew I needed to act quick. I yanked Violet's hand out of the popcorn cone and held it in the air, waving it around like she was extra-excited for this opportunity, more so even than the mob of little kids in the front rows squealing *me-me-me-me-me-me*. She wiggled her wrist limply in my grip, and that told me she was in, because I knew she could break my grip and also every bone in my body if she wanted to.

Salvador looked beyond the clamoring sea and pointed without hesitation to Violet. She rolled her eyes at me as she stood, but the corner of her mouth was curled upward. I knew what that meant. I sat back and prepared for her to steal the show.

Onstage, Salvador had Violet sit in a baroque chair with its original legs busted off, replaced with the taxidermied limbs of some cloven-hoofed creature. He announced something or other to the audience, but I wasn't listening as much now that Violet's skin was lit up under the stage lights. I looked at her and could feel how much she belonged there. It reminded me of looking up at the sky at the precise moment when a flock of birds passes over. And how you can only see the sky a patch at a time. How the flock feels like a pressing into place, a reminder. If I squinted a little, the black glitter backdrop blurred to a starry night, and Violet could have been in outer space. She could've been anywhere.

The hypnotist produced a big fake green gem dangling from a long fake gold chain. This he swung in front of Violet's eyes. It was uncreative, an exact replica of every story I'd ever heard about hypnosis. He told her she was becoming sleepy. He said she would snap out of it when he said a special word. He asked the audience what the word should be, and because the average age in attendance was like eight, they insisted on *poop* and, when that was shot down as inappropriate, settled on *toilet*.

Salvador kept bringing out more crap from his oversized pockets: oranges that he told her were fourteen-karat gold underneath the peel, blueberries that he presented as pearls, and then, to uproarious laughter from the audience, a head of broccoli that he told her was a chocolate cake.

'Which one would you like to have?' he asked after laying everything out on a table beside her.

'The pearls,' she responded without hesitation.

He rolled one to the far end of the stage.

'Retrieve it.'

She stood up immediately and started walking toward it.

'No,' he said. 'Walking backward.'

She turned around and kept walking until he told her to stop again.

'On your hands and feet,' he instructed then, 'and backward still.' I couldn't believe it when she obliged.

The next part was worse. He sat her back down in the chair and gave her a bowl of blueberries.

'You followed instructions so well,' he cooed, 'that you get to have all of these. But there's a catch. To have them, you have to *eat* them.'

The kids shrieked with laughter when Violet's face crumpled in confusion.

'Okay, fine,' Salvador conceded, 'you can keep that one you fetched if you eat the rest of them here.'

So Violet ate the blueberries, eyes brimming with tears, the motion of her jaw oddly mechanical. I was shocked. I didn't even recognize her with blueberry skins folding over and clinging to her teeth. I had never seen her capitulate like that.

The hypnotist said *toilet* when the bowl was empty. When she came to, she looked at the blueberry in her hand, then up at him and back.

'It's a reward for your participation,' he said. 'Eat it.'

She threw it on the ground instead and stomped it to a pulp.

Violet never told me for sure whether or not she was actually hypnotized. She said she wasn't, and then she said she was, but I couldn't tell if she was joking. The only thing I was sure she was serious about was leaving town that night, something that she insisted upon with her usual vehemence. But then she said it was because she didn't want to run into Salvador Dalí. That she'd rather not stick around and find out what else he could make her do.

I wander into one of the makeshift dressing rooms assembled against the side of the truck: PVC piping draped with opaque fabric, dressed up with a thick cord to tie the whole structure shut. I find my eyes in the mirror inside.

Observe your reflection as you recall: a) a memory that induces deep joy; b) a long-held anxiety that causes fear; c) a question to which you have sought, but have not found, the answer. Write a record of your observations in your log.

No one will know what I'm doing if I do just this one. Only to see what it's like to be told what to do, and then to do it – with someone other than Violet. I approach the mirror cautiously, let my nose almost touch.

A memory that induces deep joy. A long-held anxiety. A question. I think of Violet, I think of my mother, I think of Criss Angel. I think about how sometimes when I hold my arms out in front of me toward the stage lights, if I remember to pay attention, my hands can just disappear.

I look into the mirror to see if there are any secrets written out on my face yet. I try to superimpose Criss Angel's face on my own, and it dawns on me that I can't actually picture him. I scratch away the whitened crust that I didn't realize had collected in the outer corners of my eyes. A question: what does Criss Angel look like? A question: would I recognize Criss Angel if he walked down the street?

I would like to have spent more time looking at myself in a mirror than I have, I realize as my focus wanes. Violet always does my makeup. So I look at Violet. And I look at her first thing every morning, and last thing every night. Her eyes haven't gone red and watery like mine during our time at the circus. She isn't sensitive to cheap mascara and smoke.

It's not as if I'm having a blast right now, sitting here staring at myself. It's not as if I like what I see.

I guess I would have just liked to have a reason to look.

And I would have liked having all that time.

41

I reported everything I learned from the ringleader directly to Violet, of course. I choose to adopt her perspective, that it's all part of the experience and for the enhancement of the performance, even if I can't quite believe it, since my understudy sessions occur behind closed doors.

Violet instructed me to feel flattered that the ringleader had recognized my unusual talent and told me that in fact this should make me trust him more, because she had done the same when she'd first met me. I pretended to agree, but really I was just focusing on our art now more than ever. Violet and I have an act to polish and perfect, now that we have an audience ready to receive us.

Shows are nightly, and while I haven't touched that place I reached the first night again, I feel myself growing closer to Violet with every performance. I am doing exactly what she wants, finally. I'm making her proud.

All of us are expected to go out during the daytime and hand out flyers for the show. Rumor has it the ringleader won't let you in if you come back without your hands empty, which makes me eye trash cans more than it motivates me. Violet and I usually hang around the Pine Cove, a corner dive where a depressing parade of people with vacant cow eyes trickle in and out. Violet ensures that interacting with her will be the highlight of their day. Men take the flyer and barely look at it, ask if she is in the show, smile nasty and flicker their cow eyes down-up, down-up in a way that makes my stomach awaken with a whole different kind of fire.

The ringleader has primed us on how to respond if anyone accuses us of being a cult. We have been told to go ahead and laugh, laugh in their faces, because that would be the most natural reaction to an accusation like that, right? We are to tell the person not to worry, that it isn't a religion or anything: it's spirituality. Something everyone can partake in and benefit from.

People don't understand the value of spirituality in modern society, we've been told. They just want a fat, juicy cult to point fingers at. But that's why we're here, he said. To teach them. To enlighten them as to what their lives could be, if only they opened their minds to the light.

I'm discussing this very point with Violet as we head to our most successful hotspot – in particular how it's difficult to keep suspending disbelief when you get to the subsequent-planet part of the philosophy.

'Have you considered it might be true?' she asks, instead of agreeing with me.

'Come on. Don't tell me you believe in this shit now.'

'I didn't say I did. I'm asking if you ever even considered that there's a real, important purpose to all this, because the way you're talking right now, it sounds like you never did.'

'Okay, no. My answer is no, I never considered that.'

'Why? Is it intimidating to think you might be a part of something that actually matters? Doesn't it feel good to be a part of something?' She stops walking and looks at me expectantly, but I can't formulate a reply, too horrified by the possibility that at some point, when I wasn't paying attention, she slipped from pretending to go along with Holy Toledo into somehow getting fully on board.

'You never believed in us – I always knew that. You were always just following along with whatever because you were scared to be alone, but I thought you'd finally seen the light once we got to Holy Toledo, because I wasn't lying when I said your performances have been, like... *transcendent* here.' She clamps her lips together as if regretting the compliment that slipped out. 'I guess you're a really good actress.'

'We're both actresses.' We're both liars.

'I'm not acting. I've told you this before, it isn't *acting* for me, it's *being*. How does everyone here get that except you? The ringleader gets it. Dusty gets it. The people here, they get me, Smidge, and it's actually really hard that you're still the only one who doesn't.'

My jaw clenches, ready to argue, but I keep my mouth shut. I force myself to consider the possibility that I really don't understand Violet, after all.

I think of all the times I've let her keep talking, filling the space with the contents of herself, and how I let it all wash over me like water: soothing, certainly, welcome, but was I ever really paying attention? Not daydreaming about train wrecks? Was I ever not pretending to go along with everything so as to avoid drawing any attention to myself, so that I could stay lost, stay hidden in the wide-open unknown of America – far from the coast and the redwoods; far from my mother; far from the version of myself that hadn't shed off me like a snakeskin when I ran like a coward, but had in fact only constricted tighter as I grew, creating an itch that I could no longer ignore?

'I think it's the ringleader messing with my brain,' I concede instead of saying any of this out loud. Anything to soften her up, because Violet could scare me when she was angry. 'Maybe there's something to this, but it's hard to take him seriously. Did you know he has a lava lamp in his caravan?'

'Lava lamp...'

'I forgot to tell you that, I think. It still has the tag on it.'

'So tacky,' says Violet, clicking her tongue for emphasis. I try to think of something else to say to get us back on a familiar page, making fun of the ringleader, but find that I have to focus instead on keeping my hands from shaking.

One of the men from the idle parade of daytime Pine Cove customers is mooning down at us now, as Violet twists her fingers through the newly applied blue stripes in her hair. It's high noon; the sky's a white void and looking up to meet his gaze feels impossible.

'Are all the performers as gorgeous as you two? Hell, that couldn't be possible. They'd have to call that heaven on earth.'

You have no idea, sir. I smile my best American strawberry shortcake smile instead of enlightening him. 'Bring your friends!'

He stands there on the steaming sidewalk with feet apart, making no moves to get on with his day, so I link arms with Violet and drag us around the corner.

Observe the manner in which people approach one another. Observe the reactions between groups of different dynamics. When the observation feels invasive, you are close.

I forgot to read about what *dynamics* were supposed to be. Or I just left it, figuring the ringleader would tell me everything he thought it meant in one of our sessions. After all, he wrote the book that I am supposed to be studying in between meetings with him. Violet has already read it cover to cover. She summarizes pieces of it for me sometimes: most recently, the chapter about mankind's inevitable descent into mechanization. Radio waves and, more recently, TV and cell-phone signals have established a background frequency that our brains have become used to, attuning the human mind over generations to a state of constant overstimulation. The more we rely on our technological devices to keep our minds programmed to this state, the closer we draw toward our consciousness being captured, measured and recorded onto them. No TV or radio is permitted on circus grounds, and the more established members of the circus have sacrificed their phones to the ringleader. These members can be identified by golden sashes tied around their waists. They are first in line for meals, and excused from flyering duties.

I hope Violet has no ambition to attain gold-sash status, because I'm not willing to give up our phones. Today is the first time I'm hearing that she's entertaining the idea of Holy Toledo having a purpose, though, which has me worried.

'Bad energy from that dude?' Violet asks once we're in the east-side shade.

'Sometimes I pretend any man I see is my biological father,' I say without thinking, the words trickling up like rain slipping from leaves. I haven't unlinked my arm from Violet's yet.

'What?'

I haven't thought about my father in years. I don't know him. I guess I met him when I was a baby, when he stood there next to my mother's hospital bed as they pulled me into existence. But that was it.

I don't feel the need to go look for him, the way I know other people who don't know their fathers sometimes do. I can't imagine what he could do for me. I don't have any questions for him to answer. None of the holes in myself, as far as I can tell, are for him to fill.

'Sorry, I don't know,' I tell her. 'It's like an inside joke I have with myself. I have no idea who he is, which means he could be anyone I see. So sometimes I'll just see a guy in the grocery store and think... could be him.'

'You haven't even seen pictures?'

My mother had shown me pictures when I was a little kid. Or one picture, at least. I remember her doing the showing, but I can't conjure up his face. She went into her room and closed the door behind her afterwards, and I kept waiting for her to get up to make dinner. It grew dark and eventually I opened a can of chicken noodle soup and ate it cold, avoiding the floating bullets of congealed fat. I didn't want the sound of the microwave to wake her up, so that she'd come out and cry about not having heated it up for me.

'He looks like nothing,' is all I can say to sum up this memory for her.

Violet nods, reaching down to take my hand. 'You don't have to remember anything about him that you don't want to.'

She is using her wise voice, which is a few beats slower than her regular voice. It's a signal to pay attention and take her seriously that I don't need. I'm just grateful that she seems to have forgiven, or at least temporarily forgotten, our conversation prior to the man's interruption.

I try to look casual and to unwrinkle my face. 'There's nothing to remember.'

'That's the spirit.'

I don't want her to let go of my hand, but I don't want to talk about the dead space of my father anymore. My father as an abstract concept, as a running joke. My father as almost nothing, his face lost in the crowd of all the faces I've collected that make me feel like the ghost at the bottom of an empty cup.

I marvel, as I have often marveled, at how easy it seems for Violet to disconnect herself from everything that came before. I know her parents are still in Piscataway. Her mother was a speech-language pathologist. Her father did something with insurance. They fought and fought until Violet had had enough and left, and the way she talks about them, it seems like her leaving was a clean and uncomplicated break.

I mean, her mother hit her. She hit her in the face. Nothing I've ever known can compare.

But I'm uncomfortably aware that all I know about Violet is exactly what she has divulged to me, in carefully curated stories at choice moments throughout our shared lives. I can name the feeling I feel when she speaks about anything that happened before I knew her, and that feeling is longing. Longing because I want to know everything. I want to learn everything from her: how to make sure that what's behind you is behind you for good. How to remain miraculously unhaunted, when everything you touch keeps sticking like sap in the creases of your palms.

But it is getting close to warm-up time. So Violet and I start heading back to the circus, scattering flyers behind us all the way.

42

I have a memory that I return to often when the waters start feeling stormy again. In this memory, the music on the other side of the door is loud enough that I can hear every word. Loud enough to fill the room the same as oxygen, just as easy to take in and ignore.

Violet and I had escaped to the bathroom when she noticed I had panic eyes. The college kids who lived in the house we were in had spray-painted the walls and ceiling of the bathroom in shades of black and neon. A sloppy skull hovered above where we sat in the bathtub.

I tried to sense the pipes gathered in a knot below us and uncover the secrets of the house by way of the plumbing. I didn't pick up on much. Maybe that house didn't have secrets. Not like the ones my mother's had – I would lie in its bathtub and press my hands against the ceramic and feel connected to the universe.

We were still in Miami. We were trying to figure out where we would go next, after we'd been kicked out of the apartment we'd been peacefully squatting in, and were thinking about leaving Florida behind us. Violet had followed the music and lights to this house party, where the people smoking on the porch waved us in without hesitation. Violet wanted to find amphetamines. I wanted to get out of the sludge of outdoor humidity and into the sludge of compacted body heat. Since leaving the shelter, there hadn't been a lot of situations in my life that put me in close contact with a lot of people like this. It was mostly Violet and me, me and Violet, and I liked it that way. But there was something about being in a crowd that made me feel invisible and Violet seem hyper-visible, and I felt as though we sometimes needed that return to center.

It reminded me, also, of being in school. It was somehow easier to disappear back then. I could walk down the hall and never feel like anyone was looking at me, a feeling I haven't been able to recreate since.

Inside the house, there was an unsavory mix of teenagers still growing into their frames and men outgrowing their chunky hoodies pulled over neon floral caps. The teenagers were in the centers of the rooms and halls. The men were pressed against the walls. The skin smell was everywhere. I breathed it in, brushed past people as close as I could and made eye contact with no one.

I sat on a tufted purple chair that didn't look like it belonged in that house, which had been modified from a single-family home to a patchwork disaster. Posters covered the walls and even the sides of the furniture, some of them advertising events from decades prior, starting to unstick from where they'd originally adhered, curling up at the edges. Nothing was white; everything that might once have been had dulled to sleepy shades of beige and grey. I found it cozy and comforting. I chose the old-timey stuffed chair as the space into which I would contain myself while Violet snaked through the house.

I concentrated on an Alicia Keys poster across the room. Two girls took turns sucking from a dragon-shaped bong and blowing the smoke onto Alicia's stomach. One of the men unstuck himself from the wall and came over to the out-of-place chair to tell me I was pretty.

He held his hand out to shake and I shook it before remembering my rules for house parties like this, along with group therapy sessions, workplaces, and any other gatherings where you might encounter strangers. No touching anyone. No looking into anyone's eyes. I'd broken both in the space of a second, and he was grinning as if he were in on it all.

Then he asked me to stand up. I said no thank you, and he pulled on my hand as if that could pull my whole body off of the chair.

'Why are you scared to stand up?'

'I'm not scared,' I corrected him. 'I just don't want to.'

'What if I told you it would make me really, really happy, and that good things happen when I'm happy?'

'Why would that make you so happy?'

'You'll find out when you stand up.'

I stared at the man and waited for him to go away. I tried to stare like a cat does to let you know it's not bothered by your presence and is certainly not going anywhere. It's a stalemate, I told him with my cat stare. Neither of us are going to get anywhere with this.

He didn't receive the message, because he asked how old I was.

'Twelve,' I told Alicia Keys. As young as I thought I could pass for to make him feel the greatest possible shame.

His face was so close. 'There's no way you're twelve. You're not fuckin' twelve.'

His face was so close and so red, shiny with sweat and speckled with more details of his goatee than I would have liked to ever see.

'You thought I was going to fall for that? You're a troublemaker, aren't you?' he asked, and I could see every line pinching the pale skin on his lips as his mouth formed the word, *troublemaker*, which was really the word for the exact amount of noncompliance I was allowed to exercise, the word for the amount of rebellion that was still in bounds. *Troublemaker* was the word that made sure I knew that no matter how much I tried to outsmart the man, he would put me in my place.

I just kept staring past the man and his wet red head at Alicia Keys, her face like the setting sun. I asked her what she would do in this situation. *Because here's the thing*, I told her – *I like people better when they aren't paying attention to me.*

The rest of the men and the other girls shrank down and stilled to a surreal painting, and when I looked at the painting I couldn't help but notice how the men had been rendered as gigantic eyeballs and the girls just as girls, and how wrong it was that no one here took us seriously enough to see us as a threat.

I hated to think that no one saw us as a threat.

So I ran my tongue over my egg tooth.

And I remembered what the frog guts smelled like on my face when I was actually twelve. And how that smell lingered even after I ran to the bathroom to scrub my face with the perfumed hand soap and rinse it off with cold water, scrub and rinse, scrub and rinse, over and over and over until my skin was raw.

I remembered my egg tooth and Nojan's soft, young arm, and how the skin broke like sausage casing.

How I was trying to settle it like a boy, but missed the mark. A boy would have just punched him: in the gut if he was only trying to settle the score, in the face if he was really pissed. A boy wouldn't have used his teeth. He wouldn't have needed to.

And I know that I can no longer trust my survival instincts, because they're forever whirring at the back of my brain, insisting *you are in danger, all of the time.* My mind sharpens when I let myself listen to this; I start to feel like I'm more teeth than brain, more teeth than anything else, big bloodstained teeth, always chewing myself free from a trap in a burning forest, then running until I can't smell smoke.

This will not be one of those times. There won't be blood in this story.

There will only be this man, whose hair would be the color of blood if the blood were washed up and old and faded in the sun, which blood never is. There will be me feeling safe because of all the people around me and Violet nearby, and forcing myself to forget the weapon tucked under my top lip.

Because I felt safe, I smiled, and because I felt smart, I gave Violet panic eyes when she materialized across the room. Because Violet is smart, she came over and complained loudly about period cramps and how her flow was so heavy that the chunks were getting caught on the way out, and she lifted me from the chair by my hand and I let her, and we found the bathroom upstairs, miraculously empty, and locked ourselves inside.

'What did he want?'

I shrugged. 'Probably a porn recruiter. I was fine, just wanted to get out of there. Spit was flying out of his mouth when he talked.'

'This place is full of them. Sorry I left you alone.'

I shook my head at her with *are-you-crazy* eyes, so she would know there was nothing to apologize for or forgive. The recruiters hung around places like this, handing out business cards to any girls that fit their bill and telling them to call them when they were eighteen. They promised pay in the thousands, which I knew wasn't true. They paid after the shoot in cash only, no records, so no one could ever argue with what they were given. The footage was already taken. They got what they got.

The business cards were just a dude's name and cell phone number. Sometimes a logo. When there was no other information than that, you knew what they were for.

'Should we take a bath?'

I gave her milder *are-you-crazy* eyes, because of course I wanted to take a bath. People started pounding on the door eventually, but we ignored them, because what were they going to do? Break down the door of their own busted house?

Someone told us to open the fuck up, they had to piss. But I had seen everyone on the other side of the door and knew they could afford to piss on the lawn. In fact, it would do some of them a lot of good. Some of them had never pissed anywhere other than a toilet, and it showed.

The college kids were identifiable by their monogrammed sweat-shirts and, sometimes, by the careful way they carried themselves. They had a way of looking very unstable, teetering in between their childhood and adulthood, not knowing which they really wanted at any given moment. I hated looking at college kids sometimes – how they exploited the luxury of choice with no risk if they failed.

We found salts under the sink and dumped them in the tub, crumbled a bar of soap under the running water in an attempt to make bubble bath that ended up just making chunks in the water.

'I'm gonna piss under the door if you don't open up,' screamed the voice from above.

'We dare you,' Violet said calmly, locking eyes with me through the tendrils of steam. She looked at me and I looked at her, and the crumbled soap floated in the water in between us, and the lumps were like chum, I realized, something else I'd only ever seen in National Geographic documentaries. Chunked flesh kept in blood-stained buckets, thrown overboard to tint the water red and oily.

And if the soap was the chum, that meant we were the sharks.

Which meant we were wild animals after all. And some of the ones with the biggest teeth.

And that meant this feeling didn't mean I was about to hurt someone.

'We're sharks,' I told Violet and she nodded in appreciation, so I knew that it all made sense. I didn't care anymore that I couldn't pull the secrets from the plumbing of the house, just closed my eyes and relished the blood I had not drawn because Violet was there, and how the steam cast her scent all over the air, encasing my body amniotically. I felt no secrets from the outside, only my own organs bubbling to fullness inside me: poached in the water, perfectly tame with fluorescent blue aquarium light.

43

'We're going to try something new today.'

The ringleader has been pleased with my log so far, which I turn in for his review at the end of each week. I write whatever I think he would want to hear. That I've had revelations. That the exercises are making me see the world in a new light. In *the* light.

'What is it?' I make my eyes wide and round. The ringleader never notices when I make the doll face at him. It's like he isn't even paying attention.

'It's an experiment. Nothing too intense. Have you heard of the Akashic records?'

Whenever he asks me questions like this, my answer is always no. I want to hear how he will describe these things. I want to check if he will lie. He loves listening to himself talk, so mostly the dumber I act, the more time he'll take up explaining the inner workings of the universe to me.

'Hmm.' I pretend to think, letting my eyes drift above his head and to the calendar of nonsense on the wall behind him. He doesn't divide his calendar by days, weeks, or even months, but rather by some complicated system that has to do with the distance between this lifetime and the next. The units are something like steps that need to be completed as a measure of the future, and those completed as a measure of the past. I don't know how it all became numerical, but the ringleader engaged in some sort of ritual calculation that produced the figures on the calendar, some of them crossed out, none of them in order.

'I don't think so,' I conclude once I feel an appropriate amount of time has been wasted. 'What is that?'

The ringleader straightens up in his chair, palm-tree posture curving over the desk toward me. 'I couldn't possibly put it all into words, even as a master reader. But in short, it's a record of all that has ever happened in the universe of souls,' he tells me, almost sputtering. His fingers drum heavily at the edge of the desk, nearly vibrating, the crystal on the lamp shivering from the disturbance. 'Everyone and everything is a part of it. For example, all of your past lives are visible in the records, and they intertwine with the lives of other souls who you may have never met in this life, so it creates something of a web that stretches over all of space and time. Connecting all of us to each other.'

I wonder what qualifications are necessary to become a master reader of these records.

'If you've ever wondered why something felt familiar when you were experiencing it for the first time, or why you reacted in some way that didn't make immediate sense to you – or even more general things, the things we all wonder about, where we come from and what our purpose is – this is all revealed in the records.'

I recognize all of this as a trick. I have thought about these things because everyone thinks about these things, as a condition of being human. The promise of invisible answers is, of course, too good to be true. I already know that no experience can be unique anymore, no question original, that I was born at a point too late in the timeline to fulfill any purpose that can't be fulfilled by another. Violet and I will get as close as we can through our art.

'I'd like to just take a look today. We won't do a full reading, but at this stage, I think you're ready to learn a little more about the path I've chosen for you.'

He digs out a glass pipe and lighter from the top drawer of the desk. 'You'll have to trust me entirely,' he lowers his voice to disclose, thumbnail trailing lightly over the ridges of the striker before snapping a flame to life. 'What's crucial about this process is that you let me in, no mental barriers, so I can access the frequency of your soul. That's what spells out the readable part that will give us answers. You'll have to find a way to give yourself over to me.'

I would rather beat my brain with his ritual abacus.

'Wow,' I say, pursing my lips into the doll-face rosebud and letting my eyes stretch cartoon-wide. 'That will be a challenge. But I'm sure you can help me through it.'

The smoke from the pipe is thick and smells earthy, cleaner than tobacco but less grassy than weed. It does something to my nose that I don't recognize, fuzzy moss closing over the airways.

'I don't want you to feel bad about anything that might come up,' he's telling me through the haze. 'These records exist outside of ourselves. In your current form, you could not have done anything differently to change what's already brought you here, do you understand? The records are fundamental to you while remaining separate from your life, unaltered by all your choices. There's nothing else that functions this way, so it can be difficult to grasp.'

'I won't feel bad,' I promise, almost holding up a pinky before realizing that might be pushing it over the top. I try to just look impatient instead, like I can't wait to get started. The room fills quickly, and I can't tell whether my vision is suddenly losing focus or if the smoke is thick enough to transform the ringleader into the blocky cloud I'm seeing now. I try to find the corner of the room with my eyes, but everything that's supposed to be a straight line looks like it's melting.

'We start with something of an incantation, which just draws out the vibrational frequency from your body. I'll warn you, you might receive something of a physical sensation. It might feel like nostalgia, or familiarity.'

I don't remind him that neither of those are physical sensations. I mean, maybe he's about to prove me wrong.

'Why don't you look into my eyes to start.'

He leans forward and I make a point not to hesitate in doing the same, to prove his body language does not intimidate me and that my cosmic heart and soul are in this.

I see absolutely nothing in his eyes when we get up close, which is comforting. He mutters the incantation under his breath, softer than anything, and I don't bother trying to catch the words. It takes most of my concentration to ignore my peripheral vision, anyway, where the walls are still sliding into a puddle of themselves.

'Thank you, Smidge. I'm seeing it now.'

'Oh yeah?'

'Hold it right there. Whatever you're thinking right now, just hold it. I'm starting to get something.'

I look into his eyes. I search inside my mind. I wasn't thinking about anything in particular. Maybe that's the point.

I understand how people can get hooked on this stuff. I've seen the world in a circle and know in a simple sort of way how everything rolls back into itself. And that realization feels fresh every time, never gets old: some magic you can unlock over and over. I mean, I can get high on nothing – and I mean high like suspended and rising, so everything shrinks below me. Sometimes I can get so high and the world can get so small that it seems possible to draw a thick black outline around all of it.

I force my eyes back from doll to human, which means round to oval, big to small. I keep my elbows folded in, stay small, drop my shoulders when I notice they're tight to my ears, get smaller. I make myself think about small things: mice, ants, molecules. Smaller. My world has never felt smaller than it did in the forested quiet of the northern California border. I know that where I come from still owns a piece of me, whether it would show up in the cosmic records or not. The ringleader doesn't seem to notice the shifts between doll and human in my body, my performance too much a part of my person now to shed.

The months after I received my driver's permit were a time when it was easy to give myself over to the universe. There was no one and nothing to keep me from a flat sky and hills run through by interstates, signs that promised places far away while I kept returning every night to the same water-park parking lot, sitting in the car under the light that wouldn't stop blinking because there were places where things broke and stayed broken, and this was one of them. I would allow myself to become sleepy, very sleepy. I liked to watch the light strobe in slow motion over the dashboard, over the garden of dead flowers scattered there by my mother's always-collecting hands.

When I see broken lights blinking now, I know that these lights will eventually be fixed. But I trust that the one at the water park will not.

I know that if it was fixed, the already tenuous connection would have to disappear entirely. The light would have transformed while I've had to stay the same all this time: unwillingly vulnerable by design, lying for fun and for survival – always putting on an unfinished show. I'd have to figure out how I left thinking I'd freed myself of everything that bound me, but found myself still entwined by knotted rope and unable to avoid the oncoming train. Because you can't run away from yourself. But you can probably connect every place I've been by interstates, leading all the way home.

It is all very delicate, you see.

'I'm getting something, yes,' he interrupts, not breaking slitted eye contact with me. 'I see a vast abyss, and you standing at the edge of it... on a... some sort of cliff, perhaps? A natural feature. I can't quite see, it's a bit fuzzy there. But I can see you're looking down at the drop below, instead of forward, where there may be light.'

'Do you see a blinking light?'

'Blinking... blinking, no. I believe I can't see the light yet because you haven't seen it yet here at Holy Toledo. You're still looking down. You're searching for your trust, I imagine, your courage, so you can step off into what appears to be darkness.'

I wonder what he's getting out of this, and what he's actually thinking about right now, because I can't ignore the voyeuristic glint in his eyes and can't help feeling exposed. Even when there's nothing to show. This is all fake, of course. *Fake, fake, fake*, I remind myself as he narrows his eyes as if boring a hole into my body and breaking through to its trenches, seeking to extract an epiphany I know is not there.

'Don't be afraid,' he murmurs. 'The world wouldn't create so many opportunities to fall if it didn't provide just as many open arms to catch you.'

44

ligyrophobia – fear of loud sounds

Everything echoes. There's a small opening near the ceiling of the big top, just one, and it frames a perfect rectangle of tree and sky. I can't see it through the lights when we're performing, but I can during rehearsals. We don't always drop the curtains at the end, but when we do, sometimes I'm convinced there's a haunted house on the other side.

A row of lipsticks under a mirror. A tube of lipstick up Violet's sleeve. Violet using lipstick to write on a mirror in a parking garage restroom, all theatrical, all fired up, *IF YOU LOOKED IT'S TOO LATE.*

Me closing my eyes in the parking garage restroom and covering them with my hands, as a joke, and then not a joke, because standing in a self-created dark for just a second is as close to escaping to the moon as I will ever get.

I learned in school that there's no echo on the moon.

Not everything you learn in school is true, but science is.

This is.

There's no echo because the sound waves have nothing to exist within and nothing to bounce off of, so they go on forever into space.

I could say that I want to exist within nothing, and otherwise go on forever into space. I could say that my life is already crowded with too many things to bounce off of, so everything in my tiny universe creates a web, so the web doesn't stretch far and wide into the distance connecting all things in harmony, but instead into a claustrophobic net tangling all around me.

So I daydream about the moon.

Although on the moon I would technically be dead, because there's no oxygen, and my daydreams are never as simple as wanting to die.

The daydreams are inseparable from the lack of oxygen, though. Because where there is no oxygen, there are no echoes.

And without echoes, I would be free.

45

Russell bangs on the side of the sleeper bus. Violet and I had once seen some maniac kids shooting BB guns at a dumpster. That had sounded something like Russell's fist.

'Everybody up! Announcement in the big top.'

Violet presses the heels of her hands into her eyes, rummages for her phone and turns the screen toward me. It's 4.55am. We've all slept for less than four hours after the previous night's dance circle. I pull the sleeping bag over my face, every bone twinging with the small effort and digging into the muscle.

The ringleader makes announcements at seemingly random intervals, usually a bunch of the same messages about light and hauntology, transmissions he's decoded from the winds, hidden symbols in his Cream of Wheat. The frenzied passion with which he conducts our private sessions disappears in front of the rest of the circus, where he appears still and certain as an oracle as he delivers his versions of the truth. These are just about the only times that Violet and the others ever see him outside of performances.

Violet is the first out of her bunk and pulls me behind her all the way to the tent in the soggy pre-dawn. She is the pillar for my body to stay upright against as everyone else trickles in. Her index fingers press little spirals into my temples. I lower my eyes to half-lid, preparing to focus on the gentle pressure and tune the ringleader out.

He steps through the canvas door in a deep purple velvet gown that I recognize. It stretches skintight across his body, and little pearls are stitched along the hem, a painstaking addition that I remember Violet making by streetlamp one night. That is Violet's dress. Has he gone rummaging through her stuff? I elbow her ribs and point to the dress with my eyes.

'Thank you, everyone, for taking the time to gather here today. I'm afraid I have some bad news,' he begins.

'What?' Violet hiss-whispers.

'What do you mean, what? He's wearing your dress. How did he get his hands on that?'

'Why is that what you're worried about right now?'

The ringleader pauses to suck in two fat lungfuls of air and exhale heavily. He sighs so hard that I'm worried the grease from his mustache is going to fly off with the momentum and soil Violet's dress.

'I received a message last night, and the end times are sooner than we think.'

Well. Now I'm paying attention. I can tell I'm paying attention, because all my guts are twisting up against my will. Violet's hands move to the back of my scalp, rake fistfuls of hair and hold tight. I glance at the others gathered in the tent, rows of cave eyes fixated on the ringleader. When I find Deva, she's already looking over at me. She doesn't look away when our eyes meet, her expression hard and unreadable.

'The message said we have six to eight months to make the ascension, which is far, far less time than any of us could have expected. I reckon we've saved about as many people as we can, but that doesn't mean we won't keep pushing until the very end. We've got six to eight months of work ahead of us, right? Six, to be safe. We're going to keep going until then. There's a lot of work to do.'

He's tracing slow, deliberate shapes in the air as he speaks. The ringleader has a thing for shapes, all kinds of shapes, but especially circles and triangles. For announcements like this, for example, the handbook instructs the group to arrange ourselves in perfect concentric circles around the ringleader. The caravan reflects this proclivity, too. The more you look at it, the more circles you see half-hidden in the overlapping images that cover it. He can come up with a million things that a circle represents – unity, eternity, absolute balance. And, of course, the planet of light emerges in every circle he sees.

I focus on his fingertips to distract from the thought of Violet's velvet on his skin. His probably pig-sweaty skin. I'm strung out from lack of sleep, and imagining the salt and oils from his flesh contaminating the dress's royal fibers is enough to make me sick.

'That makes it March 17th. That's the day we'll all ascend, and as we draw closer, I'll announce more details as to everyone's duties. Until then, let's put on a great show, shall we?' The ringleader throws up his hands and everyone claps on cue. Even me, I realize as I look down at my hands. Violet releases my head to join in, and my skull prickles with absence.

The ringleader bows, straining the seams of Violet's dress, to which my eyes are affixed, making sure nothing rips. The crowd parts to allow his path back to the door, and I turn immediately to Violet.

'Why does he have your dress?'

'You aren't the slightest bit worried about the end times that were just announced?'

'Violet. Come on. We'll talk about that, you know, later. Is he... Is he going through people's stuff?'

'God. Again with the conspiracies. I gave it to him, okay?'

'What? Why?'

Violet shrugs. 'It was huge on me. You saw. Heavy, too. It wasn't worth carting around, and he liked it.'

Violet once found a floor lamp that she liked put up for offer under a magnolia tree in the suburbs.

It was admittedly eye-catching, with a pearly blue conch-shaped glass shade at the end of a long golden pole. Someone had kind of spoiled the regal effect by hot-gluing souvenir-shop seashells to its base, frosty tendrils of the dried adhesive still curling out from the edges. I'd bet that someone in the neighborhood had to foreclose on their beach house and was getting rid of the decor as quick and dirty as they could. Because, you know. Why would anyone have something like that in their regular house? Violet did not challenge my theory but wrapped the cord around her arm and hoisted it up by the pole, and that floor lamp came home with us, and then it followed us from Miami to Daytona Beach.

The only reason she ever got rid of it happened when we were performing on the boardwalk, before we had anywhere to stay. A man with unfocused eyes and too-tight baby-blue overalls was asking what my deal was as we were trying to concentrate on our art; he edged closer throughout the performance, and finally put two fingers under my chin and pressed upward.

'Hey,' he said. 'Can you hear me? I'm talking to you.'

Violet told him to back off.

His hand clenched around my jaw.

My body locked up and retreated from me.

'I'll back off when she answers the question,' he said, and I remember thinking that he was so stupid, how was I supposed to talk when his thumb was clamped down on my cheek like that, he was making his own request impossible, but that train of thought was interrupted when the butt of the floor lamp split a gash in his head and the blood that sprayed out landed on my face, and on Violet's arm holding the lamp, and on the lamp, and on her face too, which was the first place I looked when my body unfroze, to see her wide open and wet with raw terror.

We pulled our backpacks from the planks and ran without checking if anyone had seen what had just happened. If anyone was after us, we didn't hear them. The plug from the lamp bounced behind us like the string of tin cans on a newlywed couple's car.

Violet did not let go of me for the rest of the night.

'I'm sorry I let that happen,' was the first thing she said in a cracking voice when we stopped to catch our breath. We were in a neighborhood that I didn't recognize: neat rows of lawns contained behind the bright white sidewalks, sprinklers oscillating dutifully under the sun to maintain these perfect colors. I dropped to my knees in front of a sprinkler head and let the water wash the blood from my face, gathered the pinkish runoff in my hands and flung it toward the sidewalk.

Of course, I wanted to say no, wanted to say it wasn't her fault, but I was intimately familiar with how Violet felt about things like this and knew those words wouldn't help. *Tough* was a touchstone for Violet's identity, the glass through which she saw the world and the well from which she drew her life philosophies. But I knew she was scared all the time. There was a price to pay for appearing as free as we pretended to be, in order to create a destiny that suited us – something that she was beginning to weigh around then. She was scared of understanding just how much was out of her control.

When night fell, we went to the wharf, a different one, and threw the lamp into the water.

What I mean is, that's what it took to make Violet part with something she loved. So I cannot accept that she just gave the ringleader her velvet dress with the pearl beads hand-sewn in.

The air inside the big top feels heavy with murmurs from the crowd, which remains arranged in a circle despite the ringleader's absence. I feel compelled to be the first to leave and break the shape.

'Can we talk outside?'

The breeze carries an unexpected scent of apple blossoms. We walk down the weird sidewalk-less road, the kind that's everywhere in Texas, making everything look even more gigantic and vacant than it already is.

'What do you think he means with all the end-times stuff?'

Violet shrugs. 'I mean, I guess we'll see. I doubt anything will change.'

'I think...' My brain searches for the right words. 'I think we shouldn't wait around to see. I think we need to leave. For real this time.'

Violet studies me, waiting for evidence to support my argument. I look across the street at a faded window decal advertising spicy fried chicken.

'What if *ascending* is exactly what it sounds like?'

She blinks, expressionless, daring me to say it.

'You know what I mean,' I try again, and she waits.

'I mean, leaving this planet to get to the next one? What if it's going to be a mass suicide?' I finally ask, and she scoffs on cue, finally opens her mouth to tell me everything she knows about the paranoia and self-sabotage that plague me and inhibit my creative growth. Some of it sounds like it could've been lifted directly from the Holy Toledo handbook.

Violet's voice fades to a consistent whine. I fixate on the pearls lining the purple velvet hem and the strains in the stitches, and how the stake that this drives into me feels immediate and real, up close and personal, much more so than the idea of mass suicide.

The lights snap off behind the spicy fried chicken sticker, telling me that this conversation is over and won't be visited again.

Six months. I guess the ringleader has set a deadline for when I can't ignore him anymore.

46

Deva and I are seeing how far we can hurl coins into the parking lot behind the liquor store. We'd tried to give a flyer to the clerk, who emptied the take-a-penny, leave-a-penny dish into her hands. 'We're not poor,' Deva muttered, but shoved them all into her pocket anyway. Because, I mean, aren't we?

She flings a penny that bounces from the concave of a smashed can, rings to stillness on the pockmarked tar. She hums in response.

Being around Deva can be exhausting when she's in the mood to talk but doesn't have a topic, and I can tell she's in that mood now by the way she's mimicking the sounds around us. The worst is when we're somewhere heavily trafficked and she imitates engines with a clenched growl. I'm tired enough today that the humming is enough to blot out my brimming reserve of fondness for her.

'Hey, no offense, but I think I might want to go do some flyering on my own now. I just want some alone time. You won't rat me out?' Flyering was supposed to always be done in pairs, but I'm hoping Deva is flexible.

'Oh, okay,' she replies coolly, sliding her palmful of pennies back into her pocket. 'I can stop talking, then, but I have to stay near you.'

'Why?'

'My dad asked me to watch you. He thinks you're a flight risk.' Deva says this without looking at me or changing her tone, but I can feel myself flushing like I've been caught.

'When did he ask you this?'

'Oh, all the way back in New Orleans. When you first joined.'

The flush travels down, lights up my insides. I am, of course, disturbed by the news, but something strange is fluttering up. I realize I'm hurt that I mistook Deva's constant presence for infatuation with Violet and me.

'I thought you just liked us,' I admit, too aware of the heat in my face.

'I do,' she says. 'I wanted to be friends with you guys anyway. But it was also my assignment. Still is.'

'When you say flight risk…' I'm not sure how to put it. 'What happens when someone wants to quit?'

'Well, it's up to my dad when people come and go. Usually it's a mutual agreement when someone goes. There have been a few times when it wasn't agreed on, and we've had to retrieve people.'

'What does that mean?'

'Means a small group breaks off to go talk to them, see why they left, remind them why they need us and need to come back. He wants everyone safe when it's time. Can't stand the thought of willingly leaving someone behind, especially someone who already knows the truth. Once they're back, they're assigned a watcher. You just got one pre-emptively, I guess.'

I want to ask how they know where to find the people who leave, but can't think of how to get to that answer without revealing my own plans.

'How do you think he knew?' she asks after a pause.

'Knew what?'

'That you would want to leave before it was time?'

Anxiety surges up, paralyzing me for a second.

'Violet told me. And I told him.' She still isn't looking at me.

I am convinced that Violet would never have told Deva anything. When did they even see each other without me around? But there isn't any other way Deva could have found out, so she must have. I should feel betrayed, but I'm too tired. I'm mostly just confused.

'You know why my dad doesn't have to do this, and we do?' Deva asks suddenly, swaying toward me. Abrupt changes of subject like these are not unusual for her, but I'm still uneasy.

'Why?' I respond carefully. Flyering sucks, but somehow the ringleader not partaking has always made sense to me. Or at least, I haven't ever questioned it.

'He was touched by the divine. Which is – well, do you believe in God?'

Her floaty voice, as always, is unflinchingly earnest. Maybe that's why I don't want my answer to be no.

'I've prayed before,' I say, which is the truth.

'So, the divine is different from God. It's not a being so much as a life force. But not like the Holy Spirit. It's something that people in ancient times were intimately in touch with, and it's what made their cultures so prolific, especially in the arts. Think about the pyramids.'

She turns her flashing Jupiter eyes on me and I widen mine in return, trying to make the face of a person who is thinking about a pyramid.

'And creating a language from scratch. That's not something we've got to worry about anymore. So think about what we could be doing if we could access the divinity that our predecessors accessed to create everything that's led humankind to where we are today. I'm afraid we've gotten quite far away from it in modern society. But that's why it's so incredible that my dad was touched by it.'

'When you say "touched"…?'

'Contacted by the spirits of ancient peoples,' Deva replies without missing a beat. 'I don't know exactly how it worked, because I'm sure you have to experience it to understand, but they shared the divinity with him.' She pauses to send another coin hurtling into the empty lot. 'Seems like he could spare a couple hours to hand out flyers with the rest of us, though.'

I shrug.

'Doesn't it?' she insists.

'I don't know. Sure.'

She nods, then squints up at the sky and makes another low hum at the back of her throat.

'Listen, I don't know exactly what's going on with you, and it would get me in a lot of trouble to ask. But if you're going to leave, you'd do best to leave now, before you have any duties.'

'Duties?'

Deva nods solemnly. 'Mine is finding those beings from the other planes again. Honestly, I would never know that I could access this state in my mind without him. Your mind needs to go to the theta level, which allows your consciousness to remain at work while removing itself from your immediate physical surroundings. If you can drop into this level, you can visit other worlds. Your brain waves range from four to eight cycles per second. Some people have visited the celestial world this way, or even gone briefly to the afterlife and back. It takes deep concentration and training, and there are only so many people out there who are qualified to train you in these things, and my dad is one of them. I learned everything from him and from finding the light here, but if I leave, I'll lose it, and we'll never make contact again. I'm the only one who's ever seen them. I'm their only hope.'

Her voice lowers to a breathy whisper. 'They're in danger. I don't mention that part often because I don't want to distract from everything else, and besides, they're my duty. Mine alone. You understand?'

I nod yes and it isn't a lie because I do, in a way. I understand how it feels to have a duty.

'I know what you're thinking, but it's true. You'll understand if you stay. But I know you need to go.' She suddenly darts close, wraps her arms around my shoulders and whispers into the hollow of my ear. 'I wasn't immaculately conceived, you know. I have a mother who was pregnant with me and gave birth to me just like anyone else, but I don't know who she is or what happened to her, so I can't tell if knowing even counts.'

A little something inside me collapses then, under the unexpected weight of her words and the gentle pressure of her bones against my shoulder. Something within me would almost rather she be blissfully wrapped up in the stars of her father's lies, dim and hopeless, weightless on those other astral planes. In the next moment, I know that this is not what I want for her at all. Deva is trapped without answers, has no way of knowing where her mother is or how to find her, or even who she is – she could look directly into her mother's eyes and not even recognize her.

And then I think about my father, and how I could look directly into his eyes and not recognize him. I feel one of the holes in myself emerge. And I feel the soft sponge of myself grow too, covering over, smoothing away the empty so that after a moment of resting in this echo, it does not feel like a loss.

The truth is, I don't know a lot about what's right and wrong with families other than the general understanding that mine did it wrong. I'm not sure exactly how – just that I'm not supposed to be here in a parking lot with my legs throbbing and threatening to buckle with every step, my hair holding curls from three days ago because it sees more hairspray than shampoo, a fog in my brain where everything once felt sharp and overwhelming because I was a child – because I *am* a child, no matter how little that word resonates with me. I'm not supposed to be here. And yes, I wouldn't be if my family had done everything right. But I'm not convinced that all it would take is a visit to the celestial world to make sense of it all.

The next time she speaks, the word is so quiet that I can't be sure I didn't imagine it.

'Go.'

47

Sometimes my mother wouldn't be there when I got home from school. It wasn't unusual for me to fall asleep before she came home. One of those nights, I finished my homework at the kitchen table, ate peanut butter out of the jar and ice cream out of the carton, then searched the cabinets for snacks. There weren't any. So I took the rest of the ice cream and my fuzzy blanket into the bathtub with me to wait.

The sun had already fallen behind the trees, so there was no fading light through the window near the ceiling in the bathroom. I stared at the crack under the spout of the bathtub instead and felt that we were equals. I mean, I was feeling defective. Like anything beautiful could turn ugly in my hands.

At school that day, we'd been learning about pirates. During art period, I swirled my brush too vigorously in the plastic cup of water and accidentally knocked it across Lana's portrait of Sir Francis Drake. She shrieked that she would have to start all over now, and I didn't tell her that maybe I had done her a favor, because her portrait looked more like Mr Potato Head than anyone else. When Mrs Gallo came over and saw the mess and asked who'd done it, Lana pointed an accusatory paintbrush at me, and Mrs Gallo looked at the mess and looked at me and sighed and said, *of course.*

It was cold in the bathtub and my mother still wasn't home, so I decided to run myself a bath, even though she didn't allow me baths now that I was in fourth grade. She was always worried about the water bill, which was a concept I had yet to grasp. The stopper for the drain was missing because of the forbidden nature of baths, so I used half a lime from the collection I'd stolen from the neighbor's tree down the street. I sank my teeth into the other half, thought I tasted communion in its unforgiving acidity.

When the water approached the brim, I let it keep running. I saw a tidal wave in my mind's eye, a rebellious crash when I'd get up to open the door and set it loose into the house. It didn't happen that way. The water drizzled unceremoniously onto the linoleum and slowly made its way out the gap below the door.

When I finally shut off the tap, opened the door and crept out, the carpet was mush under my toes. The darkened carpet looked like an evil finger pointing down the hall, a black lake. It was every sinister omen in the book, and I couldn't register that I had created it. I drained the tub, got dressed in a matching pajama set that I never wore, and obscured the tight ball of my body on my bed with a heavy layer of blankets.

When I saw my mother next, the following afternoon, I told her it was an accident. I made up a story where I was making dinner on the stove and letting the bathtub fill up, and didn't want to leave the stove unattended for safety reasons. I was making Rice-A-Roni, I clarified; I was waiting for the simmer part to be over, and was trying to estimate when the tub would be full, but it was hard because, I explained, I hadn't taken a bath in so long.

I can't remember if she believed me. If she pretended to believe me.

She said, 'From now on, don't touch anything when I'm not here.'

I didn't bother telling her that was impossible. That I would have to touch the doorknob, at the very least, to get inside the house. She was hardly ever here in the first place. So when was I supposed to touch things?

It became hard to breathe after that. I had sinus congestion and a perpetual runny nose. Goo dripped from my nostrils at school, which didn't exactly help my reputation. At home, it felt like my eyes were on fire, and they itched so badly that my mother started keeping spoons in the fridge for me to press against my inflamed lids. At night, my eyeballs would light up and I would rub them until I saw the underworld and the afterlife, felt hellfire, met the antichrist, and I would fantasize about scooping them out and dropping them into a bathtub – not flooded, filled perfectly to a reasonable volume with cool ice water.

My mother eventually became concerned that I was sick all the time. My mother also did not trust doctors. She told me healthcare was mostly a money-making scheme, and that being a doctor was a legitimate profession for me to pursue if I so chose, but that all the good ones were for the rich people. When I asked why, she said it was just set up that way. I filed this away with all the other ideas she'd shared about the system being rigged, and how if she had it her way, we'd up and live somewhere off the grid and grow all our food with our hands. I asked if we could start a garden, then, once, and she told me gardens were for rich people too.

She did call a man to look at the floor. He came into the house with a cart of blades and ripped into the floor, poked at the soft layer of mush between the carpet and floorboards, and determined that it was mold. This meant we had to tear out all the carpet in the hall and my room. Everything from my room was piled into the living room, where I slept in between my bookcase and the wall. It felt like a fortress.

I was further away from my mother's room there. So when she wailed at night for me to come to her, her pleas were fainter, and I could reasonably pretend that I hadn't heard anything.

In the mornings, I couldn't look her in the eye. Or maybe it was her not looking me in the eye. I could never accuse her of abandoning me because I didn't want to admit that I needed her, even back then. So instead I flooded the bathtub. I cost her a fortune. I tore up the haunted house.

The mold was the picture-perfect manifestation of the evil I was starting to feel as a seed inside myself. It was ugly. It was unwelcome. It existed only in hiding, yet its ill effects plagued those who drew near.

I call it a seed because it felt like something natural.

And because I knew it would continue to grow.

It was a seed because it was buried deep and already sprouting roots inside of me, so that I could not dig it out without tearing myself into the shreds of a haunted house, so that I knew it was an important part of me. The seed, the mold, the evil, the mess – all critical to my composition. All there for a reason. So that I would use it all for something. The seed was my second weapon, this one invisible. I hadn't wanted either of them, but I knew they belonged with me, and couldn't help feeling braver knowing they were there.

This was what I thought about as I pretended not to hear anything at night, although the pretending was a performance for only her benefit.

I heard her calling out to me, and felt my body not moving toward her voice – instead, I lay still and stared at the dark window, every bone aching for the dawn.

48

After Deva's whisper, I know that I will leave the circus, head back toward California. I will go regardless of whether Violet comes with me, a conviction that snaps at my nerves. I think of all the times I have followed Violet into corners that I would never have chosen on my own. I am starting to question myself. I am starting to wonder why.

Perhaps the answer is simple: doing what Violet wants is easy; deciding what I want is hard. The world is huge and complicated, and Violet seems to be the only one who has it figured out.

It feels like I should make a phone call when I make this decision, but I don't have anyone to call. The only person I would call is Violet, and she's only steps away inside the truck, pressing her extra-long acrylic fingernails on.

When the truck is emptied out from the big-top pieces, every sound echoes down the chamber of its silver guts. Crates of props that we don't have space for elsewhere become haphazard skyscrapers here, the effect like the attic of a magpie hoarder or a witch. It's the closest thing we have to privacy while on circus grounds, the crates providing just enough cover to have a serious conversation, or make out. Dusty's voice is vibrating as I climb in through the back, asking Violet how long we've been using our act.

'How long have you been standing still doing nothing as your act?' is her answer.

'I'm not an act. I do fundraising, recruitment and the door,' Dusty replies, unbothered, nodding a welcome to me. They dump out a crate of spangled ribbons and turn it upside down for me to perch on, beside Violet. 'And I didn't mean it like that. The opposite, in fact – you two obviously have something. You're going to be around for a long time. So you'll need something fresh when we start circling back and hitting the same cities.'

Violet considers this. 'I have one other piece I've been working on.'

Dusty sweeps their arm toward the ten feet of space between their crate-chairs and the wall. Violet gets up and whirls around to face them, placing her hands in a cup between her legs. I recognize this already as the opening sequence from the performance on the freight train. I watch until she's offering the egg to the sun and when she collapses, signaling curtains, I clap enough for a sold-out show. Dusty has not risen for a standing ovation, and is shaking their head instead.

'I mean, Vi, that was great. We both know that. But there is something missing, and I think we also know what that is.'

They look over their shoulder and make eye contact, and the electric maggot in my stomach tells my brain that they mean me.

'Have you heard of the alchemical triangle?' they ask.

I can tell that Violet wants to say yes, so I'm relieved when she reluctantly shakes her head.

'It's for passion. Fire. And it's three points, right?' Dusty points at Violet, then me, tallying with their other hand. I can also tell that they want us to ask what the third point is.

'What's the alchemical meaning of a single point, then?' I ask instead.

They think for a minute. 'I don't think there is one. So that tells you everything you need to know.'

'Right.'

They stand up and pull a glitter gel pen from their coat pocket. 'I'm not saying you have to study the ancient texts to understand. Just think about it. The triangle is everywhere, and the single point is nowhere. The symbol for light is like this.'

Dusty takes my arm and pushes my sleeve up without asking, then draws a triangle staked on a vertical line with two shorter ones crossing through it.

'Phosphorus. It traps light and ignites spontaneously. The element of passion and absolute illumination.' They've finished drawing, but don't let go of my arm. 'And isn't that what you want?'

I can't tell if they're asking me or Violet. They're still holding my arm by the elbow, and suddenly I can't think of anything I've ever wanted.

'Phosphorus,' Violet is saying, slowly on purpose, so each syllable lands hard and trails with its own echo.

'Phosphorus,' Dusty agrees. 'My dear, if you don't keep your heart open to these things, you'll never reach your full potential. There's an opportunity for so much richness, so much depth here – can't you feel it? When you're performing, no? Can't you feel it?'

Violet looks at me and I look at her, and we each know that the other knows what Dusty is talking about. And we each know that the other does not want to admit this.

'So you have to work together, is all I'm saying. Smidge is crucial. Together, you make fire.'

Dusty takes an unwrapped caramel apple lollipop out of their pocket and stabs it into their mouth, lint and all. They always have stuff like that in their pockets. Glitter gel pens. Lollipops.

They spin the stick in circles, coating the inside of their mouth with sugar and dirt, and watch Violet and me try to have an epiphany.

I rest in Violet's familiar gaze, mind gushing with everything important I've ever seen and everything important still out of reach. All the phosphorus I haven't touched. But now I have this, at least. An alchemical triangle, a glittering sigil; I'll admit I have never really felt quite this important before.

49

I am watching Violet dance.

I am losing track of where she ends among the movements of the other dancers and the flames themselves, tonight's bonfire seeming to stretch impossibly high into the night sky.

So I am concentrating on her face. Then finding her neck, her shoulders, her arms. Her torso, her hips, her legs.

Almost all of our clothes are ill-fitting.

The gown that Violet wears for fire dances, I notice now, is not.

I have given up on counting how many hours I've slept in a week. To know the number is to confront the disbelief, and I'm afraid my body might give up if it knew. I'd rather stay in the dark and fuel myself with something other than sleep, which is unrest, which is keeping moving, which is watching Violet dance, which is making the unrest come inside and make a home in me.

Violet never seems to run out of energy. There is no lazy sway to her movements, only purposeful punches, slices, kicks, the contours of her limbs rendered dramatic as cliffs in the thick orange light. She looks like she could hurt someone. She could hurt someone.

Her face glows and expands to consume my field of vision. No – it's that she has approached me, and is leaning in close to my face. Everything behind her melts to golden flicker. She is going in and out of golden flicker too – no. It's that my eyes are having trouble focusing all of a sudden.

'Are you okay?' she asks, and her voice is clearer than anything.

I'm sure I can reply that I'm all right, just watching her dance, or maybe I've said so already. Can't remember and don't care, because her staying this close to me feels like the most important thing.

'You don't look so good.' Now her hand is on my forehead and I notice its moisture, not the usual flame-toasted layer of sweat but something cold and reptilian. I am on the ground, seated with my legs clumsily folded beneath me and my hands pressed into the cool dirt.

'Are you going to pass out?'

I don't know. I can't keep dancing, that's for sure, not even the half-hearted twist back and forth that I resort to when the exhaustion turns my body leaden.

'Ladies, is everything all right?' The voice of the ringleader cannot be mistaken.

'I think she isn't feeling well.' Violet straightens and folds her hands primly behind her to deliver her thought to the ringleader, which seems unnecessary, but then again, I don't know if I'm thinking straight.

I let my eyes fall almost to closing and watch them through the mesh of my eyelashes. Violet is nodding a lot, hands still bound to themselves, chin tilted up, looking intently at the ringleader while he surveys me. I wonder what they're talking about now, because I can hardly hear them anymore. Violet looks so little beside him, I realize as she seems to strain upward, stretching her spine to its capacity. Then darkness pushes in from all directions, zeroing out everything.

*

When I wake up, Violet's face is my entire field of vision again. She draws back; I feel arms wedging under my shoulders and knees, and then I am moving weightlessly away from the crowd.

*

Metal shrieking. The ringleader's voice, although muffled to the point that I can't make out the words. As soon as I feel matter beneath my body again, something impossibly soft and smooth, the exhaustion takes over and I fall asleep.

*

'Up. Up up up up up.' Violet is kneeling over me, jerking my shoulders up and down.

We're not in our bunk, but a cot somewhere that I don't recognize. A box fan whirrs beyond the end of the bed.

Shifting halfway into sitting up, I realize we're inside the semi-truck.

'Okay, yeah, I'm up. Why are we in here?'

'You fainted. The ringleader thought the sleeper bus would be too stuffy and you'd be more comfortable in here. He told me to look after you.'

'Oh. Well, thanks.'

'Mazzy and October had to go bunk in the sleeper bus tonight. So that you could sleep here. And be comfortable,' she adds, in a tone I could almost swear is resentment. I hope I'm imagining it.

'Thanks for staying with me.'

'I had to. He told me to.'

'Thanks anyway.'

Violet emits a tight sigh and sits back on her heels. 'Why did you pass out?' she demands.

'I don't know. I'm tired, I guess. Aren't you tired?' Memories of her dancing float back into my consciousness. How is she never tired?

'We don't have time to be tired. Sleeping too much messes with our development, anyway.'

'What do you mean?'

'The ringleader was explaining while you were out. He said you guys have been making a lot of progress on your development and that sleeping it all off now would be a huge step backwards. So I'm here to wake you up every few hours to make sure that doesn't happen.'

'What? Come on. My development toward what, Vi?'

'Don't be ungrateful right now,' she says sharply, 'or I'm going to get really angry. If you saw the way he looks at you…' She is staring at me with something unsettling in her face that I can't identify, and it's making me feel trapped beneath her. It's a small relief when she bends down to dip a cloth into a pitcher of water on a crate beside the bed, squeezes out the excess, and presses it to my forehead. 'Even when you're passed out cold.'

I had never considered that Violet might be jealous of me. *You don't want the ringleader to think you're special*, I want to tell her. But something keeps me from opening my mouth.

'When can I go back to sleep?' I ask instead.

'Later,' she says, hopping off the bed. The aluminum booms under her feet when she lands. 'Right now, let's go get you some air.'

I allow the pudding of my body to slide back into the warm cave I've created within the cot, and she completes the song and dance of ripping the blankets back and pulling me to my feet. By the time she's muscling the door open, we're both laughing despite ourselves, but I haven't forgotten the look on her face.

Violet has frequently talked about actors disappearing into their roles, and I've never quite known what she meant – when I watched the same movies she was referring to, all I saw were actors acting. I wondered if there was something wrong with me, if I couldn't distinguish between acting and disappearing. I worried that, if Violet disappeared in front of my very eyes, I wouldn't even notice.

50

'Are you feeling all right after your incident?'

The ringleader and I are across from each other at his blank desk in the caravan. I have to admit that his question takes me by surprise; he usually forgoes any kind of small talk in favor of crashing right into the day's convoluted lesson as soon as we've sat down.

'I'm fine. Thank you for letting me stay in the truck, with the fan and all – I appreciate it.' I stack my hands into a neat triangle on my lap.

'Of course. We can't have anyone in poor health. Not with so much to do!' He laughs and I can't summon the energy to join him, but manage to press out a smile.

'Really, Smidge. Are you all right? You look as though you've had the life knocked out of you.'

'I could probably use some more sleep.'

'Ah, I thought your mind might be playing those kinds of tricks on you. That's a terrible misconception, I'm afraid.'

'That you should sleep when you're tired?'

He looks at me coldly, and I regret saying anything. My guard is faltering. I am almost, almost too tired to care.

The ringleader allows a long stretch of silence to pass. I don't break eye contact, try to make my stare just as cold, hope he can see every bright red blood vessel splintering the whites of my eyes.

'I'm not sure I feel comfortable sending you out flyering if you might just keel over at any moment,' he finally concedes. 'Maybe you ought to do a different job for the time being.'

'What other jobs are there?'

'Plenty. You don't need to be doing these entry-level tasks with everyone else. You've proven that you can be trusted. You have an unusually high level of maturity and intelligence for a young lady your age.'

He pauses again, and this time I keep quiet. After a moment, he swivels his chair toward one of the filing cabinets and removes a thick yellow folder, then places it on the desk between us.

'The safety and well-being of our members is Holy Toledo's number one concern – as you are well aware. When any one of our members shows the smallest indication of being unhappy, it's paramount that we take care of the problem as soon as possible.'

As he speaks, he flicks through the documents within the folder, pulling a few aside one by one to make a small stack on the desk.

'On occasion, members will find one reason or another to leave the safety of Holy Toledo, despite knowing what is imminent, and it's our job to make sure we get them safe and sound with us again. With these members, we need to make sure we are giving them special attention and an adequate support system, which includes a mentor of sorts.'

The ringleader fans the stack out so that all of the documents he's selected are visible.

Each one lists a name, address, email address and phone number, plus a list of family members and corresponding addresses and phone numbers. There is a box labeled *STRIKES* with a tally, and a column titled *INCIDENTS*. I skim the document closest to me:

Requested meeting to end contract with Holy Toledo; we communicated during meeting the need to stay on due to contract not yet fulfilled. Early AM watch reported a car arriving and departing; later identified as his wife. Retrieval successfully performed by October. Retention program commenced the following day.

I'm aware of the ringleader watching me read, so I keep my expression neutral. 'So you want to put me on the retrieval team?'

'Not quite. You see, when those who have made mistakes like this return to Holy Toledo, it can be immensely helpful for them to have someone to speak with openly who is wholly committed to the mission. We need empathetic listeners to hear them out and, most importantly, to become a trusted friend. And if I may be frank, Smidge, there's no getting around it – nice young ladies are the best suited to this role. You're welcome to become very friendly with your assignees.'

My skin is prickling with resistance to his words, to the slow crawl with which he emphasized how very friendly I was welcome to be.

'What's the retention program?' I ask, as much to end the moment as out of curiosity.

'I'm afraid I can't go into too much detail, as that's rather private and we prefer to respect the confidentiality of participants. But I can say that your role will be absolutely key. Especially for the gentlemen I've selected for you. Smidge, not everyone possesses your level of intelligence, unfortunately, and men tend to have a different way of looking at things. They are more likely to lose sight of why we do what we do, and to need a more immediate reason to stay.'

I swallow and am surprised that it hurts; I hadn't noticed all the moisture leaving my throat as he spoke. 'So what am I supposed to do?'

The ringleader smiles approvingly, as if we're following a script and I've responded to my cue with the appropriate line. 'I'm sure you know how to capture a man's attention. And hold it.'

I do. He knows that I do. It dawns on me that maybe this is the extra-special talent he identified within me as warranting special attention. Nothing about my performance on the stage but rather my performance everywhere else: a nice young lady, someone who can play along.

'I want to impress upon you how effective our system has proven,' the ringleader continues, not dropping the smile even as his voice lowers distinctly. 'No one who has left Holy Toledo has stayed away. We have rescued each and every one of our wayward wanderers.'

I wonder whether this is true or if it's only the story he tells to discourage anyone from leaving. My skin prickles again when I consider the possibility that the ringleader has somehow caught on to my plan, and that this is a performance of his own for me. My mind races with possibilities: that the files are fake, that these members never tried to leave and were instead assigned roles to play, that it's all to convince me that I would be retrieved just like them.

The other possibility, of course, is that the system is real. That escape is impossible, and – somehow worse – that the ringleader has actually hand-selected members for me to deploy my special talent on. If the latter is the truth, the selections on the desk reveal how the ringleader has come to see me: as a whore who will do anything.

My mother decided I was old enough to be called a slut in the seventh grade.

I decided I was old enough to make money off of my body when I was fifteen and walked into the Miami nightclub with the permanent now-hiring sign glowing in its window.

I have intentionally flirted with the ringleader all along to endear him to me. I batted my eyes and stretched them wide when he spoke, as if to drink in every word he said, doll-wide and doll-empty inside and welcoming him to fill me up. Like a whore who would do anything.

He has seen me for what I am. He has caught on. But why do I care what he thinks?

Settling into this realization takes the rest of the meeting. The ringleader is business as usual while wrapping up, snapping the binder closed and standing in one motion.

'Thank you, Smidge. Why don't you give the retention program a good long think? Go ahead and finish up your flyering assignments for this week in the meantime.'

It makes me deeply uneasy that I didn't even realize I'd started feeling special until this moment, now that I have stopped. What else has changed during my time at Holy Toledo? I don't want to admit to myself that the sensation coming over me is betrayal. Betrayal occurs when trust is broken, and any nugget of trust I've been harboring so far was unbeknownst to me. But if I couldn't call it betrayal, it was at least something edging dangerously, confusingly close.

51

Deva corners me as I'm exiting an outhouse after morning circle.

'Are you going to do what you need to do?'

I look around. No one else is here and it doesn't seem like we need to speak in code. Still, I nod silently instead of answering to maintain our cover.

'I have an auntie in Fort Worth. She's not really my auntie, but I'm supposed to call her that – you know how it goes.' She pauses. 'Well, maybe you don't. Anyway, she can provide a landing spot, if you need it. She'll give you money, too, if you tell her you're my friend. I swear on my life.'

I want to tell her I believe her, no need to swear on her life. 'Thank you,' I tell her sincerely. 'How do I find her?'

'I haven't got her number or anything, but I know where she lives. She sent me this once.' Deva slides a postcard into my hand. It has two oranges on it, ringed by white blossoms. 'She hid it in a fake credit card bill and sent it to our PO box in New York a while back. I can't say who, but the person processing the mail gave it to me last time we were passing through the city instead of turning it in to my dad.'

I turn over the postcard in my hand – it has a return address.

'How do you know she still lives there?'

Deva shrugs. 'I don't. But what's your plan otherwise?'

Steal a car. Jump a train. Crawl. I should accept this help, I know. I should let things be easy for once, as easy as they could be.

I've done enough bellying up to a tough-shit world and taking the hard way out. Besides, I have all but drained my savings. Even if I stitched together a route on buses and trains, I doubt there'd be enough to cover the tickets. Plus, I'm worried about feeding myself – have never shoplifted without Violet, the two of us taking turns keeping a lookout or occupying store attendants when needed, and am not sure it'll be so easy on my own.

'She'll help you, I promise. Give her this and tell her you're my friend.' Deva pulls one of her necklaces from the thick tangle around her neck, a shriveled-up rat's foot on twine. 'She gave me this last time I saw her.'

'Yeah? When was that?'

'She came to the show when we were in Texas last year. She found the back door of the big top, but we could only talk for a few minutes before they found us and made her leave.'

'Who found you?'

There's a silence, and when I look over, Deva's eyes are clouded and strange.

'I don't really remember.'

I'd question her on that, of course – how could you not remember? – but I also understand how the brain picks and chooses what to swallow into hiding. Some details scored viciously like still-fresh scars when they float to the surface. Others lost in the smear.

'Well… what happened then?' I ask, and then immediately regret treating her life like a storybook.

'The important thing is that you go – like, soon – and get there safely,' she says, and I nod, pretending I didn't ask anything at all.

I collect the twine of the necklace into a tight, important-feeling ball in my fist. I will go.

But before that, I need to do the hardest thing of all. I need to tell Violet.

52

Dusty had suggested that we go flyering together. I'd wanted to go with Violet, of course, but couldn't think of a believable reason to refuse Dusty's invitation.

'So.' We've just been chased out of a diner by a man with a body like a steaming enchilada. The stack of flyers in our hands is still thick.

'So,' I reply.

'You don't have to tell me anything specific – in fact, I'm sure you can't,' they begin, squinting past me at the nothing over my shoulder. 'But how have you been liking your sessions with the ringleader?'

'Oh. Uh, they're fine.'

'Are you learning anything?'

'Definitely.'

Dusty's nails dig into their folded arms a little, but they continue coolly: 'Okay, my dear. So what are you learning?'

'It's hard to explain,' I say, borrowing the favorite phrase of everyone here. 'But I'm catching on, for sure. There are many avenues to the light – I understand now. Mine is just highly unusual.'

Dusty is eyeing me now, still unimpressed.

'It's because I'm so gifted,' I continue, trying to think of anything believable, and to spin enough material that I'll be the one talking and not them. My arms whirl like generators, and I realize I'm emulating the manic gesturing that the ringleader always succumbs to when we are sealed in the privacy of his caravan. 'I mean, that's what the ringleader theorizes. I'm not saying I'm that gifted. But I'm starting to understand some of what's going on inside me while we're performing and, you know, like you said, I can't say exactly, but basically what that means in terms of... of the universe.'

'Mhm.'

I can't tell whether they're not buying it, or if they weren't actually interested in the first place. Then they answer the question for me.

'Sorry, darling. I'm just thinking about something else. I wanted to talk to you about something I've been feeling for a while now. Which is... Well, I'm just wondering if you remember when we met, back in New Orleans? When you were the swan girl.'

'Of course I remember. That wasn't that long ago at all. You're the only one who ever referred to me as the swan girl, by the way.'

'It was so fitting.'

'Why?'

'Because... Do you know what swans symbolize? In folklore?'

'Nope.'

'They're...' Somehow I can tell that Dusty is blushing, even through the statue makeup. It's something about their face. 'I've been meaning to say, I miss getting to spend that much time with you. I feel like you and Violet are always together these days. Which is great, I mean, of course, you two are a powerhouse together. I just miss that time.'

'Wait, what do swans symbolize?'

Dusty continues as if I haven't asked anything. 'Basically, I feel like I need to tell you that I think you're special, and you bring out the best in me, so I think maybe you're my muse.'

Muse is a word I have not been called before. It feels like *enigma*, the first word they chose for me. It feels like something powerful and good, maybe a little mysterious, but perhaps that's only because I don't know what it means.

'We don't really talk as much now, so I was wondering…
if you felt this, too,' Dusty is saying, appearing to select each
word cautiously.

'Felt what? What's a muse?'

They look at me with an expression that says *come on, keep
up*, but I don't even know what I've missed.

I try again. 'What does a swan—'

'I'm trying to say I might have feelings for you.'

Oh. Feelings. I can say with confidence that no, these are not
something I have experienced when thinking about Dusty. I was
grateful to have met them in the very beginning. I was comforted by
their presence. And although I've been thrown off by their refusal
to answer my questions about what is happening at Holy Toledo,
what all the secret programs are and why we need to convince our
audience that we are hurtling toward imminent destruction, they
have a way of making me feel like we've been friends for a hundred
years, and that everything will be okay if I follow their easy lead.

I need to get myself out of this one carefully. I've never had to
do this to someone I cared about before.

'Dusty, thank you for being brave and telling me this, but I
don't feel that way.' There. That sounds mature. As patient and
mature as any muse before me.

'Because you're in love with Violet?'

Their voice is suddenly so sharp that I wince and wonder if that's
what jealousy sounds like. The only time they've been sharp before
was when their hand slammed the truck in front of my face on
opening night, after I found the pamphlet of esoteric secrets that I was
apparently not ready for. I remember vividly their hand and the sound
it made against the metal. But the fraction of the pamphlet's contents I
managed to glimpse are already hazy at the back of my mind.

'What? No. I mean, I love her, obviously, but it's not like that,'
I insist. I think of Romeo and Juliet and how wholeheartedly that

does not fit, Bella and Edward and how wrong that feels too. This makes me feel like what I'm saying is definitely not a lie. 'It isn't that simple.'

'It is simple, though,' Dusty argues. 'Love is the easiest thing in the world, if you don't make it so complicated in your head. Everyone wants to feel like their experiences, their feelings are so unique because that makes it feel special, but it's universal. That doesn't have to be a bad thing, see? It's what brings us together.'

'You don't understand.'

'And Violet does, right? Violet is the only person who understands you?'

No, I think. *Yes*, I think. It's not like I can even put it in those terms. It's more like I am the roof and she is the house. She is the wagon, I am the wheel.

'You need to give Holy Toledo a real shot, Smidge. Take something seriously, for once. I know it's a lot to absorb right now, but you'll understand if you stay.'

This is exactly what the ringleader has told me, and even Deva has told me, I realize. And I also realize, for real this time, that there is nothing to understand.

As soon as my mother got back from rehab, she tried to convince me it was mind control. She begged me not to make her return there, as if it were my choice. As if anything were my choice. She told me that each of us had the strength within us to overcome whatever life dealt us, and according to her, life had dealt us in particular a disproportionate amount of shit.

'Don't ever let anyone tell you that you need anything, because you don't. You don't need anyone else, you don't need programs, or medicine, or God. It's all in here,' she insisted, vehemently tapping her chest. 'Everything you need is in here. They're gonna try to sell you a lot of bullshit out there, so just be careful and remember that.'

Years later I found her in the empty bathtub with my fuzzy blanket tucked into her sides. She was fully dressed, black tights inside her black shoes, thick lipstick even in the winter. I sat on the toilet next to her once I realized she couldn't hear me asking what she was doing, and waited for her to wake up.

I look at Dusty and feel the invisible canyon expand between us. Who knows how high my mother was when she told me that, but she was right. It's what Violet had always lived by before Holy Toledo, too. It was the truth.

I tried on all of my mother's lipsticks that day, too, and the mascara I found in one of the drawers. There were two little fake diamond earrings in there too, which I just held in place against my ears because they weren't pierced yet. I let the temptation to stab them into the flesh anyway wash over me and quietly pass. I stared at the mirror in the meantime, searching for anything from her face in my own.

'Plus, Violet isn't going anywhere,' Dusty declares with a mellow smile that doesn't make that sentence sound like less of a threat.

They pull open the door of our next destination, a Burger King that looks like it hasn't been updated since the nineties. I hesitate before following them inside, considering how you can tell which truth is the real truth by how it stitches itself close against your bones, and by how it is heavy like gold, leaves traces, leaves echoes. I think about all the weight I've been asked to carry. When I catch the door that Dusty holds open to me and look at where their eyes should be behind their sunglasses, all of my trust dissolves.

53

Violet and I sit on the curb with our legs in the dirt. The night seems especially spooky for some reason, the moon dull white-gold and knowing behind her head. I know what I need to do.

'I need to go back to California.'

I don't look at her while I say this, just cast my gaze on the crisscrossing phone lines and try to find little creatures scaling their lengths to focus on instead. Small birds, or maybe rodents. Geckos with roving eyes. I don't see anything to break up the stillness. Even Violet is too quiet. Silent.

'My mother. I've been thinking I need to go make sure she's okay.'

She still doesn't say anything.

'Violet? I'm saying we need to go, okay?'

'Why?' Her voice is electric in the flat hush of the night. 'Why would you ever go back to that?'

I know she means it by the look in her eyes, and that look makes me feel all alone again. I mean, of course it's lonely to feel misunderstood. But there is something comforting about wafting through a constant state of discomfort, too. It makes distances like the one I sense now feel justified. And each one that we cross is a revelation.

Of course she doesn't understand. No one does.

'Because it's my duty,' I tell her, hesitantly borrowing Deva's word. 'She loved me, too, you know. And I've told you... I'm all she's got.' It's eerie to pull those words from years ago out of my mother's mouth, the ones I'd sworn would never come true because they made me feel ill with responsibility. Some still-soft part of me knows that they are the truth, the real and heavy kind that I will need to weigh someday, so I have scratched and clawed my way out of that possibility and poured all of my love into new people's blood. And my mother I picture in the same spot on the couch, frozen TV dinner tray crusting over on the empty cushion beside her. I left her with no one. I left her with Salisbury steak. I left her with my worst fear.

'What if she's not okay?' Violet asks. She's lying down flat on the sidewalk now, staring up at the sky.

'What do you mean?'

'You feel like you have to go make sure she's okay. But if she isn't, what are you going to do?'

She isn't being mean. She's really asking, and I wonder what kind of weight that question holds for her. The question flutters through the air and into my lap.

I haven't thought about *do*, have only thought about *go*, just like how we lived for months before coming here. The *do* would come to me when I got there, I figured, or at some point along the way, or Violet would tell me – I didn't know, just knew I needed to not be a person who had left her mother to die alone. Needed my mother to not be alone.

So I try to think how to explain to Violet how I realized I needed to go. I try to remember what I was thinking underwater, and in the dusty confession box, and looking at the purple velvet where it did not belong. And in the bathtub, and on the moon – pretending to be on the moon, where nothing would matter. How the moon was the only one that was imaginary because everywhere else the echoes were deafening.

I know that I will not make Violet understand. That I am not capable of doing so. The realization punctures the soft sponge, my protective layer, and makes me want to go back to the time when listening to her came naturally – when it guided my life, because she was my light. And I want to explain that she is my light. And I don't know how to make it sound different from what Dusty said to me. Because what I feel is nothing like love, I think. Or it's something like love, but nothing so simple. It's outside of feeling, of *having feelings*, and more like a pulse I've always sensed in the background of everything, requiring certain conditions to remain steady. I thought I'd found them. I thought I'd found her.

Because I want... because I need... and this isn't the right way to say it, not even close, *because you are the house and I am the...* no, *because you are the sun.*

'You've been manipulated by her. You're choosing blood. That's bullshit. That's one of the biggest lies they feed us, that the people who gave birth to you mean something more than anyone else out there because you share DNA.'

'I'm not, and I'm not choosing. I want you to come with me.' I force myself to say *want* and not *need*.

'Well, I can't. If you're leaving, you're choosing blood. I can't stand for that. You know I can't. You need to move forward with your life – there's nothing good in going back. I'm right here, Smidge. I would never hurt you like she did.'

I can't find the words, again, to express that this is something I need to do, something for which I am responsible. It isn't about sending a message, like Violet just made it sound. I can't afford to keep up the jig, to make my life into constant art. I fucked up, sinned, whatever the right word is for my transgressions, so now I have business to take care of. I can't run around in torn-up fishnets forever. Violet's refusal to understand this is starting to feel like a gap we won't fill.

'She's my mom,' I say, words like bricks, too plain, but all I can come up with when her disapproval is staining the open air, suddenly claustrophobic.

'That doesn't make anything she did okay.'

'I know.' But so many things have happened that were not okay, and I don't remind her of any of them. There have been too many messes and not enough opportunities to make anything right, something that never seems to bother Violet the way it bothers me. The seashell lamp opened a gash in someone's head, and his blood was all over us. Nothing will make that okay.

I feel my insides creep to the exterior again, watch the particles of myself detach and reach toward Violet and disappear before they can settle into her skin. I recognize the particles to be everything I can't make her understand: how many things are not okay, and cannot be made okay; how my mother is not innocent but neither am I, and if she doesn't deserve to be forgiven, then I don't either.

I want to explain all of this to Violet, who is still waiting for an answer, crossing her arms triumphantly because she thinks my silence is her victory. Maybe it is. After all, what do I know about forgiveness or innocence or all the infinite degrees of love? These things are only visible from the tippity-top of the sunny clouds, and I have only ever seen the world from my place in the dirt between the train tracks, the loamy earth below the tracks, and further down, the wet black toxic waste coating the ocean floor.

'I'm going,' is all I tell her.

'I can't stop you,' is all she says in return.

We let the silence shrivel up and turn cold while the deep purple fades to black. I tip my head back for the stars that materialize but do not twinkle in the sky. Almost lazily they're suspended, blurred by the leftover smears of cloud, cold and utterly aware of just how present they can be even from so far away. I'm sitting right there next to Violet and becoming aware of my own lack of gravitational pull.

'I could never,' I try to joke with the stars to lighten the mood, prepare for liftoff.

'Could never what?'

Have that much gravity, I think but do not say. I know I wouldn't be able to explain the joke. And since I've broken the silence, she's asking if we can go already.

Go already, go already – I make sure I don't say it out loud as I lift my legs from the dirt, because how would I explain that I wasn't telling her to go and leave me behind? My first steps feel like slow motion, so I break into a run, telling myself that it's because I want to be the one doing the leaving: making the choice, taking the steps, holding the power in my body and its impending absence. I just want to test my gravity. I want to master a distance and so have resorted, as always, to the physical when that other one feels too big and complicated to contend with.

A sky full of stars could almost have been designed to make us feel inconsequential. I know I will never have a presence like that, never have a pull like the tides or the planets, because I take up so little space, my life like the evanescent blip of an exploding star. This knowledge is how I become convinced, as I run, that I need to master at least one thing with my relatively small and relatively lightweight non-celestial body, at least some distance that someone could later measure and write down, like data, like science, like *xyz*, like I care about any of that, like I care about anything, just want to be one of those people who don't give a fuck about anything as I run further and further away from her.

I run until I get to a hotel, and enter the lobby as though I belong there. The inside reminds me of a casino we auditioned in months ago, carpeted pillars stretching up toward golden bulbs in the ceiling. Fluted vases taller than I am fill the corners, holding crisp palm fronds high above the smooth leather armchairs. The effect like an ice-cream cake for a king.

Excessive. Imperial. The elevator doors are mirrored and I watch myself watching myself. The person in the mirror looks nine years old, the rich honeyed light from the chandelier softening her face to a moon. Then I blink and she looks ninety-three. On both sides of the blink she looks the worst possible thing, which is scared, so I scowl like I'm the scary one until she scowls back.

I take the elevator to the top floor, where the elevator opens to an empty hall flanked with locked doors. There are placards promising ballrooms behind those doors, and I try every handle. I could dance slow and easy in those ballrooms until whatever I am supposed to do next dawns on me. I could look through the grand windows down at the city, and be so high up that I'd see the stars and the ground all at once, and surely then I would know exactly what to do.

The only door that opens for me leads into a laundry room. The smell of clean hits me like a tidal wave, and the big blue laundry baskets look just roomy enough to hold me. I climb inside and curl up, suddenly willing to give up everything I've ever known for a nap in this clean, warm place.

The scent of fresh towels is heady, perfectly engineered pleasantness. I think of the scientists who created this, pouring one bubbling test tube into another with wise and righteous hands that only ever wanted good things to be born of them. The low rumble of the laundry machines, like that of trains, gets my senses purring as I imagine my body tumbling around and around the soapy chamber, being wrung clean and emerging brand new. It has been a long time since I've had a good night's sleep.

I close my eyes and conjure the big ballroom windows in my head, where I would have seen the night sky and the city below at the same time. If those doors hadn't been locked, I know I would have finally made sense of it all. Sometimes when I can see big things from far away like that, it feels almost possible to understand how everything connects to each other, and to me, and to every person I have ever touched. The vastness of all that I know is out there, and that I know I'll never see, fills a small but ready space in my chest, somewhere between regret and relief.

But I am always so tired, far too tired for that kind of clarity.

Who knows how long I am out before I'm woken up by a woman with a pale blue apron and a metal name tag that says Ruta. She cluck-clucks at me like a mother hen and says something that has the cadence of a question, but I miss the words. Ruta calls to the other women in the laundry room, and they gather around to peer down at me. Their heads form a ring around the warm yellow light directly overhead. *Please refrain from disrupting my incubation*, I want to joke. *Like I'm an egg, get it? Freshly laid.* But I don't think anyone would laugh. So I just reach for Ruta with both arms and smile radiantly when she gives a disbelieving shake of her head and reaches back, as if this is what was supposed to happen, in the end, as if I'm clean and new, her own little miracle.

54

The last great escape of our lives, from the shelter in Miami, felt like nothing short of flying. Without Violet, my departure feels more like boarding a sinking ship.

After I made my way back to the circus from the hotel, Deva, Violet and I made a plan. We have to go flyering in pairs, per the ringleader's orders, so I suggested that on the day of my escape I would go with Deva, and have her report that I'd gone missing when I said I was going to the restroom. Violet was appalled. 'Fuck no,' she said. 'It's going to be me doing that.'

She steps out of the gas station food mart we have chosen as the scene of my disappearance with a bunch of Slim Jims in her hands.

'For the road. I probably shouldn't walk all the way to the bus stop with you,' she says, staring past me down the empty street. 'In case someone is watching.'

I accept the meat bouquet. 'That makes sense. Well... I'm going to use the bathroom real quick.'

Her stare scoops the core out of me. 'You know I don't agree with this.'

'I know.'

'You know I love you more than anyone.'

My core is gone and I want to cry. I want to tell her I love her too. 'I know,' I say.

'So you're breaking my heart right now.'

'Thank you for the Slim Jims,' I respond inadequately, then walk into the restroom and close the door behind me.

It smells like mold and old paper and faintly like fried corn in here, and the light tints my reflection sea-monster green. I lean against the door and watch myself eat a Slim Jim. It tastes like nothing.

I peel each one open and bite it down, peel and bite, peel and bite, one by one, feeling ritualistic again. This time, I immerse myself in the thick and heavy sludge of the ocean floor and make each Slim Jim the blade of a harpoon sent to impale me. But I will not allow it, so my ten-foot teeth reduce each one to harmless meat paste. Because I can't afford another hole, no space left for another thing that sticks and can't be removed.

By the time I'm out of meat, my hair is damp seaweed stuck to the back of my neck. When I open the door and round the corner, Violet is not where I left her. I feel the tide of panic rising, as if this weren't the plan all along. Did I say goodbye? Is that even as important as everyone seems to think it is? What about telling her I love her? I know she knows. So is telling her as important as it feels right now?

I've circled the block now and Violet is still nowhere, of course, because I'd eaten seven Slim Jims in the gas-station bathroom, and she was getting as far away from the bus depot as she could. I'd looked scared again, according to my reflection in the few inches of the dull, scratched-up mirror above the sink. I turn another corner, glance fleetingly into the windows of a pawn shop, a party store, a restaurant supply store and a pastel ice-cream shop with flies smeared against the glass of the cooler. I feel like a child about to cry because they got lost in a theme park. Someone should ask where my parents are soon, so that an announcement can be made on the loudspeaker to unite me safely and ceremoniously with my family. No one does.

In the bus terminal, a woman with a braid as thick as a horse's tail is arranging a tangle of children into a line. Most of them hold onto a rope, but some of them keep letting go, so she's tying the disobedient ones by the wrists. I remember what it was like in elementary school: I never wanted to draw attention to myself, but always admired the disobedient ones.

A navy-blue double-decker bruiser of a bus screams to a stop on the curb outside. Bodies flood out and disperse toward the city. One woman sits down in the seat right next to me, even though every other bench is empty.

'You should keep your backpack in your lap,' she advises me. 'Not at your feet like that. Someone could grab it and run real easy.'

If they want my snacks and toothpaste that badly, they can have it, I want to tell her. I keep my cash tucked into my bra and socks, like Violet taught me. But I pick up my backpack and place it on my lap anyway.

'It's scary here, isn't it?' she murmurs, eyes darting around the terminal.

I look around again, searching for anything scary. The rope of children has wriggled away by now, and the man at the Subway window is leaning on the counter, absorbed by his Nintendo. The trash kicked in from the street is minimal. The newspaper stand is non-threatening.

'Here in the bus depot?' I ask.

'The... Well, the *bus*. Maybe the buses in Dallas, I don't know if they're always like this.' Her own purse is perched dutifully in her lap, both her hands clenched over its zipper. Her rows of knuckles are tensed into a snow-capped mountain range.

'You just never know who's going to...'

She closes her jaggedly red-lined lips as a man with his daughter walks by, and finishes her thought once he's out the door.

'You just never know what people's intentions are.'

'Well, yes. That is technically true. No matter where you go.'

She just bounces her knees on nervous toes and roves her eyes around and around the station.

'What are you looking for?' I finally ask.

'What?'

'You keep looking around. Just wondering what you're looking for.'

I can feel the current from her head when she snaps her neck to look at me straight on.

'What do you want me to say?' she snarls, suddenly angry with me.

'It was just a question. I thought maybe I could help you find it.'

'Well, what do you expect me to say to a question like that? Are you crazy?' Her voice suddenly booming. I don't know what this lady wants from me. Reassurance? Confirmation that the world is large and unknowable? But it's become clear that I can't provide her with whatever it is.

'I don't think so,' I answer truthfully, and then get up to pretend to read the Subway menu.

The Subway man looks up from his Nintendo to offer me a conspiratorial little eye-roll when I approach the counter.

'Yo, don't worry about Cathy,' he assures me. 'She calms herself down pretty good if you just ignore her. You can hang out here as long as you need.'

'Thank you,' I reply as his attention returns to the Nintendo. My voice comes out softer than I intended.

I train my gaze on the perfect disks of cucumber, slippery mound of banana peppers, soft pale turkey slices in their factory stack. Each component divided into its own container, colors and textures of the sandwich made homogeneous, and buckets filled almost to the brim. A veritable bounty. I look hard at those meats and vegetables and know that they were prepared without love, but can see that they each occupy their space with purpose. Cathy is screaming about having everything taken from her, and the scent of manufactured bread swirls over my head and into my lungs, the vegetables are tidy and self-assured beneath the glass, and I am concentrating hard, devouring it all, just grateful to be this close.

55

thalassophobia – fear of deep water

His hands on each side of my head. The blood on the shell-shaped lamp. The geyser erupting from my stomach. I know how to name these things now, and their name is violence.

My mother drowning in a million different ways – in her tears, in her vomit, in her desperation. I don't have a name for that yet, and the light through the bicycle spokes is blinding.

56

The trailer has clearly been lived in for a while. Potted flowers line the steps up to the porch, where bougainvillea is hanging down in a poofy poodle curtain around the front door and windows. The entire place is populated by frog figurines, wearing little sunhats and holding watering cans or garden shovels.

Fort Worth was easy to navigate. I gave a man at the bus depot the postcard, and he told me off the top of his head which local line to take. I was almost impressed enough not to mind that the route included two hours of walking under the open sun.

A small, heart-shaped sign of hammered tin stakes its claim at the edge of the garden, and I bend down to read it.

FROGS DON'T FALL IN LOVE.

THEY FALL IN HOLES.

THEY FALL IN HOLES THAT I DIG SO I CAN CATCH THE FROGS.

'Can I help you?'

A woman in a floor-length yellow slip is standing in the doorway, peering at me through the screen. All of her hair is piled on top of her head and tied in place with a floral scarf, creating a teetering mass that looks like it's ready to come undone with every tilt of her head. And there are a lot of head tilts as she looks at me, then into the distance, then at something behind her, then back at me, then down at a frog, then back to me.

'Oh, sorry. Hi. I like your sign. Did you make it yourself?'

Her head tilts down to look at the sign, then her eyes rise slowly to mine.

'Did you need something?'

'Um.' I fumble for the rat's foot and pull it out from under my shirt to show her. 'I'm a friend of Deva's. From Holy Toledo.'

She nods approvingly, as if I've taken a wild guess at a *Jeopardy* question and gotten it right, opens the screen door and motions for me to come inside. The interior of the trailer is surprisingly cool and dark compared to the desert heat outside, and positively claustrophobic with figurines.

The frogs outside were only a preview. Inside, every surface is crowded with figurines, and I can see that extra shelves have been installed to create risers of more figurines all the way to the ceiling. Mostly frogs, but also pastel ceramic angels and cats, wooden carvings of totem poles, and tough-edged sculptures of insects welded from screws, washers and wires.

Sloppily painted rocks overflow a flower vase on the table where she offers for me to sit. The rocks are painted to look like eyes.

The intricacy of her self-made surveillance impresses me. It's a world made only for her, as far as I can gather from the batik curtains obscuring all the windows. Every tiny face on each figure still manages to be illuminated, if only intermittently, by candles nestled into any spaces left between the stones and figurines. Individually, each one might technically be cute, but the effect of their congregation is ominous. The shadows in between them look like a million tiny portals into the void.

'You must need to dust a lot,' I say unhelpfully to make it feel less heavy in here.

She places a thick clay dish on the table in front of me.

'Is there anyone after you?' she asks in a low voice.

'After me?'

'From Holy Toledo. Did anyone follow you?'

'No,' I reply before realizing I don't technically know if it's true. 'I don't think so,' I add to be extra covered repentance-wise, just in case.

'It's burfi. It's a sweet. Eat it.'

I dutifully take a bite of the small white diamond in the dish. Sugar crystals and pistachio dust dissolve over my tongue.

'So. You're Deva's friend.'

'She told me you might be able to help me get to California,' I say too quickly. 'My mom is there, and she's, uh, she's sick.' My throat twists up on cue. Still not the right word. And why did I explain all of this before even giving her my name? Did she notice?

'Okay,' she says slowly. 'What's your name, hon?'

She noticed. 'Smidge,' I respond, and it sounds like a squeak.

'It's nice to meet you, Smidge. My name is Lady. So. Your mother is in California?'

My face feels like its own sun under her deep-set eyes, outlined with mahogany kohl smudged to the temple. I nod, studying the gentle contours of the clay dish, the only thing in here that doesn't seem like it's watching me.

'And Deva's sending you back to her.'

Not exactly, but I don't feel like explaining the whole thing end to end.

'That's right.'

Lady laughs a weird short laugh, and I can't tell what her expression means. She lights a lumpy cigarette without opening a window, and the musty scent of clove fills the space between us.

'So, you're Deva's... aunt?' I venture.

'This is all very interesting to hear, Smidge,' she cuts in on the word *aunt*.

I wait for her to explain why. I avoid eye contact with the rocks peering out at me from the vase.

'I'm going to tell you what I know about the ringleader, okay? But not today. You've had a big day, haven't you, baby? When's the last time you ate?'

I don't want to tell Lady about cramming Slim Jims into my stomach in the gas-station bathroom. When I don't answer right away, she nods knowingly and opens up the fridge.

'Beans and rice,' she declares, slapping a few tupperwares on the counter. I swallow the rest of the burfi while she prepares a bowl for me, the clove-scented smoke further perfuming the flavor.

'Well, Smidge, I think I can help you get to California. I have a neighbor who owes me a few favors and collects trucks like postage stamps. I wonder if we can't convince him to lend you one for the trip.'

'Good morning,' chirps a high, sweet voice from the next room before I can reply, followed by a stream of clicking noises. Lady stabs the stub of cigarette against the aluminum doorframe and drops it into the wide-open mouth of a ceramic frog next to the sink. She hands me the warmed meal, which I accept gratefully.

'I'm not hiding anyone in there,' she assures me. 'That's my bird.'

'Oh, cool. A parrot?'

'Yes. An African grey. Mona. I've had her almost ten years now,' she says, a little glitter of pride in her voice.

'Can I meet her?'

She shrugs a little performance of nonchalance, but I can tell she's pleased by the request. 'Eat first. But sure. You can try feeding her these,' she says, rummaging around her fridge again, then pulling out a container with a few blueberries rolling around inside. 'I mean,' and she looks self-consciously over her shoulder at me, pulling the berries closer to her chest, 'if you want.'

'It would be an honor.'

The bird is skittering up and down her suspended branch with her meaty talons, nodding vigorously to herself. It's nice to see eyes with life and intelligence behind them, and the smooth white feathers surrounding each are gleaming with health. I probably stare too long. When I hold the container of berries out, she snatches them one by one.

'Wow. She's an incredible bird.'

'She is. She was bred to work for an artificial intelligence lab for the first three years of her life,' Lady explains, 'before I rescued her.'

'It's sub-optimal! I'm sorry!' Mona interjects.

'What's she sorry about?' I ask, half-joking and half not.

Lady extends a slender, elegant finger to scratch Mona gently on the side of her head. I didn't notice her tattoo before, a lotus floating in the tributaries of veins on her wrist.

'Her background has given her an interesting vocabulary. You can't put too much stock in anything she says, or you'll just go crazy. Especially if you're an old lady who lives alone like me,' she adds, with a smile that I wouldn't exactly describe as not crazy. 'Anyway, Don's off work tomorrow. I'll give him a call, and we can probably go look at the trucks first thing.'

'Who's Don?'

'The guy with the trucks. There's one he never drives because he's embarrassed about the stickers that melted and fused to the windows. I mean, he's never said that out loud, but you know. The previous owner was clearly very into Satan.'

'Submission! I'm sorry!' Mona insists.

'We'll convince him to lend it to you, okay? Now that you're a friend of mine, he'll do anything for you, trust. You just give me your word that you'll bring it back in one piece someday.'

'That's... so generous. Thank you, Lady. Seriously.'

'It isn't really. That truck needs some loving, anyway. You know how to drive stick?'

'Sure,' I lie.

When night falls, Lady pulls a mountain of pillows and blankets out of closets and makes a nest for me on the floor directly next to the door. She pointedly tells me that she's left the door unlocked and while she is very glad that I've come to her, I am absolutely free to leave with no repercussions if I wish.

The blankets are scratchy but heavy and warm, a weathered smell of clove and juniper lingering in the fibers. I try not to think about how many eyes are surrounding me in the dark, try to imagine hearts into the center of each figurine and divine the value that their presence holds for Lady. They have been unchanged throughout the years. Eternally in their arguably beautiful, specific forms. They have kept her company. I still can't sleep after making these stabs in the dark and it appears that neither can Mona, because her muttering travels easily through the silence.

'I could contaminate you if I wanted to,' she murmurs. 'I could, I could, I could.' Click-click-click.

'Nothing wrong with that.' Click-click. 'Nothing wrong with that.'

57

The light from sunrise comes in diffused through the batik curtains, barely illuminating the trailer with a faint pinkish glow. My legs are aching, as usual. I bend forward as soon as I'm awake enough to move, stretch each hamstring until it will yield no more, until it feels like a steel cord supporting the weight of a bridge.

I'm sitting on the porch with the frogs when Lady comes outside with two bowls of porridge. Someone's put on a jazz record, and the wailing notes leak toward us, just perceptible enough to let us know that someone was sad once and we are not alone.

'How did you sleep?' she asks. Her eyes seem rounder without the smudge of dark kohl around them, but still intense, owl-like as she turns them on me.

'Really, really well. Thank you so much for letting me stay here.'

She waves away my gratitude with a flat palm. 'I'm glad to hear it, baby. Now, I bet you're wondering who I am.'

'Well...' I hesitate to agree, even if it's the truth. 'I mean... yes.'

'Of course. So. You met the ringleader. I fell for his act real hard years ago. I was convinced I was in love with him because he told me that I was. During that time, he convinced me he'd received a message that we needed to have a baby, that soon we were to ascend to the planet of light and there would be no hope for a family after that. We needed to have the baby here on Earth and then take it with us there, for some divine reason that I'm sure he made sound immovably important at the time.

'When I went into labor, he took me to a river, and when the baby started crowning, he dragged me into the water. I thought he was trying to kill us at first, but he held my legs open and my head above the water. It was freezing, and the water numbed my body so much that I almost didn't feel it when the baby was born against the current.'

Lady lights another lumpy cigarette and takes a long pull, which makes her cheeks cave into shadow. They are so hollowed out already – not like a corpse, but like a sculpture of an unknown queen chiseled from sandstone.

'I'll never forget the look on his face when he cut the umbilical cord, like... I don't know, like he'd won something and he was going to eat the prize. And then the funny thing, the terrifying thing is that I don't remember anything after that. Nothing at all before waking up in a motel with nothing on me, no suitcase, nothing. I had no idea how I'd gotten there.'

'And you didn't have... I mean, what happened to the baby?' I ask, already knowing the answer.

'Yes,' she says, turning to look at me for the first time since starting her story. 'It's Deva. I'm her mother.'

The silence is cloying, sticky, while I try to think of what to say. 'Oh. So, you've been trying to...?' I don't know what to call it. *Save her* sounds melodramatic. *Get her back* makes Deva sound like an object to be repossessed.

'Her father has a powerful hold on her. I mean, she knows the immaculate conception lie is a lie, but these visions, she thinks she really has them. The aliens, or whatever they're supposed to be. I mean, maybe she does have them, I don't know.' She rests the cigarette on the edge of a terra cotta planter pot so its lit end sends a whisper of smoke between us. 'But I do know it's not her father teaching her to have them, if she does. She has a savior complex and he knows it. She thinks if she ever leaves and gives up his teachings, these... these creatures are going to starve or die or something. And it'll be her fault, because she abandoned them.' She shakes her head, and the pile of hair finally tips over and tumbles to her shoulder.

'So she's not willing to abandon the creatures,' I say carefully, 'but sounds like that means she had to abandon you.'

She doesn't say anything and I suddenly feel the need to convince her that I'm totally on her side here. 'And the creatures aren't even real!' I add, trying to imitate her weird laugh.

'She didn't abandon me. She was a baby. Still is a baby. It isn't her fault. They might be real to her. I have no idea what the truth looks like to her.'

'Do you think she at least knows you're her mom?'

'I don't know. I've told her her birth story, but why should she believe it's true? I'm lucky she'll agree to even talk to me when I go to see her, even if she never comes home with me.'

I fight off an overwhelming urge to lean over and embrace Lady. I want to cry. I want to ask her to come with me. I want to go back to Holy Toledo, retrieve Deva, retrieve Violet, and bind all of us together into a protective circle with no space in between our bodies, and no room for anyone to break free. I stab a blueberry open with my spoon.

'Anyway,' Lady says, 'Don's a good guy. He's lived here since before I moved in and before anyone else in the park, actually, far as I know. Not without his quirks, though. He had this phase of proposing to me every time we ran into each other. It was something of a joke at first, so I could laugh it off. After a while, though, you know. I couldn't.'

Don's unit is a mint-green mobile home with white trim. It has the same rock-rimmed patch of dirt for a garden as all the others, but this one is filled only with sea glass creating a vague mosaic of an American flag. The half-curtains are star-spangled too, and the mean eyes of a taxidermied bald eagle glare at us from the front window.

'Patriotic guy,' I comment unnecessarily.

'He thinks he spent his whole life demilitarizing explosives for the government,' Lady says. 'So if you've ever wondered what that does to a person, it's your lucky day.' She knocks on the door.

It swings open immediately, revealing a short, stocky man with a face almost entirely obscured by puffs and wisps of hair and beard. Smiling big enough to see both rows of teeth, though.

'I heard that!' he announces. 'I was waiting on you to come visit me. Not waiting. I meant, I could sense your presence, so I got up here to wait for you to knock.'

'So you heard us coming?'

'Not heard. Sensed you were near.'

'Huh. That's quite a funny coincidence, because I see your front window's open.'

Don smiles harder and turns to me. 'And who's this?'

He's wearing a Motörhead T-shirt with the sleeves cut off so generously that the armholes hang to his waist. I try not to notice his nipples.

'This is my friend Smidge. We really need your help, Don, okay? You're the only one who can help us, baby. Smidge has an emergency situation and needs to borrow the orange truck that's sitting out there collecting dust. Can she use it for the next couple weeks?'

Don holds up both hands. 'Hey, whoa there, why don't you come in first? I ain't even put on a pot of coffee for us yet.'

'No need,' Lady begins. 'We're in a bit of a hurry anyway, so if we could just walk and talk—'

'At any rate, it's going to take me a minute to find the keys to that thing,' Don says, 'so why don't you come sit down in the meantime.'

Lady turns toward me with a question in her eyes. I shrug. Coffee sounds pretty good to me after the morning beverage we shared earlier: citrus peel, sage leaves and cinnamon boiled in water.

'Forty-seven years, by the way,' Don corrects as we follow him inside. His hair is thinner at the back, silver threads gathered into the whisper of a ponytail at the nape of his neck. 'Not my whole life. But enough of it!' He laughs, hard, as if someone made a joke.

'There's a lot more that goes into it than you'd think,' he remarks once the laughter has subsided. 'I'd tell you, but I still ain't allowed to say. I had level-three security clearance.'

'Of course,' I pipe up. 'Only share what you're able to.' This earns me an appreciative glance as he scoops coffee from a tin.

'Well, I can tell you the bunkers had more than just ammo inside. But I can't tell you what.'

'Don't you think the keys are in the drawer with all the other keys?' Lady asks.

'What I *can* tell you is we weren't far from the coast, okay? Plenty of stuff would wash up and give those guys some cuckoo ideas about what was out there. Not me. But those guys, they'd bring the tanks out and haul carcasses back to the bunkers like they were proof of something. I'm telling y'all, there's no such thing as unknown creatures of the deep. The ocean has a floor, see? They've got it all mapped out. Ain't been no mysteries for centuries now.'

He pauses rattling his hands through a cupboard and looks at us hard, as if to emphasize his point. Lady opens her mouth again and he continues.

'In a way I can't blame those guys – they'd grown up in places like Idaho and Nebraska and had probably never seen something decayed by the ocean before. Sperm whales, for example. When they decompose in the water, the blubber comes off the body and what's left is a big gelatinous white mass. No features you could point at and say hey, that's a whale. So instead they would point and say hey, this is something the scientists don't want us to know about. You see what I mean? Could hardly blame them.'

Don pauses and cocks his head for a pitch that I don't hear. He opens and closes a drawer without looking inside of it, then moves on to the next one.

'You know what? I've said too much. Well, the sperm whale information is fine. You can take that to the bank, in fact. But forget what I said about hauling carcasses.'

'With pleasure,' I agree, and smile with both rows of teeth. I want to keep him talking about what he saw dragged out of the ocean, but Lady wrangles the conversation toward neighborhood gossip then. They place bets on the father of someone's nanny's new baby while I drink coffee with great focus, searching for decomposed creatures shifting in its steam.

Don looks over to me. 'I don't mean to be rude, sweetheart. When you get to be our age, this is all you got to look forward to most of the time. Anyway, what's this emergency situation you're in?'

'It's a personal emergency,' Lady says quickly, placing her hand over his. 'I can fill you in on the details later, if it's okay with Smidge.'

They both look at me: two adults, two wise, safe people that I somehow trust with my life. I resist the longing to burrow in between their safe, soft bodies, and make my best attempt at a normal-looking smile instead.

'It's okay. Don, I'm on a mission. I ran away from home last year and realized it's time for me to go back. My mom is waiting for me.'

'Now, that is an undertaking if I ever heard of one for a pipsqueak like you,' he snorts, not disrespectfully. 'And your mama's just sitting back waiting for you? Didn't she want to go looking?'

'Well, she...' I falter, not wanting to lie to Don. Wanting to make it the rest of the way back without lying. 'I'm sure she did. She just hasn't found me yet.'

'I never had kids. Never met the right lady in time. If I had them, though, there'd be no letting them out of my sight. I got the means to ensure no kid of mine would go missing, you understand? I got connections, I got—'

'Don.' Lady stops him with a tight-lipped shake of her head.

He shrugs, throws up his hands as if to say *what's the problem, we're all friends here*. 'Just saying, that's all. Hon, what'd you go running away for in the first place? Don't you think your mama's gotta be scared half to death?'

I think of my mother's wet face drowning in the dark, her arms locking me into place against her chest. *I know she's scared*, I want to confide in Don, *and I'm scared too*. But the fear had always been there, intrinsic to her personhood. I was introduced to it early on. I was raised with it. My leaving had nothing to do with it.

I'm still trying to think of how to reply when Lady speaks up again, her voice tender this time. 'That's the personal part,' she explains. 'Smidge has her reasons, but what's important is that she's doing the right thing.'

'Can't argue with that,' he says, taking the hint as I'm still absorbing this new concept that Lady introduced with such nonchalance: that I am doing the right thing. I have the sense that Lady's moral compass is immaculate, so her assessment must be true.

Don opens a drawer and plucks a key easily from the top. 'Gotta warn you, this truck ain't hardly a washing machine on wheels,' he says, jittering the brass between two fingers. 'But you give me your word you'll take good care, and that thing's all yours.'

'You have my word,' I respond earnestly, hoping I've done it right, hoping it means something. And beneath that hope, nursing a secret thrill that it seems like my word will be enough.

58

There's a road in Norway that has the Atlantic Ocean on both sides of it. Michael from the group home showed me this during supervised computer time. The road swooped across tiny rock islands, held up by what looked to me like some pretty flimsy bridges. Michael was going to travel to Norway to drive this road, he told me, after he got out of there and got his certificate to become a 911 dispatcher. He showed me drone videos that rich people had uploaded, and checked my reaction. I could tell he wanted me to say *beautiful* or *breathtaking*, would even settle for a *wow*.

It looked like a serpent to me. It looked slippery and ridiculous. 'If it was dark,' I heard myself saying, 'couldn't you so easily go flying off the edge?' I'd never driven a car, and I guess Michael wasn't in the mood to explain headlights to me that day.

I looked it up again later, when Michael wasn't around, and skimmed over the sunny drone videos to get to the ones of violent waves breaking over the tar. The area is prone to unpredictable snowstorms and blizzards, an article told me, so plan ahead and check the weather.

I imagined a car being miraculously lifted by the screaming winds, rolling through the air as a split-second holy vision before being hurled into the jaws of the sea. And then I watched it sink.

In my fantasy it would be winter, so that the sun would not rise the next morning to reveal the uncanny absence. I'd read up on the winter twilight, sunrise and sunset lingering in the sky as one slow burn of muted color. You can't even see the sun, just have to trust the colors changing to mean that it's doing its thing somewhere over the visible horizon. The polar night, the forever night. I guess it was the perfect place for a death trap, after all. Everything about it beckoned to you to disappear.

I'm white-knuckling my way out of Fort Worth in the Satan-worshipper's truck. Lady wanted me to stay another night with her after Don had finally handed over the keys, but I reminded her what she'd told me the first night. Free to leave.

I know why I thought of that road in Norway, because this is just how I'd imagined it. The sun has gone down, and there is nothing as far as I can see in either direction before the mountain outlines in the distance. It might as well be ocean all around me.

The desert is cold as hell at night, and I'm grateful for the clarity this imparts. I'm aware that I should feel lonely and maybe small and insignificant again, that perhaps I should look up to the stars for a push in that direction. I stare ahead instead and conjure a phone booth magically at the side of the road. I could pull over and call 911 over and over until I recognized the voice asking me what my emergency was.

It's me, I'd say. *Just wanted to let you know I'm not scared of that Norwegian sea serpent, I mean road, anymore. I'm ready when you are.*

I conjure the phone booth, and then Michael's voice, and then the aurora splitting through the pitch-black sky. I make it purple and then green and then both, make it so bright and close that it illuminates the empty highway-scape in garish detail. In the dappled light, I can see that I'm surrounded by choppy waters after all, churning with sea creatures and slicking the road with crashing sheets of foam. The wheels tangle up in the carpets of seaweed left behind and start to veer off course, out of my control, but I have bigger things to pay attention to. The strange part is that I can't identify any one animal, as I search the mass of thrashing fins and tails and teeth for anything to make sense of – even a blob of white jelly that I could point at and say *hey, I know at least* that *is a whale.* And why didn't I notice how loud it is before? I can't hear myself think. I can't hear my teeth chattering.

As soon as the vision is here, it's gone, and I'm driving alone in the dark again. I can't hear anything because there isn't anything to hear, just me and one engine that's been whirring below me for so long now that my ears don't register the sound. Just me and my engine. I guess I've found the pit of loneliness now, after all that, and I settle in to make peace with the feeling.

I don't look at the speedometer as I press my foot deeper into the pedal, and enjoy how reluctantly it gives way to my weight. I wonder how air takes on color like that. I wonder what has to happen to air for us to think of it as light. And I know that there are scientific explanations for these things, but they live somewhere over the distant mountains, far beyond the puny universe of tiny, simple things that are within my understanding.

The light through the stained-glass Jesus in New Orleans made beautiful everything it touched – even me, probably. God is allegedly all-knowing, but light is unknowing, so I got to bathe in its warm amber glow with all the rest of the sinners. The aurora, the real one, feels smarter than that, withholding itself and its cool, eerie brilliance from those of us who do not deserve to drink from its quiet power. The distance between myself and the aurora stretches longer the further I drive into nowhere, and this distance feels correct, because when I think of things like glowing red glass roses and dancing pillars of light and supplicating hands reaching down from the sky, I know they are not made for me and my puny universe. That nothing so beautiful is for me to perceive.

59

ichthyophobia – fear of fish

'It's their texture,' Amy told me as she looked pointedly away from the goldfish tank that had shown up in our third-grade classroom that day, as a way of explaining her aversion to fish. 'They're so... wet,' she elaborated.

'Yeah,' I tried to agree, instead of clueing her in on what would happen to her if she spent all day, every day completely submerged in water. The previous year, Amy had raised her hand to ask the teacher to switch desks when she was seated next to me. 'She smells,' she declared loudly in front of everyone, voice nasal because she was pinching her nose shut.

We named the fish Harold. Amy complained to Mrs Yanai that the fish freaked her out, purposely calling him *the fish* instead of using his name.

Mrs Yanai asked if it would work to move Harold to the back and Amy to the front, so they would never have to look at each other. Amy said no, and that she would tell her dad what was going on, and that he wasn't going to be happy about it. Her father did show up to the school the next day to object to Mrs Yanai exposing his daughter to her greatest fear. And because Harold served no particular purpose that parents and teachers could understand, by the next day, he was gone.

I had really been looking forward to watching him circle the tank and send tiny bubbles to its surface when I couldn't concentrate. I put Amy on my enemies list and promptly borrowed an illustrated encyclopedia of fish from the library that afternoon. In the following weeks, I carefully copied the photographs of fish into my notebook, capturing every detail that I could manage for peak realism. These sketches I left on Amy's desk, like stink bombs, and the more I did, the better I got at drawing fish, so in the end this meant I hated her even more for getting to keep the drawings that I had worked the hardest on.

No one ever caught me, which meant I didn't get a call home reporting my delinquency, which was as good as it was going to get for me. I was aware by then that I needed to keep school and my mother as separate as possible, and that she would never change the tides of my life the way Amy's father could change hers. I drew fish blowing bubbles in the margins of my notebooks for the rest of the year, daydreaming about what it must be like to have all that power.

60

Without Violet, no one is around to stop me from acting on my terrible ideas.

The man is running after me with a rifle. I run in the opposite direction of the truck, toward the open fields of glorious nothingness, because I don't want to give him any excuse to put bullet holes in the sides. I am going to get that thing back to Lady and Don in mint condition, polished and better than it was when they handed me the keys. Later I will pretend it was the big old untamed sun making me delirious, and I'll perform this pretending for strangers in one of those almost unmarked strip-mall bars, while simultaneously pretending that one beer slowly sipped is making me drunk enough to tell the story. I'm alone in Nevada somewhere. It feels like I can outrun anything.

Clarity descends on me as I run: I'm the stupid kind of smart now, or at least the smart kind of stupid. No longer the dangerous kind of stupid that drove my life to what it is turning out to be.

Before all this, it was the sign that got me to pull over after there'd been nothing else for miles.

PYRO MANIACS. THE LARGEST SELECTION OF EXPLOSIVES IN THE U.S.A. CHEAP AND LEGAL.

Cheap and legal. I had to see whatever it was that advertised those as the top selling points. The trailer was garishly yellow against the dry desert expanse, perched in the dirt like it was just visiting momentarily before erupting back into outer space. No one greeted me when I stepped inside, although a man sat behind the register. The screen door thwacked into place behind me.

As soon as the cashier took a look at me, though, he got real chatty. I could tell he felt, as many before him had felt, that he had a lot to teach me. I wasn't sure exactly what he was trying to convince me of, but for a while he got stuck on insisting that all human advancement in the sciences had come from reverse-engineering alien technology. I guess in his world, the military had been covering up all UFO contact with the Earth while secretly distributing foreign materials to the national laboratories.

'What are they doing with it in the laboratories?'

'Well, they're studying it. They're figuring out how to weaponize it, how to turn it against our own enemies in case an extraterrestrial nation wages war on the Earth someday. They don't want regular citizens to know about their research because they don't want folks doomsday-prepping or nothing, but believe me, there's a whole mess of plans going on so the president will be safe at least – him and all his cronies.'

Shouldn't have asked. It reminded me of what I'd been taught in the Christian youth group that came to the group home once a week. I'd only gone once out of pure curiosity. The leader dude told us so many times in that single hour to check ourselves every time we felt proud of an accomplishment, because it was God who had given us what we needed to make that accomplishment. So all the glory should be given to God.

I know that if I wanted to, I could make myself believe in God pulling human limbs with invisible puppet strings or alien technology colliding with the Earth and being stolen away into military pockets. I could make myself believe in anything. But I am a little more suspicious these days of humans telling me what God is about.

Buckets of fireworks lined the walls, all the different colors of cellophane crackling and winking. I wondered what Violet would think of this place. I imagined her reading every single printer-paper description for every variety as if she were at an art museum. Hunched over, squinting. Index finger and thumb thoughtfully wrapped around her chin.

Astra Mars Rocket, one package screamed in shiny red letters. *Dazzling effects*, the description promised, *including silver strobing willow, brocade crown to red stars, gold glittering with blue stars, silver crackling with green stars. An out-of-this-world experience sure to delight and enthrall.*

'I suppose they aren't teaching you this in school,' the man said.

'No way. We'd all become too powerful.'

When he wasn't looking, I snatched a fistful of Astra Mars Rockets and slipped them into the band of my skirt, same as I'd done with hundreds of Slim Jims before them. I pulled my shirt down and turned to leave.

'Nothing catching your eye? Really? Did you see the Infini-Lasers up here? Had to special order them from Romania. They've got the longest comet tail for an explosive of their size. Not technically certified for use on these shores, but I'm telling you, no one's ever checked up on that for as long as I've been in business.'

I wondered if he'd made that up. Romania sounded like a country someone would pick if they needed to pull somewhere far away and mysterious out of thin air.

'I don't have anything to celebrate.'

'Every day you wake up is something to celebrate, no? But I hear you. How about this. If you're interested in learning more about extraterrestrial contact with our planet, I got a book. I wrote it.' He flapped a Xeroxed, spiral-bound stack of papers at me.

'No thanks. I don't know if I'm ready.'

'How about you give me your email? I got all the pages scanned onto my computer. I can send them for free. I'm only charging to cover the cost of printing for these copies – I just want the truth to get out there, you know?'

That's when one of the Astra Mars Rockets slipped out of the elastic and hit the ground with a loud-ass crinkle. I looked at it and everything in the trailer stood still for a second: the man behind the counter, me in front of the counter, and all those reflective surfaces around us clutching onto the light. I knew I could get away with apologizing if I batted my eyelashes and twirled my hair like Violet did to get men to buy us drinks and take our flyers, but those promised glittering stars prickled insistently at the edges of my vision. I had to see the silver strobing willow, the brocade crown, all of it. So I snatched that unborn beacon from the ground and sprinted to the door in one motion, and only when I glanced over my shoulder for half a second as it was closing did I see him yanking out a gun.

A gun. A gun for a stolen firework. But he wasn't running all that fast and I knew the gun was just for show, while I was a real-life bullet. So when he didn't shoot for a few electrifying seconds, I knew it was over. Harmless. See, I was training myself all the time to lose the fear of guns and men. *Hoplophobia* and *androphobia*. Capitulating to these things was the same as keeping my mouth graciously shut, putting the rest of my body on perpetual display, or all the other things that I'd grown to learn were simply perform-ance art pieces, hollow chocolate bunnies. Men were the stupid kind of stupid. They'd had it too easy for too long. Harmless. I kept running just because it felt good.

61

I get away from the man with the fireworks still in my hand. The grasses are tall and I lie low until well after the sun has set and the desert cold threads through my bones. I am shivering but doing so as honorably as a noble baby deer, here in my matted-down deer bed, just waiting for my mother deer to find me and lead me quietly into the woods: where a deer belongs, and where a person could get lost for real.

He hasn't even keyed the truck, punctured the tires, anything, I discover when I carefully creep back to where it's parked. Maybe the stickers deterred him. He seemed like the type to be afraid of devil worship. *That's something else that's different about us*, I think to myself as I start the engine and rumble back toward the highway. I am no bark, all bite, and he hasn't even keyed the truck. Stupid. Harmless. All the things I have outgrown.

After the one beer in the one bar I could find whose bartender would pretend to believe I was twenty-one, I cruise down quiet residential streets. The houses here are at the end of long, wide driveways like red carpets rolled out to welcome whoever lives inside. Vampires, probably, judging by the architecture. Imported straight from Romania. Everyone has their lights out, and the windows feel like dead eyes staring down at me. I park under a bare tree, its jagged fingers pinching at the dark sky.

It's too cold to sleep, even under the thick wool blanket that Lady stashed beneath the passenger seat. I rummage around behind me to see if the Satan-worshipper left anything useful in here. All I find is a pill bottle full of crispy dead flies. I wonder if it was the Satan-worshipper or Don collecting dead flies, and can't help admiring the way their crackled wings distort the light from the streetlamps in their little orange coffin. I lay them to rest in the cupholder next to me.

I can't hear the highway from here. This neighborhood is shot through with an uncomfortable stillness, nothing to lull me to sleep. No Violet next to me. It feels like I'm waiting for something and I crave a cigarette, even though I've felt like gagging every time I tried to take a drag from one of Violet's.

I pick up the flies again and pop the lid to see how they smell.

Once, many years ago, I pulled my mother's cigarettes from the center console and crushed them one by one, then sprinkled their remains outside the open window. I wanted to antagonize her. I was nine and starting to realize that something was wrong, that my mother and I were not the way a mother and daughter should be. This was long before I'd hear words like *family dynamics* and *addiction* – and in their absence, I had only the unformed sense of a secret I needed to carry, one I couldn't share even if I wanted to.

She had gone inside the IHOP after making me promise to stay in the car and not come into the restaurant under any circum-stances. *What if there's a murderer out here*, I had wanted to say, but instead I nodded sullenly. I'd looked around for a big hulking man with a long knife, begged him to notice my pretty little face and make my mother sorry.

The tobacco coated my palms. It smelled exactly like her. When the last cigarette was crushed, I threw the box out the window too, as hard as I could, like maybe if I threw with all my might it would explode against the door of the IHOP with such an earth-shattering impact that my mother would hear it and remember that I was important and come out and wrap me in her arms before the murderer could emerge from where he was surely lurking in the dark to stab me dead.

The box landed silently a few feet away from the window and I slumped back in my seat, turned my attention to the highway and its never-ending procession of light. It was all I could do not to climb out of the window and scamper unnoticed across the parking lot and into the thicket of trees, past the solemn congregation of dead-eyed high-rises and into the dark.

I closed my eyes and did what I always did, which was pretend I was someone else, somewhere else. This is how you use your imagination as a defense mechanism, as a survival instinct. That night, I was a clean and tidy little rat who could go quietly from this place without anyone blinking an eye. And once I'd imagined this, I longed for the wail of a police siren and the flash of red and blue to flood the parking lot, while a big bad lady cop busted down the door of the restroom before my mother could fold away whatever she had come here for into an Altoids tin.

The flashing lights and siren never came, and my mother walked out from the restaurant grinning and waving a takeout bag at me. Her smile faded fast when she saw my handiwork strewn on the ground, and the way she said my name made it sound like a curse word.

She stamped around and cursed for real and raked her fingernails into the flimsy plastic of the bag instead of just untying it, opened the styrofoam box inside and pushed it right up in my face.

'I was going to treat you for letting mama make a stop on the way home. Chocolate chip pancakes for dinner, and this is how you thank me. Well. Guess what.'

She emptied the box on the ground. Two pancakes, one luminous little container of syrup, and a gold-wrapped pat of butter joined the tobacco wasteland.

I looked her in the eyes and detected the animal gleam that was visiting more often those days.

'Do I get three guesses?'

Sometimes she would laugh at something like that, and sometimes it would just piss her off even worse. I never knew what I was going to get with my mother, but it was always worth a try. This time she just accused me of thinking I was smart, and I pressed my face to the cool window when she finally got in the car and started driving us home. She was driving too fast, like she always did, and I wasn't saying anything to make her slow down, like I never did. This was another one of our private games, this one so secret that she never even had to know about it.

I turned my mind to one of my favorite distractions around that time, involving an imaginary aisle in a mostly empty party store. I'd walk down the aisle slowly, swinging a toy princess wand like a baseball bat, scanning the shelves for something I knew was not there. So I'd just drink up all those plastic, glittery things for free.

In real life, the world tore past in streaks of light and I tried to hold on to the smell that had wafted up from the styrofoam box, beguilingly sweet and warm in a trashed parking lot that otherwise reeked of piss and tar and wet-ass misery. This was the smell of a soft, safe canopy of love, I decided, the kind I knew I would escape to find someday. It was out there and this smell made it real, and it would be everything I had ever dreamed of.

62

A kid is mashing all the slots of the sticker vending machine by the window of the diner. She leans in with the full force of her tiny body, like three feet of it. I want to give her a quarter so that she can actually get a sticker from the machine, but then I notice the concentration in her face as her fingers play the slots like an unforgiving piano, and realize that getting a sticker isn't really the point.

I woke up in the truck this morning with what felt like an armadillo trying to claw its way out of my stomach. My back hurt. The sun was pounding down through the window onto my face, unobstructed by clouds, and there was a dude across the street spending way too long rolling his garbage can to the curb, squinting at me. I squinted back until the hunger won, then headed into town to see about a Slim Jim or two.

The diner had a sign out front that said *HUNGER WILL KILL YOU*. Then I blinked and it said *HUNGRY? COME IN*.

I don't touch the menu that the waitress places in front of me.

'Do you have chocolate chip pancakes?'

The kid is crying now and holding her tiny wrist with her other tiny hand. Some man who's probably her dad gets up from the counter, where a mound of ice cream is melting over a banana. He kneels beside her. I watch the man's mouth form the words *what happened* and the kid start crying harder instead of explaining herself. *Did you pinch yourself?* he asks, and she nods so hard that

I'm worried her neck will snap, and then both of them would have real problems.

I'm due to arrive in Redding tonight if I make good time. The last time I was in a diner like this, with all the smells and people like this, I was watching a waitress bang around the kitchen, and when she dropped a plate, it hit the ground so hard that I couldn't tell if it had been on purpose. She bent over to clench the shards from the floor, cutting her hands on the sharp edges, and glared up at the manager when he came out from some back room already looking pissed. She waved her bloody palms in his face, more violently as he cringed and leaned away. 'Is this up to code?' she asked, loud enough for me to hear every icy syllable from where I sat by the window. 'Send me home.'

The diner was near a highway that wound through forested hills, which had once been so rich with cinnabar that people came from all over to dig it out and turn it into money. I was sitting in a booth, imagining the hollowed-out tunnels underneath me where coveted minerals had once been. I was watching a couple get into their car outside, not speaking, not looking at anything, their flat eyes like disks of onyx in the absence of sun.

I noticed all this while waiting for my mother to come back from the restroom. Played xylophone with the silverware and the metal container holding all the pastel packets of fake sugar in a neat row. I vaguely remember the manager asking me what my relationship was to the woman I had come in with, before he called 911. The waitress had lost all of her fire by then, was somberly pressing her hands into a towel, bird eyes flitting to the manager, then me, before eventually sliding into the booth across from me and telling me everything would be okay. I don't remember much of what happened after that, but all of the before is trapped in glass: white shards and cinnabar, the blood-soaked towel, onyx, xylophone taps.

In the diner I'm in now, the waitress who brought me the menu returns to my table. She sets the pancake plate and napkin-wrapped utensil bundle in front of me, clink clink, and I unwrap three golden pats of butter. It's too much butter. I swirl it around the surface of the pancakes until it absorbs and they disintegrate like wet couch foam under my fork.

'I don't let her go walking out there anymore. It's not just the coyotes. Maggie got attacked by a Saint *Bernard*. No leash. High-school girls with no fight in them bringing that thing along on their hike. It was bigger than both of them combined.'

I feel like I'm sitting in between the men in the booth behind me. That's how well their voices carry.

'You gotta teach a woman to protect herself for when you're not around,' one of the men continues. 'Otherwise, guess what? You've always gotta be there and that's only gonna set her into worse trouble when you can't.'

'Oh, no, she's tough. And she's smart,' the other responds, driving his voice downward on the *smart*. 'Got her arm in there up to the elbow and pulled the jaws apart. She was fine – it just got her in the ear. She can't wear earrings no more.'

They go on like this as I let the couch foam slide luxuriously down my throat. It's all so wet that I don't have to chew. The molten chocolate burns the back of my tongue on its way down, but I keep eating until the pancakes are gone, and then I lick the film of grease from the plate. I want to set the men behind me straight, but more than that, I want to walk out of here without paying, because I'm burning through my cash quick with all this gas. *I'm sorry*, I write with the table ketchup on my empty plate, and then I head for the door.

'Excuse me, ma'am? Excuse me?' a voice calls out when I'm halfway across the parking lot, and I break into a sprint. It's the waitress, who I realize pulled off the whole breakfast without saying one word to me while I was inside. She overtakes my stride easily, and perches her hip on the Satan-worshipper's truck so I can't leave.

'It seems like you forgot to pay your bill. It's eight dollars fifty and that ain't including the tip.'

I don't bother with a buttermilk smile. She means business and she is mean, I can tell, and I admire her for it.

'I don't have anything. I'm sorry,' I say, stalling.

'Yeah, that doesn't work for me. Sorry don't pay my wages. You can't get away with nothing just because you're cute.'

She looks older up close, gentle lines visible around her eyes and crevice of a mouth. Little wisps of hair that have escaped her ponytail catch the sun and glow orange and gorgeous. I want to tell her that she's cute, too.

I study the waitress and wonder what her life has been like and whether she's happy with it. I'm impressed with her passion for her workplace, running out here, chasing me down for that eight dollars, fifty cents. What if I were crazed, a killer? What if I'd pulled a gun? But no one is ever scared of me.

I'm bending down to pull some bills out of my sock when one of the men from the booth behind me comes out the front door, waving a ten-dollar bill and laughing.

'Hey, hey, Miss Firecracker, let's get this settled the easy way,' he says to the waitress, my waitress.

No. I want to pay her. I want her to hold my money in her hand and know that I had made a mistake and fixed it because of her, so she would have a lesson to share with her two kids that night. She would have let down her ponytail by then and her hair would spill wild over her shoulders as she sat down to dinner with them, a dinner she had cooked from scratch even though she could've just brought home food from the diner. She'd make sure they'd done their homework, then she'd tell the story of the scrappy little punk she'd caught and turned into a law-abiding citizen, and I could only become that to make this story come true if I gave her eight dollars and fifty cents and two more dollars for her tip right now.

'No, I don't want—' I try to explain.

'Don't you go worrying your little head about it,' he interrupts, pressing his bill ceremoniously into my waitress's hand and winking at me.

'No, I mean I'll—'

'I'm happy to do it. I only ask that you promise me next time you need some help, you just ask for it, okay?' He gives me another wink, big soggy eyes asking for a gouging, and is walking away before I can refuse to ever promise that. Especially not to him. With his savior complex that I hadn't agreed to indulge. I would stake my life on never owing him shit, under any circumstances.

My waitress rolls her golden eyes and follows him back inside with a flat *thank-you-sir* and not a single glance back at me. So I will be the unreformed asshole, if she even tells the story to her kids now, because what's the point of telling a story if there isn't a lesson, or at least a happy ending? I slide into the driver's seat with face aflame, unable to scrub myself clean from what I just caught myself up in.

I got away with it because I'm *cute*, and I know I probably can't count how many times I've gotten away with something that I shouldn't have because I am small and white and pretty enough to play a doll. I feel the pink streaks, the black freckles materializing on my cheeks, but I didn't mean for this to be a performance. *Look!* I'm just a poor little girl, *incredible!* The world could so easily break me! *Help*, I'm so small and *yikes*, there are so many dangers out there for you to save me from, but *abracadabra, voilà*, at least I succeed at the one responsibility I am trusted with, which is to occupy exactly the space I am meant to, and not an inch more.

63

I can tell I'm getting close to home by how the jagged line of pines closes off the sky. The last long stretch of road before my house is an uncanny valley of semi-familiarity. After what feels like a lifetime of being away, every detail matches my memory but seems off-center somehow – colors one shade wrong, everything a little closer to the ground. All of it: big things, like the mountains shoving rock into the skyline; little ones, like the corner store that's been hollowed out of everything except a thick carpet of trash, still lying about the GAS MILK GROCERIES promised inside.

I thought the house would look extra-haunted when I arrived, but it doesn't. It looks the same as it always did: regular haunted, just like I remember from all those days coming home from school and slipping inside, unsure what scene would be waiting behind the door. We didn't have a tree in the front yard that has grown taller or anything. I mean, it looks exactly the same – like no time has passed at all.

'Phoebe?' a voice calls out.

My skin prickles. No one has called me that in a long time. I turn around and see our old neighbor opening her screen door, coming out to see me. Her name floats fuzzily to the surface.

'Hi, Deanne.'

She wraps her cardigan more tightly around herself, a gesture that gives me secondhand comfort. She's shaking her head. 'I wasn't sure that was you.'

I nod, not sure how to continue this conversation. I hadn't spoken to Deanne much when I lived here, though I remember my mom sometimes chatting with her on good days. Her face and her husband's face were sometimes visible in the window facing ours. Somehow I know his name was Larry.

'How's Larry?' is the only normal thing I can think of to say.

'Oh, he's with the Lord now. The cancer got him. It was his time, honey,' she says with a puckered smile that doesn't look like anything more than a shape.

'Oh my God. Fuck. Sorry. I mean, I'm so sorry.'

'No sorries. But thank you. The world done us right after all. Toward the end he was praying to go.'

She's still smiling but I hear the wobble carrying the words. She's looking at me intently, though, a big fearless stare that I can't match.

'Phoebe, I was real sorry to hear about your mama.'

'To hear what about her?'

She is silent, and when I finally break my gaze away from the house to meet her eyes, her face is frozen. Wide round eyes and perfect O mouth – *I should see if she's looking for a job in the circus*, my dumbass brain thinks even as my heart is sinking.

'Well, hon, about her passing. I didn't realize you didn't... I mean, I thought you was off to college or something after I stopped seeing you around.'

Everything goes cold at once. The dead flame in my stomach, the missing part at the back of my throat, the moldy seed still buried inside me. *So she overdosed and I am too late*, whispers some functioning cavity of my brain. *So I left her to meet her death all alone, after all.* Her *passing*, Deanne said, a word too matter-of-fact for what it means, and I wonder how big this is for her, and how big I should or shouldn't feel, and if I am allowed to not be crying right now. I can't think in a straight line. I have driven nearly 2,000 miles in a row to get here, and now my brain is a burned-out matchstick barely still burning inside.

Deanne is speaking again, softer than ever now. 'It was just last month. She was drivin', hon, and a car ran a stop sign and hit her. She was just a sitting duck – there wasn't nothing she could have done different. The Lord took her too early, but we got to believe she's in a better place with Him now, isn't that right?'

I wish she would shut up about the Lord, because that has made my brain catch fire again. Car. Stop sign. Duck. None of these words match up with what I have just grieved.

It doesn't make any sense. The web of my mother's tiny and claustrophobic universe had limits that I'd drawn in for her, and an end like a black hole: as dark and scary as it was unconfirmed and far away. This is not that end. My mother could not have gone that way. After all the time I'd spent scared, that *she* had spent scared and perpetually shackled by more shame than probably anything else. We had lived our lives this way, and she died from some asshole hitting her with his car? That can't be true. I won't take it.

Somehow my skin registers warmth, and I find myself wrapped in Deanne's arms, shaking and snotting all over her shoulder. She's murmuring, *I'm sorry I'm so sorry and I'm so sorry you had to find out this way, so sorry Phoebe.* I wish I could remind her *no sorries*, but to do so would be to ignore the incredible difference between the losses we have suffered. She stayed by his side to the bitter end. I fled. Her grief is pure and honest and mine is stolen, an appropriation. *No sorries*, she can say as she pictures her husband under the loving care of a benevolent God, after having driven him to his doctor's appointments and fed him his special diet and put their favorite programs on the TV at night to distract from the fact that he was dying, and when he remembered this and grieved, she was there to grieve with him, and when he did finally go, she was there to be the last image his mind would process before shutting down for good. He was loved and lost and no one could be sorry for that.

My mother, she died alone and I have to be sorry for it, because I would have been the one to be there with her and I wasn't; her life might have been different if I had stayed in it and I hadn't; and by the time I realized my mistake and came all this way to pull off the grand finale of fixing the mess, I was too late. She is lost and I'll never know if she knew she was loved.

Her universe shrank quickly. I watch a piece of mine go, too – one star blinking out, casting all the others in sympathetic shadow. Because I did love her, despite everything, even if it was in a way that I couldn't always understand.

I love her because she tried and tried and tried, and failed just as many times, and now I know how that felt. I tried so hard for this final trick, this grand reunion, and for once – when it matters the most – I'm not going to get away with it.

64

Deanne opened a can of chili and boiled a potato for me, kept bringing more and more little things to have on the side. Clementines. A box of wheat crackers. Ginger ale, then a weird chunky fruit tea. Like she was trying to fill up a hole. I was the hole.

I could see into her living room from where I sat at the corner of the kitchen table. There was a photo of her and Larry, clinging on to each other and laughing, looking like one of those stock photos that come already inside the picture frame. I didn't have any pictures like that. I made a mental note to take one with someone, someday, because when I saw that picture, a steel coil sprang to life inside my chest. It twisted up my windpipe, wrapped around my lungs and squeezed.

Now I am lying in between unfamiliar sheets, in a room that Deanne introduced as the guest bedroom. It's so comfortable that I realize I don't know what it feels like anymore to sleep in my own bed. I've lost touch with the concept. There have been too many beds. A framed painting of teddy bears wearing knitted sweaters hangs right where they can watch me sleep. Surveillance. I slide out of bed to take it down from the hook and lean it facing the wall.

The echoes aren't painful. I lie in the dark and do not pretend I'm in outer space. Instead, I pull away the sheets and the quilt and lie bare to the shallow, still air. I want to feel everything, and I do. The weight of the world not on my shoulders, but evenly distributed down the length of my body. My nerves stand up straight and raw and ready to receive, and the weight presses back as a guiding hand – *this is where you end*, it tells me. *You're right here, right here, right here.*

I'm right here, I hum along in my head, trying it out. Then I remember the fireworks stashed under the passenger seat and sit up at once. In the perfect silence, by the faint bluish glow from the nightlight beside the bed, it seems possible that they will solve everything. Tiptoeing into the living room, I find a candle lighter and carry it outside with me. The Astra Mars Rockets crinkle with promise and hope in the moonlight, and I tear away the packaging impatiently to reveal the dull cardboard cylinders inside.

I line them up in a row in the empty flat space of the street, and set fire to each fuse. They ignite eagerly, and the sound they punch into the silence is purifying as their stars crack the sky.

After a while, people come out of their houses to yell at me, but I can barely hear them. I forget what the fireworks promised: raspberry dazzle? Diamond catastrophe? But what they're giving me is violence without the destruction, just catharsis after catharsis, clarity. Ash rains down and I think about all the people I've ever seen and how once, when we were traveling, I had been awake for two days straight and realized, for the first time, that the particles of other people's presence detached from them and stuck to me just like this – that they would stay with me forever and not feel heavy at all.

Every person. The ones who I had never spoken to and only seen from a distance, and the ones who had been inside me.

I knew I wasn't crazy because I felt their essence all over me like a coat. I could walk naked in the streets.

I knew I wasn't crazy because I told Violet what was happening, and she felt it too.

And I know I will call Violet in the morning to remind her of this.

I envision my mother in her final seconds of life, driving down a familiar street. In my head, she didn't notice the car until it hit, and she was gone on impact. After this life she'd lived, agoraphobic and submitting to a hunger inside of her that she was terrified of but couldn't control, she died without fear.

I'm still not sure about the afterlife, but I hope this means she will never be scared again.

I'm right here, I try again, and no weight presses down as the ash clears my lungs, my mind – *right here, right here, right here*. I know I've started screaming because I can feel it vibrating in my throat, nothing missing back there anymore, and the neighbors are asking me what my problem is, but it's because they don't know that I've just now proven myself infinite. Which means that they are too.

I've heard that the meat from animals who know they're about to die, who can see their brothers and sisters strung up by the ankles in the slaughterhouses before them, tastes different from the meat of an animal who is hunted without knowing what's coming. Unnoticed bullet to brain. So I guess, whether or not souls exist and hers is at peace, at least after all those years of acrid tension, the meat of my mother is sweet and tender at last.

It's a silver-spangled tendril of hope, if nothing else; something that finally makes sense.

Acknowledgements

Thank you to my parents for raising me with the freedom to be myself, and never making me feel that being an author was not a goal worth pursuing, nor one that was out of reach for me. To my sister for remaining my best friend and stable counterpoint throughout the unpredictable life that's resulted so far from the pursuit of this goal. To my family at large, I love you and I'm proud of you.

To all the friends who have supported me and taken me seriously as a writer even when the silliness of my personality prevails. Randy Bucky, I owe so much to our accountability sessions wherein you studied for law school in order to protect our youth and save the world, and I wrote my deluded circus-cult novel. Those times helped me reconnect with the joy of writing when getting to the end of the first draft felt like hard work.

To my teacher Melissa Gallo for quietly but firmly planting the seed of the idea that I could one day write books early on, such that my life path was decided by the end of fifth grade. And to the teachers and professors who noticed and believed in me since: Jennifer Touchton, Richard Ajlouny, Adrienne Eastwood, Paul Douglass and Samuel Maio. Luke Goebel for helping me publish my first ever story and, with that, affirming that anything I wrote was worth publishing at all.

To my fellow commune members at the Muse for sharing and co-creating a space bursting with creativity and chaotic energy. I don't think this story would be half so juicy and flavorful without the unique environment into which it was born.

To my readers Geoff Medhurst and Jennifer Dwight for slogging through the earliest drafts of this novel in all their convoluted, unhinged glory. Your feedback did the readers of this resulting novel an invaluable service.

To my editor Sarah Shaw at Fairlight, who guided me every step of the way in bringing my very first novel to its final form.

About the Author

Jennifer Love is a writer from the Bay Area who currently calls Oakland, California home. Her debut short story collection, *Punch a Hole in the Sky to Let in the Light*, was published by 5ever Books in 2023, and her short fiction and poetry have appeared in *X-RAY*, *Minola Review*, *Storm Cellar*, *Autre* and elsewhere. *Please Fear Me* is Jennifer's debut novel.

PHOEBE WALKER
Temper

There's a gap where my sense of place should be. It's quite a useful one sometimes. It allows me to sit on the cusp of an opinion.

Following a move to the Netherlands, a young woman dissects the developments of her new life: awkward exchanges with the people she meets, days spent alone freelancing in her apartment, her confrontation with boredom and unease. In her newfound isolation, she develops an unusual friendship with Colette, a woman she neither likes nor can keep away from. As her feelings of dislocation grow, larger anxieties about her purpose – or lack of it – begin to encroach. And underneath it all, a burgeoning frustration bubbles.

Intimate, incisive and brilliantly observed, *Temper* explores loneliness, self-worth and disconnection with head-nodding accuracy.

'*Stark and brilliant*'
—Jessica Andrews, author of *Saltwater* and *Milk Teeth*

'*A quietly devastating debut*'
—Naomi Booth, author of *Exit Management* and *Animals at Night*